Silencing Memories

by

Desiree Holt

Guardian Security Book Two

This is a work of fiction. Names, characters, places, and incidents are either the product of the author's imagination or are used fictitiously, and any resemblance to actual persons living or dead, business establishments, events, or locales, is entirely coincidental.

Silencing Memories

Contact Information: info@thewildrosepress.com

Cover Art by *Diana Carlile*

The Wild Rose Press, Inc.
PO Box 708
Adams Basin, NY 14410-0708

Visit us at www.thewilderroses.com

Publishing History
First Scarlet Rose Edition, 2017
Print ISBN 978-1-5092-1636-9
Digital ISBN 978-1-5092-1637-6

Published in the United States of America

Dedication

To my team, without whom nothing would be written—Margie Hager, Janet Rodman, and Joseph Patrick Trainor.

Prologue

This has been so easy I almost laugh. This is so delicious. The prey has no idea that my eyes follow her everywhere. Her office. Her appointments. Casual lunch dates. I watch her avidly while she shops. Even when she has her car washed. I coordinate everything with her office routine, which has been simple for me to learn. Watching her with her dinner dates, the well-dressed professionals who court her, is almost a joke. She always keeps them at arm's length, thinking she's too good for them.

That little piece of nothing who ruined my life. Why would anyone want her, anyway?

Sometimes it's hard to contain the suppressed rage that has always lived within me. It grows constantly, fed by the hate and jealousy that has been my lifelong companions. I can feel the hot fury thrumming through my blood, racing through my body from head to toe like a wild wind. It isn't fair. It just isn't fair. None of it.

Bitch!

There. I've said it, but it doesn't relieve the awful feeling of hatred, the bile that rises when I think of her name or hear it mentioned.

Bitch! Bitch! Bitch!

That's what you are, Lindsey Ferrell. You've had all the advantages and deserved none of them. And you came by them so damn easily. Well, it could just as easily be taken away. How would you like that? I even found a doll that looks like you, and at night, I amuse myself by dismembering it. One of these days it will be your turn.

I lift the camera again, focusing on her walking down the street. What an easy capture for the camera's eye, the pampered princess always walking so freely, moving about so easily. She never suspects that my eyes are always vigilant, always watching.

Sometimes the urge to kill is so strong I can barely control it. But the time is not yet right. I still have work to do.

But soon, Lexie. Very soon.

It will all be over but not until you know the fear and pain that should be yours.

I focus the camera again.

Click!

Captured.

Chapter One

Lindsey Ferrell strode down San Antonio's Commerce Street, her high heels clicking like castanets. Designer sunglasses shielded her eyes, and a classic suit hugged her trim, five-foot-two figure without being too revealing. Thick, shiny dark brown hair swung against her shoulders with each step. A single pin on her lapel and tiny gold earrings reflected back the hot Texas sunlight. Definitely dressed for success.

And why not.

Tucked in her purse was a contract and retainer from the wealthy industrialist, Richard Marquez, to design a new home for him and his wife. A few more contracts like that and her reputation would be solidified.

Twisting her way through the sidewalk crowds, she realized just how much she loved San Antonio. Austin had been great, and she'd had the chance to cut her teeth at two prestigious design firms, but coming back here was a no brainer. If only it hadn't been prompted by her mother's sudden death from a stroke and heart attack. She was still adjusting to that tragedy, one that left a huge hole in her heart.

The heart attack had been completely unexpected. Her mother had been making great strides at the nursing home, working hard with the physical therapist to recover her motor skills. Every day, she showed more and more improvement, and her spirits were high. Lindsey was looking forward to bringing her home. The day she went to visit her mother after work to find the room crowded with medical personnel and a crash cart was one of the worst in her life.

The medical staff tried everything to bring her mother back, but in the end, even Lindsey realized it was futile. For days, she badgered everyone for answers, doctors and nurses alike. But all anyone could tell her was that it wasn't uncommon for someone to be nearly recovered from a stroke and then suffer a fatal heart attack. She couldn't explain why she had a weird feeling about it. No, unsettled, as if she'd missed something. No matter who she asked, no one could recall any incident that might have triggered the heart attack. She finally just chalked it up to a generally uneasy feeling.

Tired of arguing with her, the doctors gave in when she insisted on an autopsy. Unfortunately, the results were inconclusive and left her even more unsatisfied. She finally backed off, but the whole episode continued to niggle at the back of her mind. That made her mother's death even harder to live with, though. Somewhere deep inside, her subconscious told her there was an answer, and she'd find it no matter how long she had to look.

At least, the revisiting nightmares had finally stopped. Again. She hoped for good this time. They'd first hit when her father died, visions of her swimming under water, nearly drowning, fighting to get her breath. They disappeared when she moved to Austin, then roared back to haunt her with her mother's death and her return to San Antonio. For weeks, she'd been skewered on the twin agonies of grief and fear, until they'd buried her mother at last. The nightmares had ended as abruptly as they'd begun and she was looking forward to a good night's sleep.

And today was Friday. That meant tonight she'd be going home to the ranch. Week nights she often stayed in the apartment she'd created out of the space adjoining her office, but she loved being pampered by Ruben and Mary Medana. They'd run the ranch for her family as long as she could remember and were now all she had left. She was really looking forward to riding Jingo, her bay, and indulging in one of Mary's fabulous meals.

Her thoughts were disrupted by the ringing of her cell phone. She fished it out of her purse, noting the call was from her office. She stepped out of the path of the foot traffic to answer it. "It's me. What's up?"

"Lindsey?" The voice of Brianna James, her assistant, was unusually tight and strained.

"What is it?" Her hand tightened on the phone. "You sound weird?"

"Are you finished with your meeting?" The words rushed out. "Are you on your way back here?"

"Yes." Lindsey frowned. "Why? What's going on?"

"Just get back here right away. There's something you need to see. Right now."

Brianna hung up without saying good-bye.

Lindsey's stomach knotted with anxiety. Brianna never got rattled about anything. She shifted direction at once, crossing to the opposite corner to catch a VIA trolley, then fidgeted until it stopped directly in front of her office building. She could not begin to imagine what was so urgent. Her next appointment, a short one at that, wasn't scheduled until after four o'clock, and she couldn't think of any emergencies waiting to ambush her.

Inside her building, she impatiently watched the numbers change as the elevator rose to the fourth floor.

Mark Hatcher, her draftsman, and Brianna stood at the desk in the reception area. Both wore strained expressions, and Brianna held a large envelope in her hands.

"Okay, kids." Lindsey dropped her portfolio case on the floor. "What's the big deal? I didn't even get to have lunch."

"You won't want any lunch when you see this." Brianna's voice was tight with anxiety as she held out the envelope.

Lindsey felt her own surge of apprehension when she opened it. Inside was an eight by ten photo of her leaving her building, swinging her portfolio. Across the bottom, someone had written in black marker, "I'm watching you."

She dropped both envelope and picture on Brianna's desk as if they'd burned her hand. Someone was spying on her, and she felt a total loss of privacy. Violated. Was this some kind of sick joke?

"Where did this come from?" She tried to swallow back a bubble of hysteria. "Was it in the mail? Did someone bring it?"

"I found it when I came back from getting a sandwich." Brianna couldn't seem to stop twisting her hands. "Mark was right behind me. Someone must have slipped it under the door while we were gone."

Lindsey picked up the envelope again and turned it

over, but nothing there gave her a clue. In the same marker, someone had lettered Lindsey Ferrell, Architect, and her address.

"I opened it because I thought it might be from a client," Brianna said.

Mark stood wordlessly watching the two of them.

"I can't imagine who sent this." Lindsey forced herself to look at the picture again. Her stomach pitched, a queasy feeling crawling through her. Someone was obviously paying enough attention to her to take this picture. The thought of a stranger spying on her was unsettling. Why would someone do this?

"You need to call the police," Mark told her. "This should be reported. You don't know what kind of nut is doing this, or how much further he could carry it."

"Yes, yes," Brianna added quickly. "I agree. This is from some psycho, I'm sure of it. You need to let the police know about it."

"I don't know." Lindsey frowned. "Maybe this is just someone's idea of a prank. A one-time thing." But even as she said the words, her gut told her she was wrong.

Mark shook his head. "This is no joke, Lindsey. Someone did this deliberately. You shouldn't try to laugh it off."

She stared at the photo again. "I guess you're right," she sighed. "Bri, get me the number for the San Antonio Police Department, would you, and buzz me with it?"

After a couple of false starts she was finally transferred to a detective. It was hard to miss his obvious lack of enthusiasm with her sketchy information. She wondered again if she should have just ignored the whole thing. He did, however, ask for her address and said someone would be along to take a report.

"Probably thinks I'm some kind of crackpot," she muttered to herself, then buzzed Bri. "I got a feeling the guy at the SAPD thought I was having some kind of spat with a boyfriend, but he grudgingly agreed to send someone over here. You'd better reschedule my four o'clock, anyway."

"That's ridiculous," Brianna blurted out. "You don't have a boyfriend." Then she sucked in an embarrassed breath. "Oops, that didn't come out quite right. Sorry."

"No problem." Lindsey shook her head. "It's only the truth. Anyway, call the client, then hold any calls. Maybe I can get some work done before whoever they send gets here."

No boyfriend for sure. Maybe not ever again, after the last few disasters. Her 'problems' seemed to chase people away faster than if she had an STD.

For the next couple of hours, she occupied herself with busy work. But her eyes kept straying to the envelope with the photo, sitting at the corner of her desk. Maybe whoever showed up would dismiss this as the work of some harmless crank, like the policeman on the phone had wanted to. Then they could all forget about it.

At quarter to four, Brianna buzzed her to say a Detective McCune had arrived, and Lindsey put away her work.

She judged Patrick McCune to be in his late forties. He had a stocky build, graying hair, and was neatly dressed in a sport jacket, tan slacks, a button down shirt, and a tie that one of his kids probably gave him. His air of quiet competence immediately put her at ease.

She held out the envelope to him.

"Let's protect what's left of the surface," he smiled, pulling a pair of latex gloves from his pocket.

Lindsey motioned for him to sit down on the couch with her.

"I feel really stupid and somewhat embarrassed about this." She smoothed her skirt nervously over her knees. "It's probably nothing, but my staff insisted that I call the police and report it."

"They're right about that. Let's see what we've got here." With his gloved fingers, he carefully removed the photo. "How did this get here?"

"No one seems to know," she told him. "We were all out of the office. I had an appointment, and the others were at lunch. Someone slid it under the door when the office was empty."

"There's no postmark, so it didn't come through the mail." He turned the envelope over in his hands, examining it carefully from all angles. "And there's no indication of a messenger service. Tell me again exactly who found this and how."

"Brianna James. My assistant. It was under the door when she came back from lunch."

He studied the envelope again. "Then I'm going to assume everyone in this office has their fingerprints all over it. But we'll see what we can get "

"I'm sorry." She tugged at her bottom lip with her teeth. "My assistant thought it was a regular delivery. By the time we knew what it was, three of us had handled it. I thought maybe it was just some prank."

"No problem. I've got a small fingerprint kit I carry with me. I'll print you and your staff so we can eliminate all of you." McCune shook his head. "I've been doing this a long time. Unfortunately, I have to say this doesn't feel like a prank. Someone definitely has his—or her—eye on this place and knew exactly when no one would be around."

"Then you think this is serious?" She locked her hands tightly together to control their trembling. Fear and anger boiled inside her, fear of the unknown and anger that someone was disrupting her life this way.

"It may well be. The way things are these days, we can't afford to discount anything." McCune took a small notebook out of his jacket pocket and began to make notes. "Have you had any arguments or disagreements with anyone lately? Maybe a disgruntled customer?"

"Client," she corrected with a smile, his matter-of-fact attitude easing her tension. "And no, my client base has been extremely pleasant to deal with."

He rubbed his chin, thought lines creasing his forehead. "Nobody mad about what you did to their house or anything?"

Lindsey actually laughed. "No. And anyway, I just design them. Once they leave here and take the plans to the builder, it's on his shoulders. I'd know before we finished if they were unhappy."

He studied the sketches on the wall, drawings of her most recent designs. "What about the builders? Any of them have a beef with you for some reason?"

"No," she said again, shaking her head. "It's not that kind of relationship. If they have questions about the specs, they call me and I give them whatever information they need."

"Okay." McCune flipped to a clean page in his little note pad. "What about socially? Maybe a discontented boyfriend in your past? Something like that?"

She sighed. "Detective McCune, my social life would bore anyone to tears. My mother passed away recently, and between settling her estate and developing my practice here, I haven't had a date in so long I'm not sure I'd know how to act."

He smiled. "Old boyfriends? Or just someone who wanted to be one?"

"Not even a hanger on," she told him. "If I'm not in town working, I'm home in Cibolo, on the ranch my parents left me. And before you ask, I have two employees out there who have been with my family since I was born. Besides, Cibolo is a very small town. If anyone there had it in for me, I'd know in a minute."

Closing his notebook, he lifted his gaze to Lindsey's face, studying her as if seeking some kind of answer, some clue to the situation. "Well, someone appears to have something against you. This may just be a one-time thing. If so, good riddance and you can put it out of your mind. I'll start a file, just in case." He picked up the envelope and photo. "And I'll take these with me, although I can almost guarantee you we won't get anything usable from it."

Fingerprinting took only a few minutes. Brianna and Mark were eager to cooperate and offered no objections. Finally, McCune put everything away.

"Thank you for your time, Detective." Lindsey held out her hand.

"No problem." He reached in his pocket and

handed her a business card. "I'll check back with you in a few days, just to follow up. Call me if anything else pops up or you think of something."

Lindsey studied the pasteboard rectangle. "Of course. Thank you."

"If you get any more envelopes, don't let everyone handle them," he warned. "Tell whoever finds it to pick it up with a tissue or paper towel and set it aside until I can come over to get it."

Lindsey nodded. "I understand. We'll be careful handling anything that shows up. Although I hope this is a one-time thing."

They shook hands, and she walked with him to the reception area. When the door had closed behind him, Brianna said, "Well?"

"Well, nothing. I told you." Lindsey shrugged, trying to appear more nonchalant than she felt. "It's just one episode, and it may never happen again. He took down all the information, but I really didn't have any to give him. We'll just hope this is the end of it. I'm sure it is."

"Lindsey, you shouldn't brush this off so easily," Brianna protested. Her forehead wrinkled with worry. "Someone could mean you real harm."

"I don't think so. Like I told Detective McCune, I really can't think of a single soul who would be after me like this. I'm chalking it up to malicious mischief."

"Still," Brianna said, "you need to be careful. Are you leaving to go to the ranch now?"

"Yes. I might as well cut out early. Everything I have can wait until Monday when I can really get into it." She grinned. "This new house is going to be fun to design. The Marquezes are nice people, and if we do a good job for them, they'll refer us to others in their circle."

"Well, you pay attention this weekend," Bri cautioned. "I still don't feel right about all this."

"Nothing will happen at Cibolo," Lindsey assured her. "A stranger would stick out like a sore thumb. I'm just going to relax and ride and try not to think about this."

Chapter Two

The minute she turned off the Interstate and onto the two-lane country road, Lindsey felt the coil of tension in her body unwind. The road led directly to the ranch, which sat in solitary comfort unfettered by neighbors. This place was her sanctuary, her protection from the world.

The scene as she pulled into the gravel parking area was better than a tranquilizer. The sun bathed everything in a late afternoon glow, the prairie grasses like strands of gold dancing in the breeze. The smell of horseflesh, combined with sage and sycamore, created a scent better than the most expensive perfume.

The big two-story ranch house sat like a queen, its gabled windows looking out like knowing eyes over the landscape. The downstairs windows were open to catch some air, and the aromas coming from the kitchen made Lindsey's mouth water.

In the barn to the left, she could hear the soft nickers of the mares penned with their new foals, two of them spindly little things that trembled when they stood. The breeding business her father had begun continued to thrive under Ruben's guidance. The other horses romped outside in the fenced pasture, enjoying their playtime.

Here she could shut out stalkers and pranksters and every other kind of disruption. Except for the nightmares. They seemed to follow her everywhere. Death seemed to be the catalyst for them, first her father, then her mother. Only the death in the dreams seemed to be hers. She hoped they didn't start up again.

Shrugging off her pessimistic thoughts, she waved to Ruben, who was walking toward her from the barn.

"Go on in," he hollered. "I'll put your car away and get your horse ready."

"Thanks."

She called to Mary to let her know she was home, then hurried upstairs. By the time she changed into jeans and boots, Ruben had Jingo saddled and set to go. He handed her the reins and gave her a leg up into the saddle.

"This horse has been feeling his oats today," he told her, "so he should give you a pretty good ride."

This was exactly what she needed. Sitting comfortably in the saddle, as if she were one with the horse, she kept Jingo to an easy lope as they crossed the closest meadow. But when they hit the next piece of pasture, she let the big bay have his head, and he raced full out. She didn't pull him up until they reached the creek at the back of the property. Then she slid off his back and let him drink the cool water while she leaned against the trunk of a tree.

Unbidden, the picture from the office intruded on her thoughts. *"I'm watching you."* Who had written those words? Why was she being watched? What did this unknown person want with her? She looked around nervously, as if a stranger might pop out of a copse of trees or from behind a giant boulder.

Climbing back on Jingo, she tried to put the situation out of her mind while she finished her ride.

The unsettled feeling lingered, even through dinner and into the evening. She tried to go through the bookkeeping records for the ranch but found it impossible to concentrate.

The episode still nagged at her the next day while she talked to Ruben about some of the things she wanted done around the ranch and checked the vet records for the horses. And it rode on her shoulders Saturday night when she had dinner with Quinn and his wife, Kate, two of her closest friends.

Quinn had been a prosecutor for Bexar County when his first wife was brutally murdered seven years ago. He'd hunted the killers down and exacted justice, then closed himself off from the world.

Kate had quite literally dropped into his life one night with her own problems. By the time Quinn resolved them for her, they had fallen deeply in love, and Kate had been able to bring him back to the land of the living. Now he had a law practice in nearby Windswept that covered most of the county. He and Kate had an adorable little boy, barely two, and she was expecting again.

Marriage and motherhood more than agreed with Kate. She radiated happiness, her eyes sparkling, an air of vibrancy surrounding her. She could say the same thing about Quinn. No more darkness and sorrow for her good friend. He looked like a man who had life by the tail. She wondered for a brief, dark moment if she would ever find that kind of happiness for herself. So far it didn't seem likely.

No matter how happy she tried to convince herself she was, those nightmares kept dragging her back into the darkness. When she wasn't having them, she was worried they'd return. Even the growing success of her client list wasn't giving her the peace she hoped it would.

She was relaxing on the back porch with the Quinns, enjoying coffee after the meal, young John Quinn safely tucked in for the night.

Quinn finally broke the silence. "All right, let's have it."

"Have what?" Lindsey worked at keeping her face a blank.

"I know you too well, Linds. You've got the fidgets about something. Out with it."

Lindsey sighed. "I'm sure it's probably nothing, but something very weird happened yesterday." In brief sentences she told them about the picture and the message on it, and about filing the police report.

"You really need to take this more seriously. Someone could be stalking you." Kate turned to Quinn. "Aren't I right?"

"You are. And Lindsey, I'm glad you called the police. There are all kinds of nuts out there in the world today." He took a swallow of his coffee. "Want me to call Jake Garza and see if he can check on the police report? He's still on the staff of the prosecutor's office in San Antonio." Quinn and Jake had been close friends since college.

"No." Lindsey shook her head. "Not yet. Let's wait and see if anything happens again. I don't want people to think I'm a Nervous Nellie old maid."

Kate laughed out loud. "The last thing anyone would ever call you is an old maid. And take it from someone who knows, you can never be too careful." Her eyes caught Quinn's.

None of them would forget when she and Quinn met, she'd had killers hot on her trail and had run out of options.

"I promise I'll be careful," Lindsey assured her. "Truly. But it's only one incident. I'm hoping it's just some prank and we won't ever hear from whoever it is again."

Quinn frowned. "Linds, you can't just blow this off the way you tend to do with things. You're so determined to control every aspect of your life, but this may well be beyond your capabilities. Again, you don't know what kind of weirdo sent this."

"I don't need help yet," she insisted. "And I refuse to run scared because some idiot sent me a picture of myself. I just wanted a sounding board."

"I want you to let us know if there's another incident," Quinn insisted. He and Kate exchanged meaningful glances again. "I'm not without resources, you know."

Lindsey knew all about his contacts. If this turned out to be more than a casual incident, Quinn would be first on her list to call.

Again, she tried to wipe it from her mind. But that night when she finally went to bed, the sleep she fell into was troubled and restless.

****

She was drowning, water filling her lungs and her nostrils.

"Help me! Help me!"

She thought she was the one screaming, but the voice was thin, younger, far away. She tried to push through the water, but her arms and legs were like lead weights.

"Help me! Please!

She opened her mouth to answer, and water flowed in, choking her. Her lungs were bursting, and her head pounded. One more push and she could reach the top. Then she was falling away, falling down, tumbling, her breath gone.

"Help me!"

Lindsey sat upright in bed, drenched in sweat, the sheets twisted around her. Dragging in huge gulps of air, she managed to get her racing heart under control. Yanking the sheets away from her body, she stumbled into the bathroom and splashed cold water on her face and neck. When she raised her eyes to the mirror, she saw such a haunted look that it frightened her. She popped two aspirin into her mouth and swallowed them with water, then made her way back to the bed. Straightening the covers, she lay down again, but fear kept sleep at bay.

She hadn't had the nightmare in so long she'd thought—hoped, foolishly, it seemed—it was gone for good. After her mother's death, they returned with a vengeance, then unexplainably went away again. Until now. What had triggered them this time? Could the photo be another trigger that kept them recurring? Was any emotional upheaval the ignition switch? And why was she drowning? What was the significance of that? So many questions, and no one to help her find the answers.

She lay staring at the ceiling, wondering if she was losing her mind. Finally, at five o'clock, she fell into a fitful sleep. When she awoke, it was late morning, and she felt as if a truck had rolled over her and dragged her down the highway.

Mary cast a critical eye over her when she came into the kitchen for breakfast but said nothing, just plied her with food and shooed her outside.

Lindsey usually loved sitting on the front porch, her feet up on the rail, the house comfortably shaded by giant ancient oaks clustered here and there. Sometimes she read, but today her mind wouldn't settle down enough to concentrate on anything. Her mind was a whirling cauldron of unanswered questions and fear of everything she didn't know.

She was still sitting, staring at nothing, when Mary brought her a glass of lemonade and some molasses cookies.

"What's going on, Lindsey?" Concern lined the woman's face. "I hate to say it, but you look a wreck."

Lindsey forced a smile. "I'm fine. Just a little tired. Busy at work."

Mary shook her head. "You don't fool me, *niña.* Something's troubling you. Your mother would be very sad to see you like this. "

"I miss her." Lindsey squeezed back the threatening tears.

"I know you do." Mary brushed a stray curl back from Lindsey's face. "We all do. But life goes on, you know. She didn't want you to live like a nun."

"I'm fine. Really." Except for recurring nightmares and a possible stalker. "Let it be, okay?"

But thinking of her mother brought something else to mind. She had yet to go up in the attic and haul down the boxes of photos and whatever else her mother had kept taped shut all these years. No one had ever opened them and shared them with her. She thought when her father died it might be the time to do so, but her mother just shook her head. Lindsey always thought the memories might be too painful for her mother, that there must have been sadness in the past both of her parents had locked away.

As she'd grown older, she'd wondered at the lack of an extended family, but her parents always waved away her questions so she'd stopped asking. Now they were both gone, so maybe the time had come at last to look through the stuff. To find what treasures or memorabilia the boxes held. She needed a distraction, and the project might just be the thing to take her mind off the nightmares and the shocking photo.

"Agitating or cogitating?"

She looked up to see Ruben watching her. She hadn't even heard him approach.

"I guess cogitating." She sighed. "Mom wasn't very big, but this place sure seems empty without her."

"Your mother was a great woman," he told her. "Her presence filled up a room. We miss her a lot, too." He leaned against the porch rail. "But she wouldn't want you moping around over her, either. She always said the greatest honor you can give someone you really love is to live a full life when they're gone."

Lindsey stared up at him. "Is that what she did when my dad died?"

Ruben nodded. "You bet. She grieved hard for him, but she had you to think of and the ranch to run."

"I'm surprised she didn't sell this place."

"Are you kidding?" He shook his head. "Your folks built their life here. She knew your daddy would turn over in his grave if she didn't raise you here and teach you to love the same things they did."

"You've been with them since they bought the

ranch, haven't you?"

He smiled. "Me and Mary. We once thought about having kids and getting a place of our own, but the kids never came and this ranch became more home to us than any other place ever could. You and your folks were all the family we needed. And you were ours as much as theirs."

"I wish I knew more about them before they came here." She sighed. "They only told me their own parents were dead and they had no brothers and sisters. I felt like I grew up in a vacuum. Everyone has family. Even distant cousins. Why didn't we?"

"Now listen here, kiddo," he admonished. "Your folks were mighty happy with things the way they were. I guess if they had wanted more family, they would have gone looking for them."

"You're probably right." She shrugged. "It just seems so strange with both of them gone and all. I feel like one of those orphans you read about in books."

"Not while you've got Mary and me," he told her and squeezed her shoulder.

Lindsey tried to put everything out of her mind and enjoy the rest of the weekend. She would leave the attic for a time when her mind was more settled, and opted instead for working in the garden and riding Jingo. She had a busy schedule ahead of her in the coming weeks and needed a clear mind.

Back at her office Monday morning she hit the deck running. She had a schedule for the day packed with client appointments that left her little time to think about the picture, her parents, or the nightmares. The Marquezes expected preliminary sketches by the end of the week. The Randolphs wanted changes made on their plans and would be in that afternoon to discuss them. The Romeros had approved plans and selected a builder. Now they wanted Lindsey to meet with him and address the list of questions they'd faxed to her.

Brianna stacked the folders for these and other clients that needed her attention on Lindsey's desk in order of priority. Corresponding sketches and information for designs were clipped to the top of her worktable. Bent over the table, light streaming in on her, she worked in complete absorption throughout the morning, everything else forgotten, including the nightmare. She was stunned to realize how much time had passed when Brianna poked her head in.

"I'm taking off for lunch," she said. "Do you want me to pick up a sandwich or something for you?"

"Is it that time already?" Lindsey looked at her watch, amazed that it was already one o'clock. "Lord, I'm on a roll here and didn't even check the time." She got up from her table and stretched, working out the kinks from sitting so long. "Can you ask Mark to come in for a minute before you go?"

"Oh, honey, he left for lunch thirty minutes ago."

"Darn. I wanted to talk to him about this project." She pushed her glasses back up on her nose. "I can do it when he gets back, I guess."

Brianna looked at her with an apologetic expression. "He had to stop for some supplies while he was out. He didn't want to wait on delivery for some things, so he'll be back about two."

"Okay." Lindsey stretched and rolled her neck. "Just leave a note on his worktable to come and see me later."

"No prob. So what about it? Can I get something

for you?"

"No. I think I'll close up and go make myself a sandwich in the apartment. I can put up my feet and veg out until the clients get here. "

"Okay. See you in about an hour." She flounced the end of a scarf playfully.

Brianna had a slightly exotic flair about her, accentuated by her choice of wardrobe and the way she carried herself. She favored bright colors and outfits that just pushed the envelope of outrageous. Her hair, a highlighted brown, was worn long in artfully arranged corkscrew curls. Bright lipstick and earrings that just brushed her shoulders completed every outfit. Without all the glitz and makeup, she would be considered fairly unremarkable, a description she seemed to do her best to defy.

With both of her staff members gone, Lindsey locked all the office doors, then went through the side door from her office to the adjoining apartment. Although the place was actually small, she had created a feeling of spaciousness, and she loved hiding away in it. The living room was all glass on one side and looked over the city, with three sets of draperies that could adjust the amount of light she allowed in. The far end of the room served as a dining nook, with a kitchen area along the wall opposite the windows. A door opening off the living room led into her master suite.

Kicking off her shoes, she fixed herself a sandwich and a glass of iced tea and curled up on the couch with a magazine. She needed this hour to unwind so she could shift gears from one client to the next. She'd just finished the tea when a sharp knock on the connecting door from the office startled her. Frowning, she got up to open it. Her staff seldom disturbed her when she was in here. She pulled open the door to find a nervous Brianna confronting her, another large envelope in her hand.

"I swear I don't know when it came, Lindsey. Or how it got here." Her hands shook as she handed over the envelope. "There's no address or messenger tag this time, either."

Lindsey took it from her, completely forgetting McCune's instructions, and opened the flap and drew out its contents, then nearly dropped everything.

"What is it?" Brianna asked. "I was afraid to look inside after the last one."

Lindsey held up a photo showing her walking away from Marquez's office building, swinging her portfolio, wearing a satisfied smile. Across the bottom, again printed in Magic Marker, were the words, "Congratulations on your new contract. Enjoy your success while you can."

Lindsey stared at the photo, shock mixing with fear. "How the hell did this person even know about the contract?"

"Are you going to call that detective again?" Bri asked.

"I guess I probably should. Apparently this isn't just a one-time thing anymore." She dropped into an armchair, her knees suddenly weak. "I entered his info into the electronic contact file. Would you call him for me? Tell him we've gotten another photo and ask him if he can come to see me again. The Randolphs should be out of here by three-thirty, so make it after that. Then bring Mark and come into my office."

Somehow, she pulled herself together. In her

apartment, she washed her face with cold water and applied fresh makeup, then popped two aspirin in her mouth in an effort to stave off the headache building behind her eyes. By the time she returned to her office, Mark and Brianna were both there waiting for her.

"Okay," she told them. "I need to find out what's happening here. Mark, you went to lunch at twelve-thirty, right?"

He nodded, looking nervous. "I needed some supplies and I didn't want to wait for the delivery. You gave me the okay to do that."

"Please," she told him, her voice edgy. "I'm not concerned about your trip to the store. What time did you get back?"

He fidgeted. "About two."

"Okay. I'm just trying to construct a time table here." Lindsey took a deep breath and turned to Brianna. "You left at one and came back at two, also, right?"

"Mark and I came back almost at the same time," she replied. "We rode up in the elevator together."

"And where did you find the envelope?"

"Scotch taped to the door. It just had your name and address in felt tip pen, like the other one."

"No other note or anything?" Lindsey persisted.

"No." Brianna shook her head furiously. "Nothing at all."

Lindsey sat back in her chair, flipping a pencil back and forth. "It concerns me that someone is apparently following me around with a camera and taking pictures at will. If that was the only thing, I might blow it off. Only how did he—or she—know about this contract? I only signed it a few days ago.

And how did they know why I was in that building?"

"I'll tell you what." Brianna flipped her head, setting her corkscrew curls to swaying. "With all those crazies out there today, I'd be plenty nervous if it was me."

"Single women need to be careful, you know," Mark chimed in.

Lindsey smiled. Mark was so devoid of social interaction she was surprised he even knew there were single girls out there. Short and stocky, he lived in chinos and polo shirts that looked left over from his college days. His curly dark brown hair was usually disheveled from his fingers running through it. His philosophy was that, since no one ever saw him at the office anyway, he might as well be comfortable. One of these days Lindsey planned to take the time to sit down with Mark and try to convince him he could have a life outside his work. His drafting skills were excellent, but sometimes she felt as if she were keeping him locked in a closet.

"I'll remember that, Mark. Thank you." She looked down at the photo again. "I guess it just makes me a little nervous that someone has that kind of information about me. All right, Brianna, call Detective McCune and see if he'll come by later."

The Randolphs arrived with a two-page list of changes and hopeful expressions on their faces. Lindsey worked hard to maintain her concentration as she reviewed the items with the couple. She liked her clients to be happy and tried to accommodate whatever she could. The Randolphs had never had the money to build a custom home before, and Lindsey thought they were like two kids approaching their first Christmas with anxiety and anticipation. She really liked them, wanted to make this work for them, and was happy when the new changes still kept them within their budget.

Finally, they were finished and, hiding her relief, she escorted them out the door.

Brianna came in at once with the list of appointments for the next day and the news that Detective McCune would be arriving in a few minutes. Lindsey fixed coffee from the single serving machine and brought a cup to her desk, plopped down in her chair, and closed her eyes. She hated to admit how this photo business unnerved her. She just hoped McCune would ease her fears by assuring her there was nothing to be concerned about.

McCune, however, had another opinion of the situation. Sitting across from her, holding his notebook, he waved away the notion that her situation was harmless.

"First of all, let me remind you that I asked that no one touch the envelope." He frowned. "You were supposed to leave it for Forensics."

Lindsey bit her lip. "You're right, and I'm sorry. Brianna didn't think, and neither did I."

"If you get another one, please remember not to destroy the evidence, okay? Not that I think we'll find anything. This stalker has been very careful about not leaving any trace."

Her eyes widened, and she felt a chill creeping through her body. Oh, God. "You think I'll get another one?"

"This is two times in seven days, Miss Ferrell," he said.

"Lindsey," she interrupted. "Please, call me Lindsey."

"All right. Lindsey. But this sure looks like someone is homing in on you. The pictures and messages are too specific." His gaze focused on her face. "Despite the fact that you say your employees aren't suspects, I wouldn't be doing my job if I didn't check them out. So, besides them, who knew about that contract?"

She shook her head. "I have no idea. It's not a big secret. Maybe someone in Marquez's office. Or maybe Marquez and his wife mentioned it to some of their friends. It's hard to say."

"It's got to be someone who can watch you enough to know your office routine," McCune pointed out. "Someone who'd know when the office is empty so the envelopes can be left without being seen." He closed his notebook. "I need you to spend some time making out a list for me. Disgruntled clients, unhappy or rejected boyfriends, people you've done business with who might be ticked off at you. Anything like that." He held up a hand. "I know you said there wasn't anyone, but you really need to dig deep and list anyone who could remotely be a candidate."

"All right." She sighed. "I'll see what I can do."

"It's usually the ones we least expect." He frowned. "Too bad you don't have a security guard on duty in the lobby during the day. Anyone could easily slip in and out of the building."

After he left Lindsey chewed her fingernail for a minute, lost in thought. Finally, she picked up the phone and dialed Quinn and Kate's number. Being brave was one thing, but she didn't want to be stupid.

"Hey!" Kate's cheerful voice answered the phone. "What's up?"

"Can I come by tonight and bring pizza for dinner? I need to take Quinn's advice, after all."

"Something else happened." Kate's voice immediately turned sober.

"You could say that. What time would be good for you?"

"John goes down at seven so any time after that. But you don't have to bring food, you know."

"Call it my fee for advice. I'll see you about seven-thirty."

She trusted Quinn's judgment more than anyone else and needed to get his take on this latest development.

"I'm leaving for the day," she told Brianna, gathering her things up and locking her office door. "It should be fairly quiet now. Check the computer for the Randolph document. There's a list of new specs we need to get estimates on. You know the places to call. I'd like to get information back as soon as we can."

"I thought you were staying in town tonight to work on the Marquez plans."

Lindsey nodded. "I'd planned to, but this whole business has me a little spooked. I want to talk to a friend of mine about it."

"Take care, then," Brianna told her. "See you in the morning."

Chapter Three

Lindsey changed into jeans and a T-shirt as soon as she got home, told Mary not to fix dinner for her, and said she'd be back sometime later in the evening.

"Big date?" Mary asked, raising a hopeful eyebrow.

"Dinner with Quinn and Kate," she explained.

"You need to have dinner with a man who's not attached, Lindsey." Mary had definite ideas about what she should be doing with her life that Lindsey found both humorous and exasperating.

"When I find one, I'll let you know." She grinned.

She kissed Mary on the cheek and dashed off to pick up the pizza. Saturday night she had resisted the idea that this was more than a sick joke. Now she wasn't so sure. McCune didn't seem too positive about getting results, but she knew Quinn would have his own ideas.

"Come on in." Kate hugged her at the door. "Quinn opened wine to go with the pizza. He thought you might need it."

"No kidding." She handed the pizza boxes to Kate and grinned at Quinn as she took the glass of wine he held out to her. "Thanks. You know how to take care of a friend."

"That's if the friend lets me." He narrowed his eyes. "Let me guess. Something else happened."

"Yes, and I just want to make sure I'm not overreacting. But food first. I'm actually hungry."

For a while, as they ate, Lindsey almost forgot why she was here and what was creating such tension in her life. But then, after she and Kate cleared the debris away, Quinn refilled their glasses and turned to her.

"Okay, you're not given to looking over your shoulder and freaking out, so let's have it. Something happened today, right?"

She took another small sip of the wine. "I got another photo today."

Quinn and Kate exchanged glances.

"Like the last one?" Quinn asked.

"Sort of." Lindsey described what this one looked like, and the message written at the bottom.

Quinn frowned, processing the information. "And Brianna said she found it taped to the door?"

"Yes. When she came back from lunch. I called the detective, and he came by and picked it up. But he didn't seem too optimistic about finding anything." She fiddled with her wine glass. "So…what do you think? Am I making something out of nothing?"

Quinn set his glass down carefully. "Someone went to a great deal of trouble to take these pictures, Lindsey. And to put personal information on one of them."

"That means this isn't random," Kate added.

Lindsey sighed. "Damn. I was afraid of that."

Quinn leaned forward. "I don't want to alarm you, honey. God knows you've had enough going on these past months with your mother and everything. But I'd say someone is going to a great deal of trouble to stalk you. That makes this a dangerous situation."

"A stalker?" Lindsey felt the blood drain from her

face. The word alone made her stomach knot and nausea bubble up inside her. “You’re kidding, right?”

“Someone’s following you and has a message to send,” Quinn told her. “Maybe even has a plan in place, one that we don’t know about yet. Don’t think for one minute that this is something to blow off.”

“I can’t even think who’d do this.” She massaged her temples with her fingertips, the headache trying to build to full force. “McCune said to make a list of everyone I know who might be angry at me for something, no matter how small. It’s just so hard to believe that someone I know is doing this to me.”

“Unfortunately, there’s only so much the cops can do until after a crime is committed.”

“Swell.” Lindsey gripped her wine glass, thinning her lips. “I don’t know what to do, Quinn. I go here, there, everywhere. Sometimes I stay in town overnight. I can’t look over my shoulder every minute, wondering who’s following me.”

“You need to be aware at all times, no matter what,” he cautioned. “But that won’t take care of the entire problem. And it sure isn’t a great idea to wait around and see what happens next.”

“So what can I do? I thought maybe you’d have some suggestions.” She slammed her fist on her thigh in a sudden spurt of anger overriding the fear that had been building. “I can’t believe some nut case is making me lose control of my life.”

“I’d take care of this myself if it were the old days.” Meaning before Kate. Between the violent death of his first wife and his marriage to Kate, Quinn had hidden up here in the hills and occupied himself doing “favors” for people. Nobody ever talked about exactly what those favors were, but she knew the people he'd helped were committed to him for life.

"Oh, I wouldn't even expect that," she said quickly. "I'm really just looking for an evaluation and some suggestions."

"I've got some thoughts about this. Tomorrow I'm going to call Nick."

"Vanetta?" Lindsey raised her eyebrows.

Nick Vanetta and his partner, Reno Sullivan, owned a large corporate security agency. He and Quinn had been friends for a long time, but Lindsey had never met him.

"The one and only."

"I thought Guardian only took corporate contracts."

"Nick owes me some favors. He'll be glad of the chance to repay them. I'll have him get in touch with you, but until then, don't take any chances."

"Oh, Quinn, I don't know if I'd be comfortable with bringing a stranger into it. Besides, even I know Guardian has a top reputation, and I'm sure they're super busy. I don't want to feel like this is an imposition."

"You won't. I promise. And it's better to be safe, honey. Trust me on that."

She nodded, still uncomfortable with the situation. "I know. I just hate letting someone take over my life this way." She paused, forming the next question carefully. "You really think you need to bring Nick into this?"

Quinn nodded. "I do. And I want you to listen to whatever he says. He's the best in the business. Believe me, Lindsey, this is nothing to ignore. I don't want to frighten you, but I've seen some of these situations really escalate."

"I'm more mad than frightened right now." She grinned. "I even thought about carrying Dad's old .38 Special with me."

"Absolutely not." Quinn shook his head. "You don't have a license to carry, you haven't practiced in years as far as I know, and you have too much of a temper to safely carry a firearm. No, no, and no."

She sighed again and clenched her fists in frustration.

"And don't stay in town again for a few nights," he cautioned. "Have you told Ruben and Mary about this?"

"Lord, no." She sighed. "Ruben would be literally riding shotgun every minute if I did. Although maybe that's not such a bad idea."

"He'll need to know," Quinn pointed out. "He needs to be told your safety is at risk. How about if I talk to him?"

"No, you'd better let me do it. Otherwise, he'll get his feelings hurt. But I want to wait until I hear from Nick, okay?"

"Just promise me you'll be extra careful until then."

"I promise to be alert and watchful." She hugged both Quinn and Kate. "Thank you so much for helping me."

"No problem," Quinn said. "You're as good as family, and family sticks together."

****

Guardian Security Services took up the entire tenth floor of the Bank of America building on Northeast Loop 410, a multi-lane highway that circled the city.

One side of the floor held the offices, including a large open area where the agents worked at their desks. The other side was all technology, containing the monitors for the security systems they installed, the labs where engineers worked on sophisticated devices, and other related sections.

Nick Vanetta leaned back in his desk chair, jacket off, shirt sleeves rolled up, feet propped on an open drawer while he studied a report. The huge oak desk dominated the office, and floor-to-ceiling windows looked out over the Interstate. A wall of monitors faced the desk. Nick liked to be able to keep track of everything from his office, and his technical staff had obligingly set it up so he could.

His specially cut sports jacket hung on an old-fashioned clothes tree in one corner, along with the shoulder holster he always wore and his Sig Sauer 9 mm. As the size of the staff had grown, he had slowly removed himself from active bodyguard work. However, years of habit made the gun a regular part of his wardrobe.

A glass case in one corner held his trophies from his days as a football jock, both in high school and college. His diplomas hung next to them. Few people knew that Nick had graduated from the University of Texas Law School, although he'd never intended to practice law. Once he met Reno, building the security firm became his main focus. He soon discovered, sometimes to his dismay, he'd become more of an administrator than an active security specialist. His background qualified him to make the right choices when hiring the agency's legal staff and supervising the work of the agents. Still, there were many days he itched to get back in the field.

He looked up at the sound of a knock on his door jamb, a slow smile creeping over his face as he saw Quinn standing there. He got up to shake hands. "What an honor. The mountain man comes down to civilization. How about some coffee?"

Quinn shook his head and dropped into a chair. "No, thanks."

"Well, you certainly are a pleasant sight these days. Never thought I'd see a smile on that ugly mug again. Life's good up in the hills, right?"

Quinn chuckled. "You're just jealous because I don't have to wear a tie to work. Not to mention going home to a great looking wife every night."

"Still trying to marry off your single friends?" Nick joked.

"Don't knock it 'til you try it. But believe it or not, I actually did come to you with a case, if you've got someone you can spare. I know you guys usually limit yourselves to corporate work now. Even the home security stuff you do is tied into it, but I figured I could call in a favor or two here."

Nick raised his eyebrows. "This must be someone pretty special."

Quinn nodded.

"All right. Let's have it."

Nick was all business now, pulling a legal pad over and uncapping his pen. He listened to the story, and then asked Quinn for his assessment of Lindsey Ferrell. Was she a nutcase? A shrinking violet easily scared? Someone who could have made this up for attention?

Quinn laughed out loud. "If she heard you ask that, she'd give you a good punch in the ribs. Lindsey is the most fearless person I know, which is why she could ignore this situation when she shouldn't. She was a firebrand in high school and still has a temper that frequently gets her in trouble."

"Sounds wonderful." Nick rubbed his jaw. "I love women who are a pain in the ass. What does she do for a living? Or does she do anything?"

"She's an architect. A damned good one, too. I've seen some of her work."

"Wait a minute." Nick snapped his fingers. "Are you talking about Ferrell Designs?"

"You bet. Have you heard of her?"

"She designed a house for a client of ours. We installed the security system. A real showplace. I understand if you want a house to blend into the Hill Country, she's the one to go to. But she hasn't been around that long, has she?"

"Actually she's been in practice for some time, but she worked with a couple of big firms in Austin. About a year ago, when her mother died, she decided to move back here and set up shop for herself."

"So this could even be someone from Austin who's followed her here, right?" Nick made notes on the pad of paper.

Quinn shrugged. "Anything is possible. That's why I thought I'd come to the experts. You know the cops won't really do anything until something happens to her. I'm not willing to wait that long."

"Exactly how special a friend is she, anyway? And does Kate know?" He grinned broadly. "Don't tell me the romance is fading so quickly. I'd be shattered. You guys are my idea of the perfect marriage."

"Get your mind above your waist, Vanetta." Quinn

shook his head. "Lindsey and I have been friends for years. Our families knew each other, and we kind of grew up together. She and Kate also happen to have become very good friends. Anyway, even without Kate, this is one spitfire I wouldn't want to get burned by." He looked at Nick. "So what's the deal? Yes or no."

"Do you happen to have a picture of this wonderful friend of yours so I can see who someone is chasing?"

Quinn pulled a photo out of his wallet of the three of them they'd taken at Christmas. "I want this back, though. You can make a copy."

Nick took the picture from him, not expecting much, but when he looked at the brunette in the middle, something slammed into him. She wasn't so much beautiful as captivating. Energy radiated from her, a zest for life. He felt as if her eyes, a silvery hazel emphasized by the sexy glasses she wore, were looking directly at him, mesmerizing him.

"Okay," he said, shaking himself. "I'll pay her a visit. Got her number?"

"You're going to take this one yourself?" Quinn stared at him. "I thought you only handled the big guys these days. Reno will have a fit."

"I want to do my own evaluation here. Anyway, Reno chooses his own cases; I choose mine. We don't throw chains on each other. If there turns out to be anything there, I'll fill him in. Besides, at the moment everything else is covered, and I'm bored reading reports."

"Aha! She intrigues you." Quinn couldn't help grinning. "You want a look at her in person. Better wear asbestos clothing. This one's more than even you want to handle." He pulled one of Lindsey's business cards from his wallet and handed it to Nick. “Let me give her a call and let her know someone’s coming to see her before you jump on her.”

“Jump on her? Is that a way to talk to a friend?” He tucked the card in his shirt pocket.

“I hate turning to the poster boy for love ’em and leave ’em ladies’ men, but I want the best for Lindsey.” The smile disappeared. “Just remember, though, whatever game you might be thinking of playing with her, this is business. And I’ll be looking over your shoulder.”

“It gives me a warm and fuzzy feeling.” Nick winked and held out his hand. “Don’t worry, I’ll behave.”

Nick sat in his chair for a long time after Quinn left, studying the picture. Why did this woman intrigue him so much? He literally had his pick of females in the city, every kind, size and shape, but no relationship ever lasted more than a couple of months. He had no intention of settling down, although sometimes he envied the depth of feeling Quinn and Kate shared. But life was a smorgasbord to Nick, one he continued to sample. So what absurd itch made him decide to see this woman himself when she had trouble written all over her?

Half an hour later, Quinn texted him that Lindsey Ferrell was expecting a call from him. He punched the number on the card into his cell and listened while it rang on the other end. Time to see if she lived up to her billing.

Chapter Four

The call from Nick Vanetta put Lindsey off balance. She hadn't expected the deep voice with the unmistakable Texas drawl, a voice that tantalized even in a business-like tone. A voice that sent unexpected feathery shivers down her spine.

When Nick asked if he could see her right away, she almost said no. She still had reservations about bringing someone into her life this way. She wavered between panic and anger every time she thought of the situation but figured maybe Nick Vanetta could at least bring some professional perspective to this whole thing. And Quinn had scared her enough that she couldn't just blow off whoever was doing this. Swallowing her reservations, she told him to come on over.

If his voice had caught her off guard, his appearance when Brianna ushered him in startled her even more. Lindsey had heard women say they were struck dumb by a man's looks, but it had never happened to her. Certainly the men she'd known, the ones she'd been with, had been appealing and interesting, but none of them stunned her with their sexuality of dark good looks.

Thick dark hair, worn just a little long, framed a face so roughly masculine it made her catch her breath. Whiskey-brown eyes gazed at her with piercing intensity from beneath thick, black lashes. His warm, olive skin was clean-shaven, but the hint of darkness along his jaw line was a sign that before evening he'd need a razor again.

A custom linen dress shirt, well-tailored sports coat, and silk slacks hung perfectly on the hard muscled shape of his tall, broad-shouldered, football player's body. Despite his size, he made her think of a jaguar stalking through the jungle. The word *powerful* flashed across her mind. There was controlled authority in his body, and his presence literally filled the room. She sensed that beneath the extremely civilized exterior he presented, he could be a very dangerous man who quite literally took her breath away.

Damn! This man was sex on a stick, and she'd stayed away from that stick for a very long time. Heat surged through her body, firing her pulse into an erratic rhythm. Her beasts felt heavy, her nipples tingled, and her panties became suddenly damp. She wanted to squeeze her thighs together to still the throbbing in her sex.

Nick Vanetta should come wearing a sign that said *Beware.*

Damn!

She took a deep breath and, forcing a calmness she didn't feel, she rose and held out her hand to him. When he took it, a sudden wave of electricity crackled between them. If she hadn't seen the sudden flare of heat in his eyes, she might have thought he was unaffected. Uh oh.

She exhaled slowly, mentally pulled herself together, and retrieved her hand.

Thank god Nick was the disciplined professional, all business. He sat in the chair she indicated, his eyes focused on her, and crossed his legs, one ankle resting on the opposite knee.

Lindsey pushed her glasses up on her nose and gathered her scattered wits. “I appreciate you coming, Mr. Vanetta, but I was under the impression Guardian no longer did individual security work.”

Nick shrugged, a graceful masculine movement of muscles. “Quinn is a very good friend. He’d do the same for me. “

“I assume he’s told you everything?” she asked.

“Yes, but if you wouldn’t mind, maybe you could hit the highlights again for me.”

She blew out her breath in exasperation. “I’m probably making something out of nothing. And I’m not all that anxious to put my life in someone else’s control. Still, I’d like to find whoever this is and kick the sh—uh, stuffing out of him.”

She saw Nick smother a grin. But then his face sobered, and he listened carefully while she told her story again, asking only the occasional question.

As she talked, he made notes in a narrow leather folder he’d pulled from his breast pocket, interrupting now and then to ask a question. Quinn said he was the best. If she had to hire someone, that’s what she wanted.

“So what do you think?” she asked finally.

“I think I’ve seen too many cases like this to tell you it’s nothing. If we’re lucky, that’s exactly how it will turn out. But stalkers, and make no mistake, this is definitely a stalking situation, are unstable and unpredictable. And dangerous.”

She wet her bottom lip with her tongue. “Are you deliberately trying to scare me?”

His smile disappeared. “I’m trying to give you my professional assessment. The police can only do so much. With no real clues, they’re pretty much helpless until a real crime is committed. By that time, it will be too late to help you.”

Lindsey fidgeted with a pencil on her desk. “What do you suggest?”

“We’ve had cases like this before,” he told her. He went on to outline the precautions she could take for her safety. “But those won’t be enough. And they certainly won’t do anything to catch whoever is doing this.”

Lindsey gritted her teeth. “So basically what you’re telling me is, some maniac has taken control of my life and there’s nothing I can do about it.” She was flipping the pencil back and forth now, so hard the slightest snap would break it. She hated this whole thing.

Nick watched her through narrowed eyes. “That’s not what I’m saying at all. What we’re going to do is take some steps to bring that control back into our hands. Your hands.”

“Exactly how do we do that?” she wanted to know.

“To begin with,” he told her, “I want to install a top of the line alarm system in your office. The fact that there’s no guard on duty in the lobby during the day makes me nervous.”

“Does that include my apartment, too?” she asked.

“Absolutely. I’ll need the address.”

“It’s the same as this one, and it’s right next door to the office.” She almost laughed at the way he stared at her. “They’re connected by a single door.”

He stared at her. “You live in an office building?”

“Just occasionally. I have a ranch in Cibolo, not far from Quinn and Kate. But my hours are often irregular and it's not always convenient for me to make the drive during the week. Having a place right next to the office also means if I get the urge, I can get up and work in the middle of the night without having to cart files and supplies around."

He shook his head. "It's absurd as well as dangerous for you to live in a building with nobody in it at night except you."

"And the odd workaholic," she reminded him. "That's why they have a guard downstairs after six, so they can keep track of comings and goings."

A muscled ticked in Nick's jaw line. "Whatever we agree to, you still need the alarm, and what we use is the best available anywhere."

Lindsey worried her bottom lip a moment, flipping the pencil again. He was right about the alarm. Even without this stalker, she needed some kind of protection better than what the building supplied.

She dipped her head once. "Fine. I can't argue about that."

He blew out a soft breath. "We'll set up the alarm in both places, but the master panel will be in your office. I also plan to get a copy of the reports you filed and check out the pictures." He looked up at her with those piercing eyes. "I'm assuming you're agreeing to hire Guardian to handle this for you."

"I think Quinn would wring my neck if I don't." Her mouth relaxed into a semblance of a smile. "He's a very protective surrogate big brother. Neither of us has any family to speak of so we kind of formed our own." She wet her lips again. "And I appreciate you taking this on."

"No problem. But I should tell you beforehand that

we don't come cheap."

"Cost isn't a problem, Mr. Vanetta." Lindsey tamped down a flare of irritation. "I make a very comfortable living as an architect. If that's not enough assurance for you, my parents left me a trust fund that will handle just about anything you can bill."

"Hold it." He held up a hand. "I wasn't being insulting here. I just like to let prospective clients know what finances are involved. That's all. We do it with everyone. And as with other clients, I just like to make sure you know my services come with a fancy price tag."

"*Your* services?" He was doing this himself? The long-missing throbbing between her thighs collided with panic at the thought of having him so involved in her life.

I can't think about sex. I'm not sure I even know what it is anymore. But certainly not with Nick Vanetta. The damn danger sign is flashing big and bright.

He nodded. "Quinn is a very good friend. This isn't something I'm comfortable turning over to one of my men. And the alarm is only the beginning."

She finally tossed the pencil down, feeling her life spinning out of control. "What does *that* mean?"

"I want to scope out every facet of this building, check your friends, your acquaintances, and your clients. And keep an eye on you at the same time."

Lindsey sighed. This whole thing was going way beyond what she'd expected. If someone wanted to mess up her life, they were doing a damn good job of it. "Is there some way you can question these people without having to give them all the gory details?"

A muscle twitched in his cheek "We're very

discreet, I assure you. We've never had a complaint from a client yet."

"I'm sorry." She rubbed her forehead. She was certainly handling this all wrong. "That didn't come out right. This whole business has just unnerved me."

He nodded. "Understandable."

She picked up the pencil again, realized she probably looked like she was losing it so she stuck it in a holder. "So will you be the one running around with the questionnaire or trailing my body around?"

"I'll be assigning someone else to do the interviews, but I promise you they handle everything very discreetly. We're not novices." His gaze raked over her. "Unless you'd rather have someone else here with you and I can do the interviews"

"No, not at all." Her face heated up. The last thing she wanted to do was insult him. Quinn was right about this man. He definitely knew what he was doing.

"Then let's get started." He unfolded the mouth-watering length of him from the chair. "By the way, what did you tell your secretary about why we were meeting?"

"That I was consulting a security firm. Why? She's certainly aware of what's happening." Lindsey frowned. "Surely you don't think she or Mark, my draftsman, could be involved, do you? They're the ones who told me to call the police in the first place. And urged me to get protection."

Nick shook his head. "That doesn't necessarily mean anything, except that one of them could be a good actor. Come on. You can give me the guided tour."

She came around the desk and moved ahead of him, inhaling his way too sexy aftershave as she passed him.

Yes, Lindsey. Go bananas for this man.

But six long months had passed since her last attempt at a relationship—if that was what one could call it. She just hadn't realized how susceptible she was to someone. No, not someone. Nick Vanetta. She didn't know whether to thank Quinn or kill him.

In the reception area, she introduced him to Brianna, then led him to the workroom where he met Mark. He spent a few minutes with each, and she was impressed with the way he turned a casual conversation into a Q and A without the other person realizing it. When they were finished with the office, she unlocked the connecting door to her apartment and he followed her inside.

While she'd chosen vibrant colors for her office, exotic patterns and things to stimulate the mind, she'd used pale earth tones in her apartment to create a place of retreat. If Nick noticed the contrast, he gave no indication, just examined every inch of the place in the same methodical manner he'd used in her office. She also showed him the apartment's back exit, so she could leave without having to enter the office at all.

When she turned from the door to go back into the living room, he was standing so close she nearly bumped into him. That same sizzle crackled between them again. His eyes blazed into hers, and her throat was suddenly desert dry.

This is just so damn stupid.

For a moment, neither of them moved. Finally, with a supreme effort of will, she managed to sidestep slightly around him and head back toward her office. She hurried to her place behind her desk, determined to put some space between them.

"So what's our next move, Mr. Vanetta?" She lowered herself into her chair.

"You know, it would be a lot easier if you called me Nick." His mouth turned up in a lethally sexy grin. "And don't be offended if I call you Lindsey."

"That's not a problem." She gave him a weak smile. "My friends do."

"We're going to be seeing a lot of each other, so let's drop the formality, if you can live with that."

"Of course." *Oh, God. Trouble."*

He smiled back at her. "Good. I hope we'll be friends. It makes spending so much time together a lot easier."

Spending time together. Right. Maybe he'd turn out to have some really bad habits that drove her crazy.

Nick pulled out his cell phone and hit a number on speed dial, speaking so softly she could barely hear his words. Finally, he disconnected the call.

"A crew will be here shortly to start on the alarm system," he told her. "I'd like—"

He was interrupted by the buzz of the intercom on her desk.

Lindsey picked up her phone. "I'm here."

"I have the list of estimates you wanted on the Randolph changes. I know you're tied up, but you said you wanted these ASAP. What should I do with them?"

"Just bring the folder in and leave it with me. I'll get to it shortly."

"You go ahead with your work," Nick told her. "I have some calls to make while I wait for the crew to get here. Which should be very soon."

Brianna came in, gave Nick a hot onceover, and

handed a folder to Lindsey. Then she headed back to her desk, but she left the office door open.

Lindsey frowned. What was that all about? The woman knew to keep the door closed when she had someone in here. She'd have to ask her about it later.

Nick sat on the couch, making phone calls and speaking in very low tones, while she went to work on the estimates. It took all her efforts at concentration to focus on her work and not him.

She was partway through the documents when the corridor door opened and two men came in. Five-ten, muscular but not intimidatingly so, dark hair clipped short, they could have been clones of each other. They carried identical aluminum cases.

"Mr. Vanetta's expecting us," one of them said to Bri.

Nick rose from the couch and went to meet them.

"Come on in here, guys. I'll show you where to get started."

Lindsey tried to ignore them and focus again on the list Bri had given her. But after she'd gone over the same item several times, she finally gave up and slid it back into the folder. She tried studying some sketches but that didn't work, either. Somehow, even when he wasn't in the same room, Nick distracted her. He walked the two men through the office and apartment, talking to them as he went. That same low, quiet voice, deep and thick like warm honey sliding over a plate was like an undertone humming in her brain.

She looked up when he walked back into her office.

"The guys will go ahead and get started." Nick stood in front of her desk. "One more thing. I'm changing the locks on all your doors so they can only be accessed with key cards. Just you, Brianna, Mark, and I will have them. And Guardian will have a master key card."

"The building management frowns on not having access to all the offices," she told him. "In case of emergency."

"I'll take care of the management. That's part of what you're paying me for. Chuck and Allen here will be working around you. Just ignore them. I have to run back to the office. While I'm gone, try to keep working as if this is a normal day. I'll be back in about an hour with a contract for you to sign, and we'll go to lunch."

"Lunch?" She stared at him. "I usually have a sandwich sent in or grab something from the apartment."

"I need to go over the contract with you," he explained, "and I don't want anything going on here to distract you."

"Oh."

The expression in his eyes was serious, even though there was still heat simmering there. Or did she just imagine it?

"Lindsey." His voice was low and patient. "Right now there's someone out there who thinks he or she is running your life. When I said we were going to change that, I meant we were going to pass that control to me. I know what to do. You don't. You're going to pay a hefty price for my services, and I want to be sure you understand how thoroughly we're going to protect you."

She wasn't sure at the moment who was making her more insecure—the stalker or the bodyguard.

"All right, then. I'd better get to work"

"Good." He flashed a brief but still lethal smile. "I'll see you in an hour."

As soon as he left, she collapsed back into her chair. There were so many feelings boiling inside her she wasn't sure she knew what to do with them. After her last disaster, she had sworn off men, but of course, she hadn't expected someone like Nick Vanetta to walk into her life. She didn't know whether to thank Quinn or kill him.

She was still sitting in her chair, immobilized by her thoughts, when Brianna buzzed her. "What's with the hunk? Is he for real from a security agency?" She lowered her voice. "He can guard my body any time."

Lindsey sighed. She hoped she didn't have to give Brianna the lecture about professional behavior. "Come on in, and I'll explain in more detail."

Brianna's eyes were snapping with curiosity when she pulled up a chair. "Okay, give."

"You told me I needed protection," Lindsey said in a careful voice, "so I'm getting some. I ran all this by a very close friend who used to be a prosecutor, and he set up this appointment. The owners of Guardian Security are friends of his and top notch in their field."

Bri frowned. "Do you really think you need to go to such extremes?"

Lindsey studied the other woman. "Didn't you tell me I needed to take this seriously?"

"Well, yes, but…"

"But what? I'm doing it."

"Doing it how? Don't you think I should know?"

Quinn had cautioned her about sharing too many details with her staff. Just to be on the safe side. But

Lindsey had no doubts about either Brianna or Mark.

"For one thing, I'm putting in a security system. After the episodes with the photos and the way they were left here, I agreed it would be a good idea. Mr. Vanetta will make other suggestions as he assesses the situation. His primary focus will be my safety."

"Uh-huh." Brianna grinned. "That's why he looks at you like he'd like to devour you, right?"

"Bri, that's absurd." She made her voice as firm as possible, even as her pulse ratcheted up at every pulse point. "He does no such thing. And the fact that he's good-looking has no effect on the arrangement at all. Would you rather I look for someone who's ugly? I just want whoever will do the best job."

"Uh-huh," Bri repeated. "We'll see.

Too bad she was a great assistant and totally dependable, or Lindsey might have told her to mind her own business. But over the time they'd worked together, the formality of the arrangement had become blurred so she held her tongue. What made it worse was the way the whole situation irritated her. Why in hell had someone picked *her* to torment this way?

"This is business, Brianna, just like I said. Nothing more. So don't read something into it that isn't there." She sighed. "I'll go over the Randolph papers again and get them back to you."

The moment Brianna walked back to her own desk, Lindsey began furiously scribbling notes on a yellow pad. Damn Quinn anyway. Why couldn't he have sent her someone middle-aged and fat?

Chapter Five

Nick pulled out of the underground garage and headed toward the Interstate. If Quinn had been sitting next to him, he would have punched Nick's lights out for the thoughts running around in his head. Certainly he had to know he was sending Nick into a lion's den to tangle with a woman feisty as well as beautiful.

In person, Lindsey Ferrell far surpassed any photograph. No picture could do justice to the silken texture of her dark hair and the way it glinted in the light like warm brandy. Or the thick lashes framing those incredible, liquid hazel eyes made all the more interesting by the dark-framed glasses she wore. He'd never seen a woman look that sexy in glasses.

Her figure, though petite, was lushly full, and his hands almost itched to touch those curves, gently explore them. Even with her anger barely held in check, the fire that radiated from her intrigued him.

But her beauty was the least of it. She was sharp, talented, a woman with real substance. Lindsey Ferrell was an enigma and a paradox. And after only two hours, she was driving him crazy.

And damn it to hell. What was with the jolt of electricity that speared through him the minute they made contact? He'd been attracted to women before, but the heat that surged through him when he touched her hand eclipsed any prior feelings he'd had for any female.

This is crazy. She's a client. And a friend of a friend. Quinn will kill me if I so much as look at her sideways.

And why the hell do I even care? She's nothing like any of the women I date.

Maybe that was the root of problem. If he was smart, he'd turn this case over to one of his agents and keep out of it.

If he was smart.

He was still mumbling to himself when he stormed into his office.

"Bad client day?" a familiar voice asked. "Or bad woman day."

Nick looked up to see his partner, Reno Sullivan, lounging in the doorway. They'd been together for a long time now, building a company they started on a shoestring. Their efforts had not only garnered them a top notch reputation, but also made them both very rich. Now they had more business than they could handle, so what was he doing back playing bodyguard?

He didn't want to admit that, not only was their client beautiful, she was smart and more complex than she looked. Something he couldn't say about the women he usually played with.

"Remind me the next time Quinn asks me for a favor to tell him I'm fresh out, will you?" Nick grumped.

"And that is because…"

Briefly, Nick related the situation to him, sketching in the bare details.

"You're doing the bodyguard thing yourself?" Reno couldn't hide his surprise. "You haven't done that for more than five years."

"So what? You don't think I can do it anymore?"

Reno threw up his hands. "I think you can do whatever you want to do. Besides, I've been waiting to see how long you could take riding a desk. You've always wanted to be where the action is."

"Are you objecting?" Nick studied his partner.

"No. Far from it. As far as I'm concerned, you need to be where you do the best work, and that's in the field. We both know it."

"This could turn out be a nasty case, anyway." Nick was irritated that he felt he had to justify himself. "Besides, Quinn came to me personally. I don't feel comfortable just handing it off to one of the guys."

"Okay. I get where you're coming from. I'd do the same thing." Reno straightened up. "I'll let you do whatever you came in for. Just make sure we know where to get hold of you at all times."

"Don't worry. I still know the drill."

Instead of having his secretary fill in the contract for Lindsey Ferrell, Nick booted up his computer and began to complete the form himself. He knew exactly what he wanted in it, and he didn't want to have to answer anyone's questions. Thirty minutes later, he ripped the completed form out of the printer. He emailed Janet a copy for the file, attaching a summary of his tentative agenda. If she needed him, she could always call his cell.

His watch showed almost one hour later on the dot when he walked back into Lindsey's office, nodding at Brianna on his way through. Lindsey sat at her worktable, and for a moment, his breath caught at the sight of the sun shining on her glossy hair where it swept her shoulders, head bent, even white teeth denting her lower lip. Jesus. What was happening to him?

Mentally he shook himself out of his trance. "Ready for lunch?"

She jerked and almost dropped her pencil, so engrossed in her work she hadn't heard him come in. "My God, you nearly gave me a heart attack." She pushed her hair back behind her ears, a nervous gesture he'd noticed earlier. "Listen, Nick, I don't think I can go to lunch. I have to get these first sketches done for a new client. Really."

"*Really* you have to eat lunch," he told her. "Besides, I want to go over this contract with you and iron out the details, and this way we can do both things at once. Come on."

He picked up her purse from her desk, moved her off the chair at the drafting table, and handed her the purse in one smooth motion. When he cupped her elbow with a hand, he almost singed his palm on the heat that flared between them.

What the fuck?

"She'll be back after lunch," he told Brianna, towing Lindsey out the door.

Brianna just grinned.

"I have appointments," Lindsey protested as they moved down the hall to the elevator. "I have people to see and things to do."

"I checked your calendar earlier. You don't have an appointment until four o'clock. Who are the Romeros, anyway, and why does your secretary have a frown next to their name?"

"God, tell me she doesn't." Lindsey sighed. The

elevator door slid open, and they stepped inside. "We designed a home for them, and they want me to meet with their builder. I know it's because they want nine million changes, and they don't want to pay for them. They think I can talk to him and see if we can alter the design to accommodate them. They are, um, somewhat difficult people."

"No kidding." He chuckled. "I hope you don't have too many frowns in your date book."

"I'll have to say something to Bri. If the clients see that, they'll be very offended."

They were out on the sidewalk now. Nick had a long stride, and even though he had hold of her arm again, she almost had to jog to keep up with him. She barely paid attention to where they were going until they had covered several blocks, and he finally stopped and opened a door for her.

"We're going in here?" she asked in amazement.

"Something wrong with this place?" The Grille, a new restaurant on the Riverwalk, had developed a reputation for its excellent food and its astronomical prices. "They have very good food. And quick service."

"I just thought we'd grab a sandwich or something. I really need to get back to the office."

"You really need to go over this contract with me, so you'll know exactly what your security options are. Come on. We'll eat fast."

She was about to protest again, but before she could say anything else, they were seated at a table and menus had been placed in front of them. They'd been given a window table with a view overlooking the narrow winding San Antonio River and the Riverwalk that bordered it. Tourists and locals combined to form a colorful pedestrian parade past the window.

"This is a great view," she told him, unfolding the napkin.

"I love the view." He looked out the window at the crowds hurrying by, people going to and from work, people lunching, tourists eating and shopping. There was always something so festive about the Riverwalk. He'd hoped bringing Lindsey here would get her to relax, but she was still wound up tighter than a drum. He had an insane desire to take her home with him, remove all those clothes from her very tempting body, and kiss every inch of her to get her to relax. Too bad his thoughts didn't make *him* relax. Or his cock, which was pressing against his fly, demanding its freedom.

Lindsey shook her head at the offer of a glass of wine. "I never drink anything when I'm working. It clouds my brain."

"Good." He grinned. "I rarely drink at all so we should make a great couple."

"You rarely drink?" Her eyes widened.

He nodded. "The business I'm in, if I'm not alert every minute it might mean someone's life. I made my choice a long time ago. I like a glass of wine now and then, but liquor doesn't actually appeal to me." He opened his menu. "What appeals to you?"

Yes, Lindsey, tell me what you like so I can make sure to give it to you in a way you'll never forget.

What the fuck? This was not him at all. He wanted to bang his head against the table.

She ordered a salad for lunch, and Nick asked for a small steak, rare. While they ate, he kept the conversation as light as possible in an obvious effort to get her to relax. He talked about himself, his degrees from the University of Texas, his family—four brothers and two sisters, all scattered around Texas.

"My parents live in Austin," he told her. "In the house where we grew up."

"They sound like a big, warm, noisy family." She almost but not quite hid the wistfulness and envy obvious in her voice and on her face. "I loved my parents a lot, but I'd give anything to have that kind of family."

He cocked an eyebrow. "No relatives at all?"

She shrugged. "None that I've ever been told about. I kept asking my mother, but somehow she always dodged the questions."

"You think there's some deep, dark family secret?" He was only half teasing. Was there something in her past she didn't know about that had suddenly, for no apparent reason, popped up in her life? Another avenue he'd have to look into. They had people at the agency who could find a relative from the Stone Age.

When the waiter set their coffee in front of them and discreetly moved away, Nick pulled an envelope from his pocket, took out the contract he'd prepared, and began to go over it with her.

The first two pages were standard, and she just nodded at the wording. But on page three she got to a clause and stopped, staring over the table at him. "You're going to be with me all the time?"

"Yes." He nodded. "That's correct." Every. Single. Minute. How the hell he was going to survive that he didn't know at the moment.

"But—but—what about at night? What about when I go to sleep?"

She frowned at him, a delicate blush coloring her

face. He didn't remember the last time he'd seen a woman blush. Of course, the women he hung out with—

"Nick?"

He realized with a start he was staring at her.

This is getting more complicated by the minute. Being with her at night could prove...difficult. I can do it, though. I'm a professional, right?

"Not to worry." He smiled. "I always figure something out."

She froze in her chair. "I didn't realize this would be...that is...I mean...I'm sorry. This is obviously a big mistake." She tossed her napkin on the table and jumped up, nearly upsetting the table. "Don't worry. I'll call Quinn and tell him I'm the one who made the decision."

She hurried through the restaurant and was out on the street before he caught up with her. He reached out and closed his hand over her arm, forcing her to stop and turn to him.

"I'm sorry, Lindsey." He wanted to tell her it would be all better, even though he knew he'd be lying. "I know situations like this can be overwhelming. I'm just so anxious to make sure we're taking every precaution necessary that I probably came at you like a freight train.

Lindsey made an obvious effort to pull herself together. "I'm so sorry. I almost never fall apart like this."

Maybe it's long overdue.

He turned her to face him head-on. "Why don't we go back to your office? Maybe you can have your assistant carve out some quiet time. We can sit down in your apartment, and I can answer all your questions. About this."

Lindsey let out a slow breath and curved her lips in an obviously forced smile. "O—Okay. That sounds like a good place to start."

At her nod, he took her arm again and started walking. "I don't want to frighten you unnecessarily, but situations like this can escalate quickly. I only want what's best for you. Otherwise, I wouldn't be doing my job, right?"

She nodded and let him lead her along the sidewalk. One tiny bullet dodged

But when they got back to her office, the question of signing the contract or not had been taken out of her hands.

****

I'm still watching you, bitch. You don't even know it's me. Everything you do. Every place you go. Everyone you talk to. You think you're so damn high and mighty. Let me tell you, it isn't that far for you to fall from that throne. And I'm going to be the one to push you.

But not until you beg me to leave you alone. Not until I put a few scars on that perfect face of yours. God, wouldn't I just love to get my hands around your neck and squeeze as hard as I could.

The camera captures it all, every second of your life. Standing still, walking along the street, working in your office. Every little detail. You can't escape me. I am everywhere.

You have a new message waiting for you, Lindsey. Will your heart pound when you see it? Your pulse race? Will the terror start to eat at you more? I must

control the rage. Rage that you feed. Wait until you are so terrified you will beg me to kill you. But this will be enough for now, to let you know I am everywhere. No one can protect you from me.

You think that man can save you? Don't make me laugh. I can deal with him easily. I'm invisible, so I can strike when no one's looking. Then you'll be alone, just like I've been for so long. Without anyone. How do you think you'll like that?

Be careful, bitch! Your time is coming.

****

Brianna pounced on Lindsey the moment she and Nick walked through the door.

"Mark has some questions on that project you gave him." Her voice was breathless, as if she'd been running, but her eyes were fastened avidly on Nick. "And the Romeros called to confirm they'd be bringing their builder at four. But—" She smiled. "—no more mysterious envelopes."

"Good. Let's hope it stays that way."

Lindsey headed for her computer to check emails before sitting down with Nick. She'd behaved idiotically, and she knew it. She'd be lucky if he didn't throw up his hands and tell Quinn he could find someone else to watch over this idiot woman. Only everything seemed to be choking her, and letting a strange man into her life and allowing him to take control of it was somehow frightening. Of course, if she had to do it, Nick Vanetta, who projected a feeling of rock solid security—besides being sinfully sexy—wouldn't be a bad choice.

While she booted up her computer, Nick went to see how the installation of the alarm system was coming along. She could hear him in her apartment talking to his men as she idly scrolled through her emails. When the last one opened on her screen, she froze in shock.

"Nick!" she screamed, unable to tear her eyes away from the image. "Nick, come here right away. Please."

She was still staring at the screen, feeling as if every drop of blood had drained from her body when Nick raced in. He moved her gently aside to get a better look at the monitor.

The body of an email was filled with a photo of Lindsey. Below it were the words, "Have a good night's sleep. I'm watching you." The picture showed her in a long T-shirt standing in her living room. The camera had captured the full length of her body as she reached up to close the drapes. A very intimate photo…and obviously meant to be just that.

"My God. My God," she whispered over and over again. "He can find me anywhere. He's invading every bit of my life. Is there any place he can't go? Damn." She dropped into her desk chair, sure her legs wouldn't hold her upright much longer, and raked her fingers through her hair.

Nick was already at her computer when Brianna and Mark rushed into her office.

"What happened?" Bri asked. "What's wrong?" She looked from Lindsey to Nick. "Did someone send you something?"

Nick turned the computer so she could see the photo.

Brianna shivered. "Whoever this is, you can see he's making it more personal, Lindsey. How creepy to think he can actually see into your apartment."

"You should call that police detective again," Mark told her. "Let him know about this."

"I'll take care of it," Nick assured them in a tight voice. "This gives me a good chance to connect with him, although I'm not sure what he can do. Brianna, how about bringing your boss a cup of coffee? Then you can both get back to what you were doing until McCune gets here."

"But—" Mark started to protest.

"Just do it please," Lindsey told them in a tired voice. "Please."

"Coffee coming right up." Bri shooed Mark out ahead of her and closed the door.

"Who did you think this email was from when you opened it?" Nick gently moved Lindsey away from the computer and over to the couch.

"I get several mails from professional organizations." Lindsey twisted her hands together. "This one said it was from the San Antonio Architects Association."

"Okay. Someone's clever enough to know how to mimic an IP address, which means this is no dummy we're dealing with."

Great. Just great.

"I don't know if that's good or bad." Her laugh was edged with hysteria.

"It just makes them harder to catch, but not impossible." Nick went back to her computer, tapped on the keyboard, then came to sit beside her. "Just give me a minute to make some calls. Will you be okay?"

She didn't want him to leave her side. She wanted his strength and power to surround and protect her. There was something intangible about him, about his presence, that made her believe she could trust him with her life. After all, wasn't that what she needed to do? And to quit avoiding the real issues?

"Yes." She wet her lips and sat up straight. "But I think I need to sign that contract right now."

He nodded, his expression solemn. "Let me make these calls, and we'll take care of it."

His first call was to McCune, the second to his office to tell them what he needed and to get things moving. The next was to his IT department to start tracing the origin of the email right away. He didn't like what this newest photo indicated, the angle and type of the shot showing how completely vulnerable to the stalker's intrusion Lindsey was.

Brianna returned with the coffee and set it on the little table in front of the couch.

Nick helped Lindsey wrap her fingers around the cup. "Think you can hold onto this?"

She nodded, dredging up a poor excuse for a smile. "I promise not to spill it on you. Or myself. I still have clients coming, remember?"

"About that," he began.

Lindsey shook her head. "No cancelling appointments. I won't let whoever this is turn my life upside down any more than he already has."

"Okay. I'll go along with that. For now. But I'm sitting in on the meetings, so you figure out some plausible excuse for me to be here."

"I hate this." Lindsey gripped the coffee cup as if it were a lifeline.

"He's playing with your mind, you know." Nick's voice was deliberately low and calm. "That's the best weapon he has right now. It's what gives him his thrill."

"Then I need to act as if he's not bothering me at all." And somehow she would. She'd find the strength to do exactly that. Her chin came up in a small gesture of defiance. "I can be a really good actress, and I'm pissed that someone thinks they can insinuate themselves into my life this way."

His mouth turned up in a slow smile that threatened to melt her panties. "I'm sure you can."

A thought struck her that ramped her anxiety back up. "You don't think he'll try to harm me physically, do you? What does he really want? To kill me? And why, for god's sake. You're going to find out what a really boring life I lead."

"It's too early to know that. Right now, he's frightening you by showing how close he can actually get without you seeing him. He's enjoying that. This is just the beginning of his campaign. We still don't know what he really wants. Or she."

"You think it could be a woman?" Frantically, Lindsey tried to run through names of women who might hate her this much. "Who have I made so angry with me? Who would hate me this much? I can't even."

"Again, it's too early to tell." He focused that dark gaze on her. "You know, it's very possible this could turn out to be someone you barely know. Someone who's developed a fixation on you."

"Oh, great. I don't know if that's better or worse." She took a sip of the hot liquid and set the cup down on the coffee table. "You're doing a lot on faith, aren't you? Where's that contract I asked for before? I want to sign it right now. This guy scares me, and I don't know where he'll intrude next."

"I wasn't worried." Nick smiled, pulled the

contract from his pocket, and handed it to her with a pen.

"Well, just to make it all legal and everything." She signed all the places he indicated, made copies at the small machine she kept behind her desk, then unlocked a drawer and took out a checkbook. She didn't even cringe at the amount of the retainer or hourly fee. Money wasn't a factor here. She filled out a check and handed it to him.

"This is out of my trust account, not the one for the business," she pointed out. "Maybe I'm getting paranoid, but I don't want anyone in the office to see the contract or the checks."

"Smart move," he told her. "At least until everyone is cleared. You're fortunate to have that financial cushion."

She couldn't tell if he was being sarcastic or not.

"My father left the trust fund for my mother and me." She stared straight at him. "It paid for my college education and gave us a nice cushion for the ranch operation if we needed it. It also paid for my mother's nursing care when she had her heart attack and stroke. I don't squander it. I worked hard for my degree and harder for recognition. That trust fund is for emergencies, which I'm sure you'd agree this is, and that's all I use it for."

"I meant exactly what I said." He looked at her with a steady expression. "You're lucky. Not everyone is that fortunate. That's all."

Quit being so sensitive, Lindsey.

Nick took the check, his fingers touching hers for a long minute, and just like that the heat was there again, replacing the cold. She snatched her hand away.

"Besides," he went on, ignoring her knee-jerk reaction, "I happen to know you have an excellent reputation as an architect and your clients sing your praises. You're smart and very together. Quinn has a lot of respect for you, and that's enough for me."

She took a deep breath and tried on a smile. "All right. And thank you for just…being you, I guess. Quinn was right. You're very good."

Nick laughed out loud. "You'll get through this just fine. My money's on you. One more question. Is your email address known openly, or is it a hard commodity to come by?"

"It's on all my business cards, so probably a million people have it."

"Let me check something here."

Nick sat down at the computer again and scrolled through the email still up on the screen. Then he printed out two copies, folded them, and put them in his pocket.

"Okay." He backed away from her desk. "McCune was tied up so he won't be here until later. Meanwhile, you need to get ready for your clients." He grinned. "But I'll be just a scream away."

"Let's hope I don't have anything else to scream about today."

He went through the connecting door to her apartment while she pulled out folders for her meeting.

****

Nick dialed his office and had Janet transfer him to the techie he'd sent the email to.

"Anything on that email I sent you?" he asked.

"Jesus, Mr. Vanetta," the guy protested. "I need a little more than five minutes. I'm working on it right now."

"Okay. I just want to make sure you know this is high priority."

The man gave a sound between a laugh and a snort. "You mean like everything else around here? Okay, okay, I'm really on top of it."

"I want you to trace the address and get me the Internet service provider of the sender. Find out how they could mimic the address they used."

"Call you as soon as I have it," the man assured him.

"Sooner rather than later, okay?"

"Yes. Okay. I got it."

Next, he called Quinn, catching him just as he was leaving his office, and filled him in on what had happened so far.

"Do whatever it takes." Quinn was instantly alert. "Just make sure no harm comes to Lindsey. Period. And listen. If you need my help, just ask, okay?"

"And have Kate after me?" Nick laughed. "No deal, buddy. Thanks, anyway. But I will keep you in the loop."

Finally, he called Reno. "I'm flagging this as a high profile case and committing resources to it. We've got a fat retainer, and I gather the fee is no problem. I'll be on this twenty-four/seven. I just wanted to let you know."

"Your decision," Reno told him. "Sounds like whoever this is has stepped it up a notch."

"Yeah. I'm worried about what might come next. Ferrell Designs is becoming a hot item with people building homes in the Hill Country, and the buzz about her is terrific. I don't want to be the one who lets some jerk bring it all down around her."

“Do whatever it takes,” Reno assured him. “Just be sure to keep us in the loop.”

While he waited for Lindsey to prepare for her client meeting, Nick checked out the view from the huge wall of windows in the living room and the angles of the buildings that faced the apartment. Guardian had sent a team to canvass the hotel, checking the logical floors and seeing what they could pry loose from the front desk. Nick called them twice to see what they’d found, but none of the information they gave him was any good. A lot of the rooms that fit the profile were vacant. If the stalker knew his stuff, he could have found a way to sneak into one of those rooms and snap his dirty little pictures.

Well, however he had to do it, he’d keep her safe. Lindsey Ferrell was more than just a client, although he’d known her for less than a day. From the moment he’d walked into her office, there’d been a visceral connection. She felt it, too, although she did her best to hide it. He was damn good at his job and had a list of testimonials to prove it. But he’d never wanted to protect a client more than this one.

His feelings baffled him and made him uncomfortable, but there they were. They weren’t going away. First he’d find this fucking stalker, and then he’d see where things went with Lindsey Ferrell.

When Nick let himself quietly back in, Briana was ushering in a well-dressed middle-aged couple with another man right on their heels. Because he didn’t want to leave Lindsey alone, even in her office, Nick had prodded her to come up with some kind of vague reason for him to be there.

“A consultant, maybe?” he’d suggested.

"Let's hope these people are naïve enough to buy that," she told him with a touch of sarcasm.

"We'll make them buy it," he insisted.

Lindsey made brief introductions. "Mr. and Mrs. Romero," she told him. "And Jordan Delaney, their builder. Mr. Vanetta is doing some consulting for me, so I hope it's all right for him to sit in on our meeting."

Nick nodded at everyone and tried to make himself as unobtrusive as possible in a corner.

Brianna returned with a tray of coffee and pastries, setting it on the low table in front of the couch. When everyone had served themselves, Lindsey opened the file on her desk and began the discussion.

Nick watched her work with sharp interest. She definitely knew her stuff. Her questions impressed him, her answers to both the builder and her clients even more. She pointed out where they could accommodate some of the changes with minor design adjustments at no additional expense. For the others, she explained why there would be a cost added. The builder also seemed impressed and agreed with nearly everything she said.

It was obvious the Romeros had expected to play Lindsey and Delaney against each other, and she'd neatly sidestepped their plan. He was amazed at how together she was considering the situation. His admiration for her was growing exponentially. This was indeed a very special, very unique woman.

At last, she deftly drew the meeting to a close, exchanging smiles with everyone.

"I'll have an addendum drawn up for each of you to sign," she said, rising to shake hands with each of them in turn. "Thank you all for coming in today."

She was so gracious about it that, when her clients left, they didn't even know they'd been hustled right out the door. Nick had to stifle a laugh.

****

As soon as everyone left, Lindsey made notes in the folder and buzzed Brianna to come in.

"Have this ready for me to go over first thing in the morning," she told her assistant.

Bri stood there for a moment, studying Lindsey. "You okay?"

"Fine, fine." She ran her hands through her hair, shoving it away from her face, and pushing her glasses up on her nose. "Just ready to end the day."

Mark brought in some sketches to be checked. They chatted about them for a moment before Lindsey put them on her worktable.

"I'll go over them again in detail tomorrow," she assured him.

At last, everyone was gone. Lindsey slumped down on the couch, pushed her hair behind her ears, leaned her head back, and closed her eyes. "All I want at this particular moment is to go to sleep and wake up when everything is over."

"I'd like to say your day is over," Nick told her, "but you have one more thing to do."

"What?" She asked the question in a voice edged with fatigue and pushed herself upright. The dull ache in her head that had been building earlier now seemed to be spreading its wings. "Oh, damn. McCune."

Nick nodded. "He'll be here in a few minutes. He's had his men checking out sites where the photographer could have been, and we're going to compare notes."

"Okay." She rubbed her forehead. "Just let me take

some aspirin and wash my face."

When McCune arrived and heard what Nick had to see, he agreed the stalker had been in the hotel that backed up directly to Lindsey's building. From the angle of the shot, the police as well as Nick's men had even figured out which floor was used.

"I don't know if that's much help," McCune began when his cell rang, interrupting him. He spoke briefly, then shook his head. "That was the team I had checking all the rooms that were possibilities. They came up with exactly what I expected. Every one of them had new occupants."

"Same here," Nick told him. "My guys have been pulling copies of the registration cards, and we'll check them out, but that will take time and I think it's probably a dead end."

"We can help, but I tend to agree with you."

"Great," Lindsey sighed. "Just great."

"I'd be sure and keep those drapes closed at all times," McCune cautioned.

"No kidding." Lindsey rubbed her forehead, wishing the aspirin would kick in.

"Sorry for the lack of progress, Miss Ferrell," McCune told her. "But I assure you, we'll keep at it." He nodded at Nick. "And we'll coordinate with the Guardian people."

It was obvious to Lindsey that Nick's presence gave the case an entirely different priority as far as McCune was concerned.

It's not what you know. It's who.

"Thanks." Nick gestured toward the outer office. "Come on, I'll walk you to the door. I need to lock up and set the alarm, anyway."

In seconds, she heard Nick's footsteps on the carpeting.

"Lindsey?"

She was still sitting on the couch, head leaned back again, her eyes closed. "Mmm? What?"

His warm hand closed over hers, flooding her with a feeling of sanctuary. Of protection. *Of trust.*

"Come on, get up. We're leaving."

"No, no, no," she moaned. "Can't I just roll through the door into my bed and go to sleep?"

"Nope. No can do. For one thing, the alarm system isn't complete. The techno twins will finish tonight and then meet us here in the morning with the key cards and the codes. We'll get here before anyone else does."

"Where are we going?" she asked, almost too tired to even care

"We're going out to your ranch. No way am I letting you stay here tonight, even with my diligent guard duty. Anyway, you need a change of scenery." One corner of his mouth kicked up in a smile. "I assume you have more than one bedroom there?"

He has the sexiest smile I've ever seen. Holy shit! What is wrong with me?

Lindsey shook herself back to reality but couldn't help smiling back. "You can even take your pick. Let me call Mary and tell her we're on the way, though. She thought I'd be staying in town tonight. She'll be ecstatic to have someone besides me to feed."

"I think it's best if you leave your car here," Nick told her. "I'm sure whoever's stalking you has it identified and will be watching for it."

Lindsey shivered, her stomach tightening in a knot. "You think so?"

"It's entirely possible. Anyway, we're not taking chances. I'll drive. You can direct me. Come on." He pulled her to her feet. "Let's get out of here."

With her hand firmly in his warm one, Lindsey felt safe and protected. Nick was smart, savvy, solid, and she'd bet, fearless. She'd be well taken care of.

Chapter Six

"Are you sure we need all this cloak and dagger stuff?" Lindsey frowned at Nick as he explained what he was going to do.

"Always better to be sure," he told her. "I want to see if there's anyone out there showing special interest in me."

"But why would this…person target *your* car?"

"He—or she—could have seen me going in and out of your office," he explained. "Maybe watched to see what car I got into. Let's just do it my way this time, okay?" He winked, easing the severity of his statement.

Lindsey sighed and made herself almost invisible in the elevator alcove while Nick drove around the garage by himself two or three times.

His precautions reminded her—as if she needed reminding—that someone was out there with a camera trained on her, maybe capturing her every move. She was glad when, at last, Nick pulled his SUV right up to the elevator door in the garage. She jumped into the vehicle, and he drove up the ramp to the street.

Adjusting her seat belt, she settled herself in place more comfortably. "I'm surprised that you drive a big SUV. I wouldn't think this kind of vehicle was your style."

"Oh?" He turned to her, but the aviator-style sunglasses he wore blocked his eyes. "Just out of curiosity, what did you think I drove?"

"Mmm, maybe a racy red sports car or a black Corvette. Something along that line."

"Those are great cars," he agreed, "but not very practical in my line of work. For one thing, they're too visible and easy to spot. For another, I need something that can go off road and also carry a lot of gear when necessary. All the agency cars are SUVs except for two pickups." A grin teased the corners of his mouth. "Think this doesn't suit my image?"

Lindsey could feel her face flush with embarrassment and stared straight out through the windshield. "I'm sorry. That was a stupid remark."

"Not at all. I get the same thing from our friend Quinn. He loves to give me a hard time, too."

"I'm not giving you a hard time," she protested. "Seriously, Nick. That was a stupid thing for me to say. I owe Quinn big time for sending you to me."

"The pleasure is all mine," he assured her and reached over to squeeze her hand.

She slid a glance at him, but didn't pull her hand away. Something was definitely happening here, something that excited her and at the same time made her afraid. Her track record with relationships was poor to say the least. On the other hand, she'd never met a man like Nick Vanetta. There was definite sexual sizzle between them, but also, she thought—hoped—a mutual respect. She just hoped she wasn't reading something into it because her emotions were upside with the stalker.

"Don't you need to get some clothes or something to take with you?" They'd headed directly out onto the Interstate.

He grinned and pointed a thumb toward the back of the vehicle. "I'm like the Boy Scouts, always prepared. Seriously, I never know when I might have to get on a plane or drive somewhere. So a long time ago, I got in the habit of keeping a travel case packed and ready. What we call a go bag."

"Oh."

They drove on in a comfortable stillness broken only by her directions until the ranch came into view.

If Lindsey had asked for a better picture to show off her home on first sight, she couldn't have gotten one. The setting sun bathed the house and surrounding land in a golden glow. Several of the horses were out in the penned area, nibbling at the grass. The soft breeze made the prairie grasses dance slightly, and all around the house, where Mary Medana had scattered seeds, bluebonnets and Indian paintbrush were just beginning to bloom.

Lindsey felt herself relax completely for the first time that day.

****

Nick pulled into the graveled parking area in front of the house, turned off the engine, and sat for a moment, staring at the view. He'd been a lot of places and seen a lot of views that took his breath away. But this? This was better than a tranquilizer. He didn't know how Lindsey ever left it to go into the city. "I think wow is too inadequate."

Beside him, Lindsey laughed, the first relaxed sound she'd made all day.

"Everyone says that the first time they see it. I think it's what sold my folks on it to begin with."

He pointed to an older couple who had come out to

stand on the porch, shameless in their interest. "Your guard dogs?"

Lindsey laughed again, and it struck Nick what a musical sound it was and how it could soothe even the most frazzled nerves. He'd love to have it soothe his nerves forever.

Hold on, buddy boy. Aren't you the confirmed bachelor? And by the way, right now she's a client. Let's save her ass first, okay?

"I think you're about to face the Inquisition," she told him. "You're the first person I've brought to the house—except for Kate and Quinn—in a long time, and their curiosity is killing them."

"That's interesting." Nick looked at her. "You don't bring anyone out here? None of your…friends?"

"No." She released the seat belt and climbed out of the SUV, the one word reply leaving no room for further discussion.

Nick tucked that away in his mind for future questioning. What kind of person never brought friends home with them? Even *he* had company once in a while, although he made it a rule not to bring any of his women into his personal space. He considered it too intimate. They left lingering traces of their presence that he didn't want to deal with.

He got out of the vehicle and followed Lindsey up the porch steps, carrying the small leather suitcase he'd retrieved from the back storage area.

"Hi, guys." She hurried up to the porch and hugged the waiting couple, then waved casually in his direction. "This is Nick Vanetta. Nick, come on and meet Ruben and Mary Medana, my family." She turned back to the man and woman. "Like I said when I called, he's doing some…work for me and will be spending the night."

Everyone did the polite thing, but Nick could tell the couple was biting back questions.

"Lindsey, honey, take Mr. Vanetta upstairs and get him settled," Mary ordered. "Put him in your old room. It's always ready for company, and nobody's stayed there since you did all that redecorating."

"Oh, I don't think—"

"And it's got its own bathroom," Mary continued, firm in her directions. She turned back to the house, giving Lindsey no opportunity to argue further.

Nick grinned at Lindsey, smothering a laugh. "I'll bet all the other guys will be jealous when I tell them I slept in your bedroom."

Lindsey didn't answer him, just marched up the stairs with her back ramrod stiff, fire sizzling from her body. Nick restrained himself from laughing. Apparently she didn't take orders well from *anyone*. Or teasing.

She ushered him into a huge room with windows that had a sweeping view of the meadows and a sitting area in front of a small fireplace. The walls were a soft shade of green, the carpet an ivory shade, and one wall was covered with wallpaper scattered with bluebonnets.

"Not bad," Nick said, dropping his suitcase next to the bed. "The ranching business must be good."

"My folks built this house when they moved here more than thirty years ago," she explained. "Apparently, my dad had investments that did really well or something. He bought the land, built the house, and went into the horse breeding business."

"Not cattle?" He raised an eyebrow.

"He said he always had a yen for horses, and

whatever he did, the business has always been profitable."

Nick started to comment, then changed his mind. He really needed to do some detailed research on the family to satisfy his curiosity about her before he said anything else.

"I'm going to change," she told him. "If you keep anything besides suits in that bag, you might want to do the same. The atmosphere is kind of hard on silk out here."

"I think I might be able to dress down," he told her with another grin. "I'll do my best."

She stood at the door, tugging at her lower lip with her teeth, her forehead wrinkled. "I haven't said anything to either Ruben or Mary about this stuff yet, so they probably think I brought you out here for other reasons. We'll tell them right after dinner. They need to be aware of what's going, and I sure don't want them getting the wrong idea about your visit. See you downstairs in a few minutes."

Nick wouldn't have minded a bit if they were out here for something other than business. The more time he spent with Lindsey Ferrell, the more he got to know her, the more he was drawn to her. He enjoyed women, no question about it, but forming attachments wasn't his style. Even in bed, he always held himself apart, his sexual calisthenics almost a dispassionate performance.

Until now.

Lindsey Ferrell was a different breed altogether. Whatever it was drawing them together made him edgy, knocking down barriers he usually kept firmly in place. He couldn't keep himself from imagining her in bed, wild and hungry and responsive. He wondered if he could convince her to keep her glasses on.

Jesus, Vanetta. Cut it out. She's off limits.

Nick could tell she was as determined as he was to keep this thing on a professional basis and try to ignore the heat blossoming between them. But he had an uneasy feeling they were quickly reaching a tipping point that neither could ignore. His brain told him to call the office and get someone else out here, but his body was winning that fight.

When he came downstairs, she was waiting on the porch for him. Her tight jeans and T-shirt, clinging to a finely toned body that was obviously accustomed to a lot of exercise, were far more revealing than her proper business suit. Nick had to fist his hands to tamp down the lust that threatened to rise up and embarrass him.

****

Lindsey's eyes skimmed over Nick. Worn jeans and a T-shirt clung softly to the muscular line of his body. Dressed up or dressed down, he was the most sinfully sexy man she'd ever met, and that alone made him dangerous. She'd have to be very careful. Her trust only extended so far. If they acted on whatever this *thing* was between them and he turned out to be like all the other men, more interested in proliferating their genetics, she wasn't sure she could handle it.

"Dinner will be a little while yet." She handed him a glass of iced tea. "Mary decided you needed more than the salad she figured I'd want, so she's pulling out all the stops. Would you like to have a look around while we're waiting?"

"Thanks, that would be great." His warm molasses voice rolled over her.

At the paddock, she stopped and whistled for

Jingo, who trotted up to the fence. The animal nickered softly and rubbed his nose against her outstretched hand as Lindsey made the introductions between horse and man. Then she led the way through the stable, the barns, the breeding barn, and the indoor exercise ring.

Nick shook his head. "This is an extensive operation. Somehow I had the idea you kept a few pleasure horses and that was it."

She slid a glance at him. "Shows what happens when you make snap judgments. Breeding and training cutting horses is a big business around here. I guess my father made a smart decision, because we've always done very well." She pointed to a medium-sized house about four hundred yards from the main house. "That's where Ruben and Mary live."

"Not in the house with you?" The fact surprised him.

Lindsey shook her head. "In the very beginning, when they first came to work for my folks, they were a lot younger, and I guess they figured they'd have kids and raise them out here. That's the way it is on many of the ranches in Texas. But they never had kids of their own, which is too bad. If ever people were meant to have children it's those two."

"But what about after your father died?" Nick persisted. "Wouldn't it have been better for them to move in with you and your mom? More protection and closer if you needed them?"

"I would have thought so, and Mom tried to talk them into it time and again." She shrugged. "But they're very specific about keeping 'their house' and 'the big house' separate. Besides, I think they like their own privacy. Who can blame them?"

"Dinner in a few minutes," Mary called as Nick and Lindsey came back into the house.

"Okay," Lindsey answered. "We're definitely ready. Come on," she told Nick. "We've just got time for the nickel tour of the house."

Nick carefully noted every detail, not just in case of trouble, but because it gave him a sense of Lindsey as a person. Twenty-four hours ago, he hadn't even met her and already he hungered for every piece of information about her. He always liked to get a complete picture of the client because it often helped to pinpoint where trouble came from, but this was different. Personal feelings were unexpectedly creeping in, and the possibilities both enticed and terrified him.

The house was comfortable, large without being pretentious, built for relaxed and happy living. A huge fireplace dominated one wall in the great room, with floor-to-ceiling bookshelves on another. A door in one corner led to a little home office, most of it taken up by an old-fashioned desk and a computer setup. It was a place that instantly made a visitor feel relaxed.

And everywhere he looked, there were pictures. Lindsey at various ages—swimming, horseback riding, sitting on the paddock fence, graduating from high school, from college. They reinforced his impression that this was a complex woman with many layers to her. A woman you didn't just rush into your bed and send on her way when the heat died down. This was a woman you built a real relationship with, something Nick had always avoided. Why, then, was he even thinking about it now?

He moved on to other pictures. A young Lindsey with a good-looking couple he guessed were her parents. In later years, Lindsey with her mother. He felt a strange sadness for her that someone who obviously reveled in family life now had none of her own. She would love the Vanetta family. Maybe when this was all over he could introduce her to them.

Now there's a scary thought.

But it lodged in the back of his mind like a barnacle on a ship, reminding him of his earlier musings. He was wading in dangerous waters.

The large kitchen had a welcoming and cheerful feel to it. And the aromas blending in the air made Nick's mouth water the minute he entered the room. He took the seat next to Lindsey, his stomach definitely ready for the feast on the table. Crispy fried chicken, fluffy mashed potatoes, corn casserole, and homemade biscuits were passed around. Dessert was an apple pie with crust so flaky it melted on the tongue.

****

Lindsey finally began to relax when she saw how easily Ruben and Mary accepted Nick and how comfortably he fit in with them. Their instincts were usually good, and she cared about their opinion. If they smelled trouble, the door slammed shut. She wanted the Medanas' stamp of approval on the man who was hopefully going to get her out of this mess. Maybe this would work out after all, having yet another stranger invade her life.

Still, she wasn't looking forward to telling Ruben and Mary the real reason for his visit.

"Heavy thoughts?" Nick asked as Mary cleared away dessert.

Lindsey roused herself. "No. Just taking a moment to regroup."

When they were sitting with refills of coffee, Ruben looked evenly at Lindsey. "It's nice that you brought someone home for a change, honey, but I get the feeling this isn't a social visit. You want to tell us what's really going on?"

"You're right. There's nothing social about it." She let out a long sigh, glanced at Nick, and was reassured by his warm smile. "Okay. I thought everything would have blown over by now or it would turn out to be just some prank, but…there are some things I need to tell you."

With Nick filling in details here and there, she told them about the pictures, her talk with Quinn, his insistence that she get someone professional to check into things and also provide protection.

"And that's how Nick came into the picture," she finished. "He and Quinn are close friends and Quinn called in a favor."

"I'll be using all the resources of Guardian Security," Nick assured them. "Here's what we've done so far."

He explained how and where they were in setting up protection as well as the process of investigating who the stalker could be. Ruben and Mary listened in silence, but Lindsey could tell they were getting madder and madder.

"Is there some reason you didn't feel you should tell us this before now, little one?" Ruben's face was impassive, but his anger was almost palpable.

"I'm sorry, Ruben." She spread her hands helplessly. "I know I should have, but I kept thinking this was just a sick joke that would go away. I didn't want to worry either of you if I didn't have to."

"This is no joke, Lindsey." He leaned forward across the table. "It's our *job* to worry about you and you'd best not forget it. I promised your daddy I'd take good care of you, but you sure make it difficult sometimes."

"You don't know all the ugliness that's out there," Mary added, getting up from the table. "I hope you never have to find out."

Ruben clomped off when they finished talking, saying he'd be right back. He returned to the kitchen with his rifle in one hand and his favorite Kimber 9 mm in the other. For a handgun, the Kimber was heavy with firepower. The snakes Ruben blasted with it usually needed a blotter to be collected.

"Good weapon," Nick commented.

"The best," Ruben said without a smile.

Lindsey raised her eyebrows at the guns. "Think we're fighting a militia here, Ruben?"

"Hope not." He winked at her, although his face still held vestiges of anger. "But at least no one will catch me off guard." He leaned the rifle in a corner by the pantry and tucked the handgun into his belt at the small of his back.

"Ruben, someone's just trying to rattle my cage," she admonished. "It's not like we're under attack or we'll be having a gunfight out here. We're just talking about a couple of pictures." She turned to Nick, expecting him to back her up.

"Right now he's just sending you pictures," Nick said. "But let's not forget one of them was taken from the hotel next door, looking right into your little apartment."

"What?" Ruben's outrage was palpable.

"Someone's spying on you?"

"Please." She wanted to smack Nick for throwing that little fact in there so carelessly. "I'm keeping my drapes closed."

"Damn straight," Ruben growled. "Whoever this is, you don't know what he or she has in mind."

"Ruben's right," Nick added, and she wanted to strangle him. "Your unknown stalker has already escalated to invading your privacy. I'm hoping whoever it is thinks it's too risky or too much trouble tracking you down here at the ranch. However, stalkers have a tendency to accelerate once they think they're achieving their objective. I for one will sleep a lot better knowing Ruben's taking care of business here"

"Wait." Lindsey held up a hand. "Don't I get a say here?"

Nick gave her a lopsided grin. "You did. You said where's the contract and where do I sign."

"Oh, for—" She threw up her hands. She couldn't argue with that. And she was torn between wanting Nick and Ruben to pull out all the stops to protect her and finding out the stalking was just someone's crazy idea of a prank.

Nick rose from his chair. "Mary, that's the best meal I've eaten in so long I forgot when the last one was. Thank you."

Mary just nodded her head, but Lindsey saw the little flash of pleasure on her face and swallowed a smile.

She glanced at Nick. "I'm going out on the porch to finish my coffee. Want to join me?"

"Sure. Just give me a minute."

She loved the rockers on this porch. They were so

comfortable and sitting in one transported her from whatever stress she was dealing with. The tension in her body finally began to release. Spending time at this place she considered her ultimate refuge always had a calming effect on her.

She had told Nick the truth. He was the first outsider she'd brought to the ranch in a very long time. Sometimes it saddened her, the path she had chosen. But she'd promised herself she'd never again be in a physical relationship that would end up leaving her emotionally bruised. Men wanted children. When they discovered she couldn't have them, they hit the road so fast they left dust in their wake. When she'd learned what her situation was, she'd anguished and screamed, but then she'd come to terms with it. But she wasn't about to put herself in the way of someone else's rejection because of it.

Nick Vanetta was not only a very good looking, totally sexy man. He was intelligent, solid, and comfortable in his own skin. The first man she'd met in ages who wasn't full of himself. But it would be dangerous if they acted on whatever had popped up so quickly between them, the sizzle of chemistry that had niggled at her all day. Even thinking about it was a luxury she couldn't indulge in.

She had no reason to believe that, in the end, he would be any different than the other men who had mocked her sterility. They wanted sons with their own DNA. It was the typical attitude of the Texas alpha male, at least most of the ones she'd met. That still didn't make it hurt any less.

Anyway, she was probably daydreaming. Nick had the look of a man who could have any woman he wanted. Despite the flare of heat in his eyes when their hands touched and the smile that woke up the butterflies in her stomach, she probably wouldn't even make his B list.

The soft murmur of voices intruded on her reveries. When she turned her head, Ruben and Nick were walking up from the barn in quiet conversation. Without being told, she knew Nick had asked the older man to show him around the immediate property and point out areas of access besides the road. He did it without involving her, aware that it might put her on edge again.

When they reached the porch, Nick thanked Ruben for his help, the two men shook hands, and Ruben went off to his own house.

"Mary left coffee on in the kitchen if you'd like another cup," Lindsey informed him.

"No, thanks. I'm so stuffed I don't think there's room even for that." He crossed his arms, leaned against the rail, and looked at her steadily. "I'd still feel a lot better if the Medanas were sleeping in this house. Ruben almost agrees with me, but you're right. I can tell they wouldn't feel comfortable doing it. So until this is over, when you come out here, I'll be coming, too."

Her body tensed. "I don't really think that's necessary. As you can see, I'm well protected here."

"Lindsey." His tone was one of incredible patience. "When I work with corporations to train their people, sometimes I'm at the site for weeks, maybe even a month. It's part of the job. Besides, that's what you're paying me for. My time is your time."

"Oh, yes, that's right." Of course. He was giving

her the services she was paying for. “Well, I think today has been long enough for me. I need to get some sleep.” She rose from the rocker. “I’m sure Mary has left plenty of towels for you and whatever else she thinks you might need. I’d like to leave by eight-thirty tomorrow, if that’s okay with you. I have a lot of work to do after today’s meeting, and I need to really dig in on the drawings for the Marquez house.”

“No problem. I have an alarm on my watch, but I’m usually up by six anyway. Longtime habit.”

“Well, goodnight, then.”

She took her coffee cup into the kitchen, put it in the sink, and turned off the coffee maker. She assumed Nick had stayed on the porch, but when she climbed the stairs, he was right behind her. He was still on her heels when she walked down the hall. At the door to her room, she turned, only to find him so close they almost shared the same breath. A warm feeling crept through her body.

“Goodnight again.”

Go in the room, dummy. What’s the matter with you?

His eyes, studying her face, were a darker brown, like melted chocolate. Her heartbeat skipped once, twice, and her breathing become shallow. She wanted to move, but she didn’t want to. His enormous image filled her vision, but his eyes were what held her immobilized.

He put his hands lightly on her shoulders and looked down at her with those turbulent eyes. “We’ll get this person, Lindsey, That’s a promise. I’m very good at what I do. I’ll take care of this.” He rubbed her shoulders gently with his thumbs. “Sweet dreams.”

Then he was gone to his room.

Lindsey stood rooted to the spot, staring after him, finally rousing herself to move. Once in her room, she firmly closed the door. He was just doing his job. Making her feel safe. She had to keep remembering that.

And the thing was, he did. When she'd looked into his eyes, she believed deep down that he was rock solid, that he would protect her, find the stalker, and make this nightmare go away.

In the bathroom, she stripped, tugged on her sleep shirt, and splashed cold water on her face and hands. Exhausted but tense, she fell into bed.

Chapter Seven

Delighted to have Nick and his appetite in her kitchen, Mary prepared an elaborate breakfast. But while Nick fed his inner man with gusto, Lindsey's stomach rebelled at the sight of so much food. Carefully seating herself on the opposite side of the table from him, she felt his eyes on her as she drank coffee and forced herself to eat some toast.

Mary clucked at her as usual, but she was in so much turmoil she was sure food wouldn't sit well on her stomach. Her sleep had been restless but at least, thank the Lord, not disturbed by the awful nightmares.

Nick had put on his jeans and T-shirt again, and she looked at him questioningly. Surely he wasn't going to wear that to her office.

"We're going to stop by my place on the way in," he told her. "I need a bigger wardrobe if we're going to be coming out here every night, and I want to ditch my dirty laundry."

"We won't be long, will we?" She looked at her watch. "I told you I need to get to the office."

"And you will. I won't be but a couple of minutes."

Promptly at eight-thirty, they pulled out through the gates onto the country highway. Lindsey glanced at Nick, and the same feeling washed over her again, the one she'd felt from their first meeting. Solid. Safe. Secure. The scruff that darkened his jaw line gave him a slightly menacing look, and she swallowed a smile. She hoped the stalker would get a good look at him this way. Maybe she could persuade him not to shave.

"Are you all right?"

With his eyes shielded the way they were, she couldn't tell if he was looking at her or not. "Yes. Fine. Why?"

He shrugged. "You just seem a little quiet."

"I have a lot on my mind."

"Of course. Let's see if I can distract you a little. What kind of books do you like to read?"

"What?" The question startled her. "Books?"

"Yes. I know you like to read. The bookshelves in your living room are crammed with all kinds of genres. Myself, I like political thrillers, histories, and biographies. So what's on your preference list?"

By the time they reached his house, Lindsey had begun to see even more of the real depth of this man, the extent of his quiet intelligence. It seemed the more layers she peeled back, the more she was attracted to him. Something she'd have to keep a tight rein on. But she realized his ploy had worked. Some of the tension had eased from her body.

Nick's house, a two-story soft red-brick Tudor in upscale Alamo Heights, had a settled look to it. Mature plantings bordered the house, and two large crape myrtle trees stood sentinel in the front yard. Someone took very good care of the magnificent landscaping, keeping it neat and fresh and well-trimmed. Not at all what she'd been expecting.

He punched a code into the transmitter clipped to his sun visor, and the garage door slid open. Grabbing his bag from the back seat, he led Lindsey inside and waved her toward the living room.

"Look around if you'd like," he said, taking the stairs two at a time. "I've heard architects like to take apart houses they didn't design. I'll be right down."

Lindsey looked around curiously. The house was impressive, with its spacious rooms, high ceilings, and wide windows. The floors were all original wood, polished to a high gloss. Crown molding trimmed the ceilings, giving them a traditional look. The furniture was masculine but not overbearingly so, mostly oak with rich burgundy leather upholstery. Everything had been carefully chosen for comfort as well as style. She wondered who'd been his decorator.

The whole traditional ambience startled her. Somehow she'd pictured him in an ultra-modern condo overlooking a golf course, with furniture that looked like something from the next century. Maybe because all the other men his age she knew found that to be appropriate, a symbol of their lifestyle. But this was the place of a man who wanted to make a home, a fact that startled her.

She was exploring the gleaming kitchen with its oak cabinets and quartz counters when she heard Nick come downstairs.

"All set," he said, walking into the kitchen. He had changed into gray slacks, a gray and white striped shirt, and a black sports jacket.

"Is black and gray the required color combination for security?" she couldn't help asking.

"Helps blend into the crowd better." One corner of his mouth turned up. "I think the FBI started it."

"Your house surprises me," she told him. "I never would have pegged you for such a traditionalist."

"It grounds me," he said. "Everything else in my life is so transient because of my job that I needed something to give me a sense of belonging to the human race. Actually, one of my sisters is a real estate agent. She found it for me and badgered me until I bought it."

Lindsey kept forgetting he had a family somewhere out there. Another interesting side to an image he tried to keep one-dimensional.

In the hallway, he picked up the soft leather suitcase and garment bag he'd left there. "Ready?"

"Are you planning on moving in?" She arched an eyebrow.

"Just being prepared." He winked. "Okay. Let's get going."

They were silent on the trip to her office, but the silence this time was more comfortable than before. She knew Nick was alert, watching for any car that might be tailing them or anything out of the ordinary, so she just leaned back and closed her eyes until they reached the parking garage.

Brianna and Mark were both waiting somewhat impatiently outside the office when they exited the elevator, Bri's foot tapping a sharp staccato. The techno twins were waiting stolidly with them, unfazed.

"We've got everything set up, Mr. Vanetta," one of them said. "We didn't want to give out the code cards before you got here. And we want to walk both you and Miss Ferrell through the setup."

Nick nodded his thanks.

One of the men opened the aluminum case in his hand to reveal a built-in machine of some sort. He took out four plastic cards and ran each through a programmer. At the same time, his partner punched something into a handheld computer. Finally, they handed out the cards.

"Each of you has your own code programmed in," the first one explained. "Whenever you enter or leave, a message gets sent to a central computer that records who it is and the date and time. Mr. Vanetta, we made one for you, too, so you wouldn't need to borrow someone's card to come and go."

"Thanks." Nick looked at Lindsey. "It's standard procedure to give the agency a code card for every system Guardian sets up."

Everyone swiped their cards to enter the suite of offices, then Nick gave them a tour of the new alarm system. He called his office to tell them he was running a test, then watched while each person practiced setting the codes. After that, Brianna went to her desk to check their messages and Mark made himself invisible in the workroom.

Lindsey was the only one Nick showed the system for the apartment. He had separate key cards for the entrances from the office and the hall and a totally separate setup for her private system.

"From here on out," he told her, "no staff in the living quarters."

"All right," she nodded. "Now, I'd better get started on those projects before my clients beat down the door."

"I'll be in your apartment working on my laptop, if that's okay. And it'll give me privacy while I call the office."

"Fine. No problem." She punched the intercom. "Bri, you need to hold my calls until lunch, unless it's something earth-shattering."

"Will do."

Nick spent most of the morning out of sight, although periodically he would silently come to the connecting door to check on her. He also strolled the corridor occasionally, pretending to search for an office or the men's room, looking for anyone or anything that appeared out of place.

The office hummed quietly with work. Even the ring of the telephone seemed muted as they all went about their assignments.

At twelve-thirty, Brianna tapped on Lindsey's door and walked in.

"Here are your messages." She handed over a stack of pink slips. "Nothing urgent, but a couple of prospective clients called for appointments. Just make a note of what you want to do with them, and I'll call them back. I sent the Randolph and Marquez documents to your computer for you to check. Make your changes, and I'll get them out. And I'm going to lunch."

"Where's Mark?" Lindsey rotated her shoulders, working out the kinks.

"He left a few minutes ago. I caught him talking on the phone just before he left and blushing." She grinned. "I think he's got a girlfriend."

"Mark?" Lindsey swallowed her amazement. "I didn't think he knew what girls were for."

"Just goes to show you, right?" She turned to leave. "See you in about an hour."

"Yes. Okay. Just lock everything on your way out and set the alarm. I think I'll eat in."

"With the hunk?" Brianna teased.

"He's working here as private security," Lindsey reminded her primly.

Brianna laughed and closed the door.

Lindsey hadn't heard the connecting door open or sensed any movement, but suddenly Nick was standing beside her.

"I checked your cupboards," he said. "I can't believe you eat some of that stuff. We'll have to do some grocery shopping."

"Maybe you'd like to give me a list," she bit off. "Or should we have put your food requirements in your contract?"

Damn. She hadn't meant to sound quite so sharp.

"One of these days that smart tongue of yours is going to get you in real trouble. You're lucky I'm such an easygoing guy." He grinned. "We can go to the Central Market later and lay in some supplies for when we stay here. Meanwhile, let's slip out the side door and go grab something quick. I've got someone keeping an eye on the office while we're gone."

"All right, but nothing fancy like yesterday. Just a sandwich. Besides, I don't need too many top dollar meals showing up on the expense account."

His hand tightened on her arm, and he yanked her around to face him. His eyes, which normally gleamed like blue fire, now looked like ice trapped on the bottom of the ocean.

"What the hell is the matter with you?" he asked through gritted teeth. "I thought we'd settled into a pretty good working relationship. For your information, when I ask someone out to lunch, it comes out of my pocket. Yesterday, I entertained a client. Today we're just stoking the engine."

She dropped her gaze. When had sounding like a shrew become a defense against her reaction to Nick? "I'm sorry. I'm just…tense."

He relaxed, nodding his head. "Understood. Now. Do you have a preference?"

She dragged up a smile. "As a matter of fact, I do. Schilo's. It's just down the street, and I could really go for one of their corned beef sandwiches."

Schilo's, a German delicatessen, was a long-standing favorite of San Antonio residents who loved the mouth-watering sandwiches, homemade soups, and great sausage platters. The place was always crowded with a mixture of business people and tourists. She hoped they could find a table. If not, they could always take their lunch back to the apartment with them.

"Let's go, then." Nick made her go through all the security steps from the office to the apartment and then out into the hall. The elevator stopped at every floor as it usually did at this time of day, but finally, they were outside and heading along the sidewalk.

As they stood at the corner waiting for the light to change someone shouted Nick's name. He turned his head to see who was calling to him, momentarily stepping away from her.

As she stepped closer to the curb to get out of the way of the crowd on the sidewalk, she felt a hand against her back. The next thing she knew, she was shoved forward just as a big VIA bus came lumbering around the corner. The fender brushed her knee, nearly knocking her under the wheels.

She screamed, flailing her arms in panic.

Chapter Eight

A steely hand gripped Lindsey's arm and roughly yanked her back.

"Are you all right?" Shock and a sick feeling at what almost happened etched deep lines on Nick's face.

"Y—Yes. I'm sorry." Lindsey pushed her hair out of her face and drew in a shuddering breath. "I think someone pushed me."

"Are you sure you're okay?" he insisted. "You nearly became a hood ornament for that bus."

It amazed Lindsey that all around them people continued to move about, totally unaware of the disaster that nearly occurred. She might as well have been invisible to them.

"Answer me, damn it." He ran his gaze over every inch of her. "Are you hurt?"

"No. I'm fine." She drew a shaky breath. "But I think I need to sit down somewhere." Her eyes were wide. "I know this sounds crazy, but I swear I felt someone's hand on my back. Nick, I think someone pushed me."

His jaw muscle clenched. "Not so crazy. Someone called my name, but I think it was deliberate, to distract me from you. I didn't see anyone I know, and no one came near me. Come on. Let's sit over here."

He led her to a covered VIA bus stop and sat her gently on the bench. Her face was white and strained, and her hands still trembled as she lifted the hem of her skirt to assess the damage. A large, ugly scrape below her knee was slowly oozing blood.

Nick cursed steadily under his breath. He took out his handkerchief and brushed off her leg as tenderly and gently as he could. The wound needed cleaning, and she would have a hell of a bruise.

"All right," he told her. "We're going to sit here for a few minutes, and then we're going to walk slowly back to your building. It's my own damn fault. I'm not usually distracted like that. I never should have let go of you, and you can bet that's the only time it's going to happen."

They sat on the bench for a few moments, Nick close to her, eyes scanning the people moving past.

"Okay." She let out another long breath. "I think I'm okay now. Let's get away from here."

"Are you sure?" He ran a critical eye over her. "Your color's better, but you still look like you're in shock. I think we should take a cab."

"For just a couple of blocks?" She shook her head. "I don't think so. We'll just walk slowly."

Nick kept a firm grip on her arm as they headed back to the office, his eyes constantly checking the crowd. She gritted her teeth against the sharp pain slashing through her knee, unwilling to admit just how much it hurt.

"I need to clean that knee," he told her as soon as they were back in her apartment.

"It's fine," she insisted. "I'll just wash it off."

"Damn it, Lindsey, you've got all kinds of dirt in it." He blew out a breath of frustration. "Quit being so hardheaded and let me take care of it. Or do you want me to take you to the emergency room?"

She looked at the wound and had to admit it was a lot nastier than she'd thought.

"Lie down on your bed," Nick ordered. "It will be easier to clean the scrape that way. Besides, you look like you'll fall down otherwise."

She realized he was right. The ordeal had caught up with her, the adrenaline high was crashing, and her legs were about to give out on her. On top of that, the pain seemed to be getting worse. She did as he told her, thankful to lie back against her pillows.

I wish I was lying on this bed with him for some other reason than first aid.

As soon as the thought entered her brain, she ruthlessly suppressed it. What the hell was wrong with her? She'd known this man for less than seventy-two hours, and she was having all kinds of inappropriate thoughts about him. Inappropriate because she was a client of his, and because she had sworn off men. Maybe this was all a big mistake, because Nick Vanetta, just by being in the same room with her, was playing hell with her hormones. Every hour they were together, her unwanted attraction to him grew and intensified.

Damn. Everything he did just increased the attraction she felt for him. Not good. Not good at all. Why couldn't he be one of those rude men who just did his job and nothing else?

Nick brought her two aspirins and a glass of water, helping her to sit up while she took them. Then he rummaged through her bathroom, found some first aid supplies and a washcloth, and carried them back to the bedroom. With great care and the utmost gentleness, he cleaned and treated her leg. But she noticed a fine tension in his body and he kept clenching his jaw so hard a muscle twitched in his cheek.

"What in the world is the matter with you?" she finally asked. "I said I was sorry I got careless."

"God damn it." The words exploded from his mouth. Then he drew in a deep breath and let it out very slowly. "Don't you understand? This was my fault, not yours. I'm supposed to be protecting you. Fine protection I am." He shook his head. "Shit."

"Nick, it was an accident." Or maybe not.

He drew a deep breath, let it out slowly. "This was no accident, Lindsey. You could have been killed because I wasn't paying attention. Because someone called out my name. And I don't know if whoever this is has someone working with him or was just clever enough to distract me and push you into the street."

She struggled to sit up. "I was the one not paying attention. Please don't keep blaming yourself. I should have been more alert, too."

"Be as alert as you want, but it's still my job to keep you safe. I don't appear to be doing it very well. I've been in the office too long. Maybe I've lost my edge. God fucking damn."

"Nick—"

He shook his head. "Leave it, Lindsey. It was my fault, and I'll make it right. Stand up and tell me how the leg feels."

When she put her weight on both feet, she wanted to tell him it felt like crap, but that was the last thing he needed to hear. "It's okay. Sore, but I can handle it."

"Tonight we'll put some ice on it. At the moment, I need to make some phone calls. Among other things, I want some backup around us. In most situations, I can take care of you completely. But if this guy is escalating and doing the kinds of things that happened today, it's stupid not to have reinforcements." He pulled out his cell phone and punched a number on speed dial, then gave her a crooked grin. "I'll get someone to bring us some food, too. We sorta missed lunch."

"I don't think I can eat," she protested. "My stomach is too tied up in knots."

"You need something," he objected. "I saw some soup in your cupboards. Can you handle that?"

"I think so." She started to get up, but he forced her back down again.

"Rest. Let the aspirins work. I can heat up a can of soup."

While he fixed lunch, he made several calls on his cell. Lindsey strained to hear what he was saying, but all that came through was the soothing murmur of his low voice. Finally, she heard him call her to come to the table and she limped out of the bedroom. He had a bowl of soup set out with crackers and sat with her while she ate slowly. The tension in her body eased as the hot liquid worked its way through her system. She hadn't thought she could finish all of her lunch, but surprisingly, when she looked, the bowl was empty.

"Good girl." Nick rinsed the bowl and stuck it in the dishwasher. "We'll do better at dinner. I have some people on the way here. They'll come directly into the apartment because I want to keep them away from your office." He let his gaze roam over her, assessing her. "Are you sure you're in shape to go back to work?"

"I have to." She raked her fingers through her hair. The aspirin had taken the edge off the pain, and the soup had given her some strength. "There are things I have to take care of. Anyway, it'll be good for me. It'll take my mind off what's happening."

"All right. But I'll check on you periodically. And don't say anything to your office staff about this," he cautioned. "I want to contain it until I feel I have a better handle on things."

"Sure. I understand. Whatever you say." She forced a smile. "You won't get any argument from me."

In the bathroom, she straightened her hair and makeup, thinking nothing would help much today, but at least it made her feel a little better. Finally, she put on a longer skirt, fuller, with softer material that hid her injury and wouldn't be rough on her skin.

Back in her office, she forced herself to go pick up the sketches she'd left, trying to wipe the incident with the bus out of her mind. But her brain kept wandering, unbidden, back to that terrifying moment. She could still feel the pressure of a hand against her back, the brush of the bus against her knee. Shivers chased themselves along her spine.

Luckily, she had a light appointment schedule for the afternoon, because she felt on the ragged edge of collapse. She had no idea how she'd handle a lot of people right now. Even so, the hours seemed endless. Her knee kept stiffening up on her, and she had to stop and flex it every so often. She needed more aspirin, too, but she didn't want to walk to get it and she felt ridiculous bothering anyone. If she could make it to the end of the day, she could lie down again.

****

Nick spent the afternoon making phone calls, asking questions, and talking to Reno about the situation. His partner agreed with Nick's assessment that the stalker's tactics were escalating. That meant the game plan needed to be changed. The two men decided which agents would be tapped as backup, and Reno said he'd take care of it.

Nick was angrier with himself than he'd been in a long time. Falling for an old, stupid, amateur trick like the one today violated a hard and fast rule of private security—never, ever take your attention away from the client. Never lose your concentration on the surroundings. He had done both. It was a wonder Lindsey hadn't fallen under the bus and a greater wonder she hadn't fired him. This was a dumb rookie mistake.

He quietly checked on her throughout the afternoon, poking his head apologetically into the office, giving her a reassuring smile. When the men he'd asked for arrived, he spent a lot of time giving them an overview of both the building and the situation and deciding who would take which assignment. He'd tapped Tony Sullivan, Reno's brother, to lead the support team. They were in the apartment going over details when he heard Lindsey shout.

"Nick? Nick, come here right away. Hurry."

The fear in her voice had a fist closing around his heart and sent him barreling into her office, Tony right on his heels.

Lindsey stood at her desk, not moving, staring at her computer. She was shaking so badly she had to hang onto the desk. Nick crossed the distance in three quick strides. On her screen was a shot of her at the corner today nearly being sucked under the bus, with Nick yanking her to safety. Across the bottom were the words, "Close, wasn't it? Remember, bitch. I'm watching you."

"It's okay, Lindsey," he soothed, his hands gentle on her shoulders. "I've got it."

Fucking son of a bitch.

Lindsey Ferrell sure didn't seem the type to generate this kind of rage in someone. He was so angry, if he got his hands on whoever this was, he might strangle him. Clenching his jaw, Nick pulled himself together to focus on what was needed. He was an expert at this. That was why people hired him, and he'd already screwed up once today. He didn't plan for that to happen again. He'd take all the anger at himself and direct it at whoever was doing this.

"It's okay, Lindsey. It's just another email. We'll identify the source and see wat we can do about blocking it on your computer."

She leaned back against him, her body fragile beneath his touch. "I trust you to do this, Nick."

Well, he damn well better deserve that trust. He stroked her shoulders for a moment, but such close contact with her body made his own behave in a totally inappropriate manner. Maybe he'd need to have a stern talk with is cock as well as with himself. He needed to stop imagining what it would feel like to bury himself in her soft, sweet flesh and—

Stop it, you asshole. Do your job.

"Let's move you out of the way," he told her in a soft, soothing voice.

And away from the temptation to take you to bed instead of figuring out what was going on here.

In all the years he'd been in this business, he'd never felt such strong temptation where a client was concerned. Not even with the women he took to bed. When he was alone, he'd give both his heads—big and little—a stern talking to.

He guided her over to a chair where she stretched out her injured leg. Just looking at it stoked his anger, and he clenched his fists to get himself under control. God, he was just losing it all over the place. Then he printed out two copies of the email as he'd done with the previous one. He handed one to the Guardian agent who was already speaking into his cell phone in low tones.

"Th-There *was* someone there today, Nick." Her voice shook. "Look how close the person was who took this picture."

"Don't worry." His voice was steady and calming, even as he kept wanting to kick his own ass for making a rookie mistake. "We're surrounding you with the best." He indicated the man who'd come into the office with him. "This is Tony Sullivan, Reno's brother. He's going to be my personal backup on this."

Tony nodded. "Miss Ferrell."

She gave him a shaky smile. "The big brass, huh?

Tony winked. "Nah, we let Reno think that's him." He studied the photo. "Looks like whoever pushed you moved back with his camera. Which means today's episode wasn't necessarily meant to kill."

"It came damn close to it," Nick growled. "Come on, Lindsey. Let's get you out of the office. Tony, get everyone back up here and get hold of our IT guy."

"Already done. You take care of the lady."

Nick led her into the apartment and coaxed her to the couch. He blotted her tears with his handkerchief, then gave her the square of white linen to hold.

“I’ll be right back.” He returned with a plastic baggy filled with ice cubes, a towel, and more aspirin and water. “Here, take these.”

She swallowed them down. “I think everything’s starting to ache now,” she apologized, lying back on the couch.

“I’m not surprised.” A muscle twitched in his cheek. “Here.” He lifted the edge of her skirt with the same gentleness he’d used earlier, placed the towel over her injury and the ice cubes on top of that. “Keep this on there. It looks swollen, and you were limping. Are you okay by yourself here for a little bit while I take care of some things?”

She nodded, blinking back a fresh round of tears. “Sorry. I seem to be a leaky faucet today. I want you to know this is not who I am at all.”

Nick swore softly and touched her cheek with the tips of his fingers. “I didn’t think so. I can feel your strength, Linds, but today would make even a grown man weep.” He couldn’t stop himself from lightly stroking her cheek. “Okay. Just hang tight here and give me a few minutes.”

He noticed her looking over his shoulder and turned. Tony had entered and stood a discreet distance away.

Nick waved him forward, then turned back to Lindsey. “Like I said earlier, Tony’s going to be the number two man on this job. I need an extra pair of eyes and hands, and these are the best available. Most of the time, you won’t even know he’s around.”

“Thank you so much,” she told them, looking from one to the other. “I appreciate everything you’re all doing.”

Like nearly getting you killed. Nick would never forgive himself for that.

"Tony and I are going back into the office, Lindsey. He's going to do some security work on your computer, and I'm going to see what Guardian has come up with. I also want to call Detective McCune, just to let him know what happened and shoot him a copy of the email. I'll be in the next room, okay? You can holler if you need me."

She nodded. "I'll be fine. You do what you have to."

"Good girl." He smiled, his heart nearly breaking at the sight of her, and went back into her office.

****

The aspirins soothed Lindsey a little, and her knee throbbed less with the ice on it. She closed her eyes, resting her head on the soft pillows of the couch, and tried to make herself relax. No good. The image of that picture kept flashing across her mind. She tried to think of everyone she knew, everyone she came in contact with, anyone who could hate her so much they'd do something this vicious. Who could want to destroy her life like this? What had she ever done to anyone to make him or her take such vicious actions?

Out of nowhere a nasty thought struck her. Did this person somehow have something to do with her mother's sudden heart attack? No, that would really be reaching. But she had yet to receive a satisfactory explanation, so was the idea really so farfetched? Maybe she could get Nick or one of his men to question the people at the nursing home again.

She rubbed her forehead, trying to ease away the tension, and felt herself drifting off.

A soft touch on her arm roused her.

"I've talked to McCune." Nick knelt beside the couch. "He was going to come by and take a report, but I gave him all the information he'd need over the telephone. There still isn't much he can do, but at least now he knows we're dealing with more than a harmless prankster."

Lindsey shuddered. "We certainly are."

"Whoever this is has planted a virus to mask his own address with one from your address book," he went on. "Tony will take care of it and put in some new security settings. They'll block out all email attachments, as well as emails from any source not already in your address book. It may be inconvenient for a while, but I don't want you opening any more attachments like that last one." His gaze scanned her face. "Can you sit up?"

"Yes." She gave him a lopsided grin and rose slowly to a sitting position, pushing the ice aside. "If I have to."

Nick helped her adjust her position so she was more comfortable. "I had to decide what the best option would be for tonight. All things considered, I don't think it's a good idea for you to go to the ranch. Ruben and Mary would wonder why you're limping, and you'd have to go through the hassle of explaining everything to them."

"Oh, Lord." She rubbed her face. "I didn't think of that."

"I don't think staying here is so great, either, but it's the better choice of the two. We're shutting down everything in the office, machines and all, for the night. Guardian will monitor the alarm, which I put on high security alert. We'll keep all the drapes closed and the lights low. Tony will be in charge of external surveillance along with a couple of other guys on night duty."

Her eyes widened in terror. "You think he'll come here, whoever this is?"

"No." He shook his head. "I don't think anything else will happen tonight. He's had his fun for the day. But just in case he's hanging around somewhere with his camera, we don't need to take any more chances."

"You're right about not going to the ranch," she agreed. "Ruben would take one look at me and know something else had happened. He'd be out in his truck with his shotgun shooting anyone who even looked suspicious." She smiled ruefully. "I think he's a little overprotective of me."

"Unlike me, who nearly got you killed today," Nick said roughly.

"Please don't keep beating yourself up about that. Everything happened so fast. How could you have expected it?"

"Lindsey, I've built my reputation on being the best in the business. When we started out, private security was the bulk of what I did. Even as a neophyte I never let anything like this happen. And believe me, it won't happen again."

She nibbled on her lower lip. "I only have the one bedroom here, though."

He thumped a cushion on the couch. "I've slept on a lot worse than this," he teased. "I'll be fine. Don't worry about it." When she didn't make a move to get up, he cocked his head. "What? Another problem?"

"I know you'll think this is way out in left field,

but something just occurred to me."

He crouched down in front of her. "Right now nothing is too wild, so let's have it."

When she finished telling him about her mother's heart attack, he frowned. "And no one could give you a reason? There hadn't been any unusual cardiac activity prior to it? She was stable?"

Lindsey nodded. "What if whoever is doing this to me somehow did something to my mother? Scared her, or something, so badly she had the attack?"

"I agreed it's reaching, but I can't rule anything out. While we're eating, tell me everything about the nursing home, and Guardian will send someone to sniff things out."

"Thank you so much." Tears flooded her eyes again, and without realizing it, she leaned forward, put her arms around his neck, and hugged him.

Heat flooded her at the intimate contact, and Nick's body tensed. They both froze, as if the wrong button had been pushed. The atmosphere between them had definitely changed.

Lindsey snatched her arms back, trying to pretend her impulsive action hadn't happened, but they both knew it had.

Nick rose slowly, avoiding her eyes, and helped her to her feet. "It's okay. Really. Now I think you need a good hot shower, and then I'm going to clean that knee again. Tony is bringing us some Chinese food. I hope that's okay."

"You sent your partner's brother for carryout?" She was incredulous.

"He'll eat while he's there so it's no big deal." Nick grinned. "He has to eat anyway and walk back here, so carrying a little sack shouldn't exert him too much. Go take your shower. I'll take one after you, so we can eat when he gets back."

In the bathroom, she stripped off her clothes and tossed them in the hamper. She'd built the apartment when she'd decided she needed a place to stay for those nights she worked late in town. Leasing the unit next door and turning it into a small apartment turned out to be a smart choice. And she'd allowed herself a lot of luxuries. One of her treats was an overlarge freestanding shower with glass blocks on two sides and a wide door on the third. Showerheads were built into multiple locations along the wall.

She turned the water on as hot as she could stand it and let it pummel her body with its jets, easing the soreness in her muscles. But the one thing it couldn't do was wash away the feel of Nick when she'd hugged him or the clean scent of his cologne that teased at her nose.

Closing her eyes, she leaned back against the tiled wall of the shower and lathered her breasts. It was so easy to imagine Nick's hands touching her as she cupped her breasts, squeezing the flesh, hefting their fullness. She pinched her nipples with her fingers, imagining they were Nick's fingers. Imagining him tugging on them before putting his mouth to them and lightly biting each one.

Heat with the force of a thunderbolt streaked right to her core, setting up little spasms in the walls of her sex. The more she tormented her nipples, the more intense the internal spasms. She wanted him inside her in a way she'd never craved another man, his cock filling her, his mouth on her everywhere.

She slid her soap-slicked hand down past her abdomen to the folds of her sex, easing one finger into the slit, and—

She jerked her hand back, breathing hard.

Stupid, stupid, stupid.

Nick Vanetta would never be interested in her that way. Imagining it would only complicate an already dangerous problem.

I should wash my brain while I'm washing my body and hope to fill it with nothing but common sense.

But when she turned off the water and reached for a towel, the pulse in her sex still thrummed with need and her nipples still ached. It was going to be a damn long night.

****

"Special delivery."

Nick answered Tony's knock and took the paper sack from him. "Thanks."

"Do I get a tip?"

"Yeah. Here's a tip," Nick said gloomily. "Take better care of your clients than I seem to do."

"I think the self-flagellation's getting a little heavy," Tony said. "We need to focus on what to do from here on in. Besides, there's a hell of a big difference between sending weird messages and trying to kill someone. I looked at the file you gave me. There's no indication of any threat to harm at all."

"Except someone tried to throw her under a bus today," Nick reminded him, still disgusted with himself.

"Yeah, right. I'll let you know if we find anything. Meanwhile, your dinner's getting cold."

Nick closed the door after Tony, set the alarm, and leaned against the kitchen counter. The one thing he hadn't discussed with his friend was his feelings for Lindsey. He was past the point of denying they were far more complicated than he wanted to acknowledge.

She was so totally different than the women he usually dated. With eyes like liquid pools of melted chocolate and hair like newly spun dark silk, this softly rounded package of dynamite was stealing his heart one tiny piece at a time. How had it happened so fast? How was it possible to want someone so desperately in so little time?

He shook his head. She was a client, for God's sake, and a frightened one at that. He would never take advantage of her in such a vulnerable state. Except he wanted her, all of her, in a way he'd never wanted anything or anyone else in his life.

Sighing, he lined the takeout cartons up on the counter and went to get Lindsey. This was liable to be a very long night.

Chapter Nine

From the bathroom, Lindsey heard the sound of voices but not what they were saying, and she guessed Tony had returned with their food. The shower had washed away the rest of the grit from her fall, but now her leg throbbed again. She'd need to put more medicine and ice on it.

In a way, that was a good thing. It distracted, as much as anything could, from the intense sexual craving for Nick that shocked the hell out of her. Like a jack-in-the-box, it had popped up and taken her over. She had to hide this from him, however she had to do it. She just hoped when she fell asleep tonight, it wasn't to dream about the two of them naked in bed.

Spraying cologne on her pulse points to lift her spirits, she looked around for something comfortable to put on. She'd hurried into the bathroom without taking anything from her closet first, and now she only had her long terry robe hanging on the back of the door. It didn't zip or button, just wrapped and tied with a thick belt. She didn't even have underwear with her. While Nick was in the kitchen, she'd have to try and slide into her closet and find something a little more respectable.

Sighing, she sat at the vanity and dried her hair, then took a look at herself in the mirror. A stranger stared back at her. The face she saw had a pinched look and world-class shadows smudged beneath her eyes.

I look like hell.

She rose to head for her closet, but when she opened the bathroom door and started to step through the opening, there was Nick, hand raised, ready to knock. They were so close a sheet of paper would barely have fit between them. He'd taken off his jacket and tie, and she could see the well-worn shoulder holster that fit so invisibly under his clothes. His collar was loose, and he'd rolled up his sleeves, revealing the fine dark hair on his arms.

They stood motionless for a moment before he moved her back into the bathroom.

"Sit down on that bench," he ordered, backing her up to the vanity. "I need to see about your leg again."

"It's—it's okay," she stammered. "I can take care of it. "

"I said sit down," he growled, then blew out a breath. "Jesus, you're stubborn,"

The bench hit the back of her knees, and she dropped onto it. She knew she should get up, but she just sat there, immobilized, while Nick pulled out the supplies from her medicine cabinet.

He knelt on the floor in front of her and reached for her leg. As he moved it forward, the edges of her robe fell away. His hand, slightly calloused, rested on her skin, and his breath hissed through his teeth.

Lindsey bit her lip and resisted the urge to squeeze her thighs together. Could he tell a wave of strong desire was rushing through her? Was the scent of her musk coating the inside of her thighs, reaching his nose and telling him how badly she wanted him? What would he think if she brushed his hand aside, opened her legs, and dragged his head down to her sex?

Holy shit, Lindsey? Where is all this coming from?

She couldn't recall ever feeling such intense desire for a man. Ever. Never. Certainly not since she'd learned about what one asshole called her defective situation. She bit down harder on her lip to distract herself from this wave of desire. Hopefully Nick would think it was just a reaction to the pain.

Nick couldn't breathe. His heart pounded so hard he was sure Lindsey could hear it. The thick layers of her hair swung forward as she dipped her head, and her eyes, behind the glasses that turned him on so much, were wide and dewy. He tried to tamp down the stirring in his groin and send a strong message to his misbehaving cock.

It wasn't just the sexual appeal that got him. She was the whole package—smart, feisty, knowledgeable, talented. Even her slight meltdown today didn't take away from her inherent and obvious strength. *That* was what turned him on.

Lindsey sat there, unmoving. She looked up at him, and he could see the erratic beat of her pulse at the hollow of her throat. He didn't know if it was his heart thundering so loudly or hers, and there was a roaring in his ears.

Don't do this.

If he did, there would be no going back. And if she pushed him away, the case would be compromised. But he couldn't seem to help himself. Taking her face in his hands, his fingers gentle on her skin, he leaned slightly forward and kissed her. He meant for it to be nothing more than a light touching of lips, but the first contact took away what breath he had left.

He watched her through slitted eyes, gauging her

response, but she didn't pull away. Heat flashed in her eyes, the warm silver darkening almost to slate, and his control blew away like smoke on water.

He touched his lips to hers again, harder this time, ravenously, and felt her mouth open under the pressure. Slowly, slowly, he intruded with his tongue, licking inside the hot, dark well, dancing across the roof of her mouth, waiting for her to back off. The kiss seemed to go on forever.

In an attempt to get his body under control, he lifted his mouth from hers and tilted his head away slightly, trying to read the look in her eyes. The hunger and need and desire swirling in them shocked the hell out of him. Now what did he do?

"Listen to me, Lindsey, and listen very carefully." He struggled to get the words out past his tightened vocal cords. "I'm breaking Vanetta's Number One Rule of Law here—don't get involved with clients. Keep the personal and professional separate. Don't get emotionally involved."

"Nick…"

He held up a hand. "You don't know anything about me. I use women and I have a reputation for it. I'm casual about relationships. I'm certainly not bragging about that kind of behavior, just stating a fact." He drew in a deep breath and let it out. "But with you, Lindsey, I don't think anything could ever be casual. This is so different I'm not sure I know how to deal with it. You have to know that I want you, but I keep thinking it's wrong. You're my client."

"I want you, too." The words sounded stiff, as if she had to force them out or hadn't said them in a long time. So now what happened?

"It scares me," he went on, "to realize if we do this, it won't be any one-night stand. Something's happening here. You feel it, too. I know it. But I don't want to take advantage of you when you're emotionally defenseless. And I don't know if I'd be any good at it. Forget about the client thing for a moment. You're not a woman a man should get involved with casually. And we let this genie out of the bottle, we can't put him back. "

"Nick…" She stared into his eyes, searching.

For what?

"Tonight will not be once and done, Lindsey." His voice was low but firm. "Not by a long shot. I have no idea where to go with this because I've never found myself in this situation before. So think very, very carefully. If it's not what you want, I need to stop right now. In another minute, I won't be able to, and I'll do something we'll both regret. If what you want is comfort in the middle of despair, I'll take care of your leg and fix you a cup of hot chocolate. But if you're willing to take a chance and see what we've got, with a man who has no idea how to handle this, now is the time to say so."

Lindsey was so stunned she didn't know what to do. Despite the nearly visible thread of sexual tension stretched so tight between them and the heavily charged air surrounding them, he'd been thoroughly professional in his behavior toward her. Until now. With that one kiss, he opened floodgates she'd kept locked since her last failed relationship.

Now, she felt like a mare in heat. If she pulled back, it would be over and done between them. He would be as good as his word. She couldn't begin to think why this cocky, arrogant man should be able to break down barriers others couldn't, but ending this was the last thing on her mind. She wanted to melt into him, let him devour her. But she didn't know what to say, how to answer him.

Nick stroked his fingers against the side of her cheek.

"Tell you what," he said. "Why don't I finish tending to your leg, I'll shower, then we'll eat? Give you some time to think about this, okay?"

"Nick, I don't—"

He touched her lips.

"Shh. It's okay. Let's just see what happens when the aspirins kick in and we've had some food."

Lindsey felt somewhat like a teenager in her first heavy petting session, but she felt both relief and regret that he was giving her time to think about this. He carried his suitcase into the closet, and while she pulled on soft sweat pants and a tank top, he took his shower.

By the time he walked into the kitchen in jeans and a T-shirt, she'd warmed the food and set it out on the table with plates and silverware.

She looked up and gave him a shaky grin. "Can't go wrong with Chinese food."

"My philosophy exactly."

The conversation over dinner was somewhat stilted, almost formal, as they both ignored the elephant in the room. But once the food had been put away and the dishes in the dishwasher, Lindsey had run out of busy work. She felt Nick's eyes on her but didn't know what to say. If she moved forward, would he think she was like all the other women he took to bed? If she backed away, would he think her an ice cube?

"Don't think so hard." He placed a soft kiss on her

forehead. "The answer has to come to you naturally. And if it's no, we'll just pretend none of this ever happened. Why don't you get some sheets and a blanket, and I'll make up the couch."

"No." She hadn't meant to shout it so loudly and lowered her voice. "What I mean is, well…that couch isn't all that comfortable."

Nick cupped her chin with his warm hand, forcing her gaze up to his. "This isn't about the couch, Lindsey. I'm not playing games with you. You know how I feel. What I want. I need to know how *you* feel. Whatever your answer is, I can handle it. Just don't beat around the bush, okay? You don't seem like that kind of person. So what's the deal?"

She drew in a long shuddering breath, released it slowly, and stepped off the imaginary cliff. "I don't think you should sleep on the couch. The bed is much more comfortable."

The smile that spread over his face warmed her to her toes. She still wasn't sure whether or not she was making a mistake, but she wanted to take this risk.

"I—I should warn you," she stammered. "I'm not very good at this."

He brushed his mouth against hers. "Why don't you let me be the judge of that?"

He lifted her into his arms and carried her into the bedroom. Sweeping back the spread and covers with one hand, he stood her on her feet and slowly eased off the tank top and sweat pants. With infinite care, he lifted her to the bed, his eyes glued to her as he stripped off his clothes.

He's magnificent! That's the only word for it.

Lindsey couldn't take her eyes from his toned and

sculpted body. And the glorious erection pointing straight at her. Heat flooded her, and her nipples were suddenly hard as diamonds. Between her thighs, she felt the pulse beat of desire and the liquid flooding her sex.

Then he was beside her, his mouth fused again with hers. She could feel its soft texture, the roughness of the inevitable late day stubble on his chin.

Lindsey could hardly breathe. She began to shake from the sensations rising through her body. The pain from her knee and the soreness in her muscles disappeared. All she could feel was the heat of Nick Vanetta's skin, the lick of his tongue, the warm fingertips seeking out the sensitive places of her body.

She shivered as he kissed the soft spot behind her ear, traced it with his tongue, and nibbled at it lightly, sending sensations cascading through her body. He stroked her everywhere, touching her shoulders, tracing her collarbone with the tips of his fingers. Her skin felt like a thousand tiny flares were igniting, and she arched into his touch, fearful he'd take it away.

But his hands moved tenderly over the slope of her breasts, his fingers lightly pinching her hardened nipples. Gently palming her breasts, he claimed her mouth again, his tongue dancing lightly as it swept the inner recesses, feeding on her, threatening to swallow her. She felt as if she'd been transported to another place.

Slowly, slowly, his hand trailed down her stomach, pausing to caress her navel, the tip of his finger circling lightly, and then drifting lower to brush the tight triangle of curls that covered her sex. For so long, she had denied herself this pleasure. No, not *this* pleasure. Never like this. Everything that had gone before was weak and pale in comparison.

With his tongue painting little circles in the shell of her ear, he moved fingers into her folds, gently separating them to probe the entrance to her body. Erotic sensations spread to every art of her as he slid one long finger into her hot flesh. When he pulled his hand away, she opened her eyes to see him stretched out on his side, looking down at her.

"Lindsey?" He sounded as if he had to push he word out.

"What? What's wrong?" She shifted her body against him, urging him on.

"Please, you have to tell me." His face was taut with the effort at control. "I know this sounds stupid in this day and age, but are you a virgin? I have to know."

"N—no." Her eyes widened, and a tiny knot tightened low in her belly. What was wrong here? "No, I'm not. What's the matter?"

"You are so damned tight." He brushed the tips of his fingers across her cheekbone. "There's no way in hell you're ready for me, and I don't want to hurt you."

In that one statement, she felt the essence of the man, someone looking for more than a good time in bed, someone who could protect and shelter her, someone with depth of feeling and emotion. It both soothed and frightened her. Soothed because this was more than just lust, and frightened her because her emotions were about to dive into a very deep pool.

Turning her head to the side, she closed her eyes. "It's…been a very long time. I'm sorry. I'm so sorry."

She waited, her heart nearly stopped, to see if he would roll away from her. If he did, that was okay. She'd handle it. But holy mother of god, she hoped he didn't because she wanted him with a hunger that consumed her.

"Shh, it's all right." Nick cradled her against him, and she could feel the tension rolling off his big body in waves. "Just relax, okay? I'll take care of you."

"Oh, God, Nick, you must think—" What? What did he think? She had to make sure he understood that this was what she wanted.

"It's all right, baby." He brushed kisses across her forehead and cheeks, stroking the length of her body with his hand. "Everything will be fine. Look at me, Lindsey."

She stared at him. The room was dark, but the light spilling through the open bathroom doorway outlined Nick's muscular, sculptured body. His eyes reflected the faint light as he looked at her with intense hunger.

"Do you trust me?"

She nodded, trembling. She *did* trust him. More than that, she realized he respected her, not just as a client but as a woman he'd obviously come to care about in a very, very short time. She wanted this so badly but her stupid body was making a mess of things.

"Then just let yourself go," he told her. "Let me make you feel good, and it will all come out all right."

He murmured in her ear, crooning to her, caressing her. Little by little, she relaxed, her muscles turning to liquid. His hand drifted over her body, touching and stroking her, all the while kissing every sensitive spot he touched. Her anxiety began to disappear as he used his mouth to coax a response from her body. He brushed his lips over her heated skin, sucking her nipples as they sprang to life under his hot, wet mouth. The scrape of his teeth on the under slope of her breasts followed by the soothing lick of his tongue made her shiver.

His head moved lower, and the tip of his tongue circled her navel, sending shards of heat through her. A pulse began to throb deep within her core. He shifted beside her, and in a moment, he was kneeling between her legs, kissing and stroking the inside of her thighs, skimming his hands over her until she couldn't stop quivering.

"Close your eyes now, Lindsey." His voice was hoarse, raspy. "Don't think, just feel."

As if she could keep them open.

"Beautiful," he whispered, his words like a soft breeze. "So beautiful."

He draped her legs over his shoulders, his thumbs opening her, and the next thing she felt was his tongue slipping inside her. At the first thrust, all her nerve endings rioted, and the heavy pulse in her core beat harder.

On and on it went, her hips thrusting at him, little cries escaping from her throat. When he flicked the tip of his tongue on her clitoris, a madness raced through her. If he hadn't been holding her hips, she'd have lifted them off the bed. He slipped his thumb over the swollen nub, drawing lazy circles over and over, while his tongue resumed its demanding assault on her hot sheath. Her body began to move with demanding urgency, back and forth, her hips twisting. Still, he kept the same rhythm, stroking, thrusting. The continued assault on her senses took her up a dark spiral of need, higher, higher, more intense than any she'd ever felt before. She tried to pull back, but Nick was relentless.

Her hips thrust at his mouth, and a hoarse scream

escaped from her throat. He held her firmly, still plundering her with his tongue, his thumb still tormenting her painfully sensitive clit. She begged him to stop. She begged him *not* to stop. She was out of her mind with pleasure and need.

He slid one long, lean finger into her again, then a second, the entry smoother and easier as the gathering moisture eased the way. His fingers curled, finding her trigger spot and setting off rockets inside her.

And then it happened, an explosion that nearly rocked her off the bed. She shattered so hard she was sure she'd come apart.

Slowly, the intensity eased until her heartbeat slowed and her body moved only with tiny aftershocks. She lay panting, astounded by the power of her orgasm. Nothing in her sexual experiences had prepared her for the stunning intimacy of what had just happened.

"Better?" Nick's voice was like warm syrup.

She could only nod.

"Hang on, then. We're far from done."

Oh, god!

He began again, kissing all the sensitive spots—where her shoulder met her neck, behind her ear, her nipples, the slope of her breasts, her navel. And wherever his mouth went, his hands followed, feathering, teasing, arousing.

Lindsey lost all sense of time and place. He played her body like an instrument, touching her in places she didn't even know existed, coaxing reactions from her she had never felt before. Her skin was on fire, and her breasts felt as if they would burst from their fullness. The pulse between her legs throbbed rhythmically, slowly increasing in intensity. Nothing was real except

Nick, and the forceful sensations that captured every nerve ending.

"Please, please, please," she begged, straining for release.

"Not yet, sugar. Not just yet."

Sweat beaded on Nick's forehead as he fought to maintain control. What the hell kind of life did this woman lead that sex had been absent for so long she was like an untouched virgin? More than with any other woman in his life, he was determined to bring her pleasure greater than she'd ever known, and that required patience. A lot of it. When he felt the first drops of her moisture on his tongue, he wanted to shout with pleasure. And when he brought her to that first shattering climax, he felt as if someone had given him the earth.

He stretched forward and snapped on the lamp beside the bed.

"Nick?" Her voice was foggy. "Don't..."

She tried to cover herself, and he moved her hands away. "I want to look at you, Lindsey. You have a beautiful body that was made for love. Let me see you. All of you."

After only a moment of hesitation, she let her hands fall away. God in heaven! He feasted on her creamy, satiny skin, the high full breasts topped with rosy, swollen nipples. His gaze swept over the indentation of her hips, the delicious navel his tongue had dipped into, and the nest of richly dark hair covering her mound.

He almost lost it right then, but he gritted his teeth and forced himself to keep a tight rein on his body. Leaning forward, he dipped his tongue into her sex, lapping at the creamy texture of her liquid, thrusting into that hungry body that beckoned his touch and his taste. Her reaction sent desire blazing through him, and he moved his tongue faster, feeling her muscles clench around it as he drove deeper and deeper.

Suddenly, she was over the edge again, shudders wracking her one after the other.

He'd had sex with many women, too many probably. But none had been so openly responsive, so unrestrained at his touch. It amazed and thrilled him. He wanted to drive her to orgasm again and again. If she thought he would let her rest, she was mistaken. His hands moved over her body again as he learned her secret places. Discovered what gave her the most pleasure, what drove her to the highest peaks.

At last, when he couldn't hold back another minute, he slowly entered her. He pushed against her tightness, easing in a little at a time until he was buried to the hilt, holding her thighs wide apart to give him total access to her.

"Open your eyes," he commanded hoarsely. "Look at me, Lindsey. Look at me now."

She opened her eyes. "Nick." She spoke just his name, a sigh on the breath that escaped her lips.

What was left of his brain screamed at him that this was far more than physical release. For both of them. Tamping down his fear of the emotional unknown, he began moving in and out of her with powerful strokes. He watched for signs that another release was building inside her. She squeezed him like a tight glove, clutching at him, holding him, the sensation beyond anything he'd ever experienced.

She wrapped her legs around him, thrust upward,

and the dance began, a rhythm that seemed to go on forever. When he felt the first edges of her orgasm, he pushed into her one last time, hard. Only then did he welcome his own release, emptying himself into her. They exploded together with a force that jolted him. The memory of every woman he'd ever been with disappeared until there was only Lindsey.

"Mercy." Nick managed the word when he could finally catch his breath. "This may be a very short lived romance because I think you're gonna kill me." He pulled her into his arms, cradling her, unable to do more than just stroke her with light caresses.

Beneath him, Lindsey lay completely still.

"I'm too heavy for you," he said.

"No, it's all right. Don't move. Not yet."

They lay there a long time, quiet, holding each other. Her hands gently explored the muscles beneath his skin, and her fingers tangled in the thick mat of hair on his chest.

Finally, with great reluctance, he slid out of her and rolled over, drawing her close to him. He felt such an unfamiliar tenderness and caring. No wonder the passion had been so volatile.

Then, like a bucket of cold water, a chilling thought swept over him. How could he have been such a fool? Taken leave of his senses like this?

"Lindsey?"

"Mmm?"

"Lindsey, honey, we have a problem." Shit. How had he allowed this to happen?

"Oh?" She tensed beside him. "What's the problem? Breaking Vanetta's Rule of Law?"

Whatever it was, she'd deal with it. And at least

she'd have the memory of this one night.

"Worse." He rubbed a hand over his stubbled jaw. "I didn't use any protection. Please tell me you're on the pill. Or some kind of birth control."

Yeah, right. Would a woman who hadn't had sex in so long she was tighter than a virgin be on the pill? Get serious.

He felt her withdraw from him emotionally, and a tight band constricted his chest. Oh, God, she wasn't. And she was abruptly hit by the consequences. That was it.

"Lindsey, what's the matter?"

"Nothing," she replied, her tone distant.

"Sugar, we have to talk about this." He tried to pull her back to him, but she resisted.

"I know," she said in a small voice. "It's all right."

"So you *are* taking the pill?"

"No, but you don't have to worry," she told him, closing her eyes so she didn't look at him. "I can't get pregnant." She said the last in a soft, tiny voice.

He frowned, feeling suddenly disconnected from her and not knowing why. "What do you mean, you can't get pregnant?" She tried to pull away from him again, but he held her in a tight grip. "Don't do that, damn it. Talk to me. What's the matter?"

She tucked her head against his shoulder, not looking at him. "I mean I can't have children. Period."

He forced her head up. "You have to explain this to me, because I don't know what the hell you're talking about."

"Can I make it any plainer than that? What don't you understand?"

****

Tell him now and get it over with.

Lindsey's infertility, the result of a physical problem that had left heavy scarring in her reproductive system, had been a major issue in the two serious relationships she'd had, and she'd learned a hard lesson. *No children? No heirs to carry on the line? Every man's dream? You've got to be kidding. Well, I guess you know this changes things. But hell, we can still have fun. And no worries, either, right?*

With the men she dated, adoption had come to be a dirty word. It was almost as if time had rolled back to a place where a woman's ability to breed was one of her greatest attributes. She never should have given in to this. Healing her heart this time would take even longer.

Her brain was sending her messages—break it off right now, fire him, go and hide until the stalker is found or finds another victim.

But Nick was relentless. Demanding information from her. "I want to know exactly what you mean."

"I have…had…a problem." She drew in a shuddering breath and closed her eyes so she couldn't see the look on his face. "I've had all the tests, and they all had the same results. No children. Can't provide the sons all you macho Texans seem to crave to carry on your name and build a Texas dynasty."

"I see." Very matter of fact. "Apparently you've been involved with some real Neanderthals. Is that why you decided to stop having sex altogether?"

"What was the point? It didn't mean anything. Not anymore." Her voice had a slight tremor. "I'm not a person who can do it just for the exercise."

"No, I don't believe you are." He put his hand under her chin and forced her to tilt her head up. "Is that why you never married?"

"Yes."

"But people adopt children all the time," he pointed out. "And the love and family bond is just as strong."

"Now there's where you're wrong," she said bitterly. "None of the men I knew wanted to raise 'someone else's brat.'"

He was quiet again, this time for so long Lindsey began to tense. She forced herself to lie totally still, her face remaining hidden against his shoulder. He wouldn't let her move away from him, and she couldn't bear to look at him.

Now what? Will he find a way to let me down easy? I thought he was different, but I guess my judgment isn't so great after all.

At last he tilted her face up, his eyes burning into hers with an unexpected ferocity. "Lindsey, we haven't known each other more than a few days, yet already I feel things for you I never thought I could feel for a woman." His throat muscles flexed as he swallowed. "Does it scare me? Yes. It terrifies me. Do I want to run away from it? Strangely enough, no." His grip on her tightened. "You don't know much about me at all, but you must have a very low opinion to believe that what you said would chase me away."

"You're a man, aren't you?" she asked, her tone bitter. "With an ego, right?"

For a long moment, Nick didn't reply. When he did, his voice was hard and grating. "I know this is all fast and unexpected, and we're both blindsided by it. But answer this for me. Did this, what we just did, mean something to you? Was it more than just that exercise you talk about? Because it was a lot more than that to me. A *lot* more."

"Oh, God. What are you doing to me?" She hardly got the words past her tightened vocal chords.

"I'm trying to get an answer from you. You don't want to look at me, and you seem to have a pretty bad opinion of me. So I guess I want to know if I've made a fool of myself here, something I don't often do."

"Yes." The word barely scraped from her mouth.

"What was that?" He turned her face, forcing her to look at him.

"I said, yes. But…"

"Yes, I've made a fool of myself? Or yes, this means something to you."

"Yes." He could barely hear her. "It means something. This was…more than just sex for me, too. I respect you and feel safe with you." She swallowed. "And care for you."

"That's the answer I was looking for." His arms tightened around her. "So we have some things to get straightened out here." His big hand stroked her back, soothing, the hot feel of his palm comforting against her skin. "Not being able to have children has to be a loss for you. It means you'll never have the experience of pregnancy and childbirth. But adoption is a very real possibility, if we get to that point."

"But—"

"Don't judge me by others, okay?" Anger edged his voice. "My ego isn't what's at stake here. My heart is. Whatever happens between us, the issue of childbearing will not be what affects it. You can count on this. I will never hurt you. Okay?"

She wanted to believe him. Badly. "O—Okay."

He sighed. "Not a ringing endorsement. Honey, do

you trust me?"

She nodded.

"Then believe in what I'm telling you. This didn't just happen because of hormones. It was another level on which we could communicate." He leaned down and kissed her. "But there's something more important than this right now. It's the reason I'm here in the first place. You've got a stalker out there somewhere that needs catching. I need to do a better job of keeping you safe than I did today. That's our first priority. Then, when this is over, you and I are going to talk about our future. Thinking about it scares the shit out of me, but I'm not running away from it." He smiled down at her. "How does that sound?"

"That sounds okay with me." Touched by his words, she managed a smile and her body relaxed.

"I'll take care of you. I promise."

Lindsey sighed and snuggled against him, warmed by his words, and dropped light kisses on the crisp hair covering the thick muscles of his chest. How amazing that disaster could bring her a man who made her feel both wanted and protected. A man she connected with on so many levels. She believed Nick and trusted him. She was safe with him. He would find her stalker and then—dare she hope—this relationship could land on solid footing.

Nick chuckled. "One thing you have to do for sure. You have to clue Ruben and Mary into what's happening. I'll be damned if I sleep alone when we go to the ranch."

Chapter Ten

I'm watching you again. So close, and you can't even see me. Fool.

Did you like my new message? I want you to know what fear is like, to realize your life is in my hands. When the time is right for you to die, you'll know it. But first I want to have my fun, my satisfaction. I want to torment you until you can't sleep, can't eat, because the fear is so strong.

Last night, I dismembered Barbie again, but a doll is becoming less and less satisfying. I want the pleasure of removing your real body parts. One at a time. Watching your blood flow out of you. Or maybe I'll just squeeze your neck in my hands, watching your eyes pop out and your face turn blue.

Pampered bitch. You have it all, and you don't deserve any of it.

I have to do something about that idiot you hired, but I'll figure it out. I always do. It just requires a slight change of plans. But I guess I'll have to stop the emails before someone tracks me down. They'll probably block your system, anyway. No problem. There are other ways.

And it's time to ratchet up the fun.

Soon. Soon it will all be clear to you.

You think you have everything. What would it be like for you to have nothing?

I'm watching you.
Bitch!

****

Nick considered them lucky that the balance of the week passed in relative quiet. The office hummed along at a fairly normal pace, if the schedule they followed could be considered normal. He had Tony run point on everything, directing the security teams, coordinating with the IT guys and supervising the research into all the people in Lindsey's life. That way he could devote himself to Lindsey and whatever was happening around her. They were all uptight—Lindsey, Mark, and Brianna—but they all made a deliberate effort to ignore the tension.

Nick spent one hundred percent of his time with Lindsey. During the day, he was in and out of her office, and at night, he locked them up together in her apartment.

"I want us to stay in town during the week," he explained, "where I have more manpower, more resources and better containment."

"And what do I tell Mary?" she asked.

"That you have several new clients with immediate deadlines." He kissed her forehead. "That's not far from the truth, right?"

While Lindsey worked each day, Nick read the reports from Guardian on her clients, her friends, her former co-workers in Austin, even the guys she'd dated. Then, leaving nothing to chance, he had both Mark and Brianna checked out. Tony brought him thick reports on both of them that Nick was careful to read away from Lindsey's curious eyes.

Brianna Moore had been raised in Michigan, her

father a paper shuffler at a large corporation and her mother a stay-at-home mom. In their late forties when she was born, they were often at a loss as to how to raise their frenzied, bright, overactive child. She aced her grades in school but took great pleasure in skirting the edge of danger. It was assumed her behavior was more to test her parents than anything else, the report read, because she was never in what could be considered serious trouble.

After high school, she took classes for a certification in business science and was working for a company in Detroit when a fire destroyed her parents' house and killed both of them. After that, she bumped around the country, working here and there, moving apparently whenever the spirit struck her. She had come to San Antonio looking for new adventures and had shown up at the exact moment Lindsey was advertising for someone.

Nothing out of the ordinary on her social life, just the usual visits to singles bars and a variety of dates. No close friends, but a lot of people took their time establishing those kinds of relationships in a new place.

And nothing that raised a red flag.

And the relationship with Lindsey appeared to be a solid business arrangement. Despite Bri's nomadic history, Nick was impressed with the efficient way she ran the office.

Nick had been in the business long enough, though, to know red flags often didn't appear until it was almost too late. It was a major reason he was digging so deeply into the lives of anyone Lindsey crossed paths with.

They also found their answer to Mark's mysterious lunch dates. Every day, he slipped out the door exactly at noon and returned on the dot of one-thirty, always with a slightly embarrassed look on his face. Tony followed him twice and reported his findings to Nick.

"Well," he told him, "the guy met the same female for lunch both times. And they always eat at the same place."

"You think she might be pulling his strings to help her with this?" Nick wanted to know.

Tony snorted. "I'd be damned surprised if either of them conjured up something like this. Think two nerds in love."

"No femme fatale stringing him along?" Nick laughed at the image.

"Nothing there, boss man," Tony assured him. "You can cross him off the list. He's too busy holding hands to do any heavy plotting."

"Maybe. But I'm not crossing anyone off just yet. Let's keep an eye on both of them as well as Brianna, just so we know where all the players are. Anything yet on the mother's nursing home?"

Tony shook his head. "You didn't say it was a priority so we just got someone loose today to get over there. Is that a problem?"

"No. At least, I don't think so. Just following up on something that bothers Lindsey. Probably nothing to it, but we can't afford to ignore anything."

Reno called Thursday afternoon. "I'm emailing more information on Lindsey's clients plus other people she's come into contact with. I thought it would be a monumental chore, but it turned out to be fairly easy. Apparently, she doesn't have much of a social life, so we hardly had anyone to check."

"Yes," Nick bit off, cursing the fact that his tone

might have given something away. "I'm aware of that."

Reno was silent a moment. "Something going on here you want to tell me about?"

Nick exhaled. "Things are…complicated."

"Listen, Nick—"

"Don't say it, okay? I'm on top of things here. And I'd like a more thorough rundown on anyone she had a long-term relationship with, regardless of how long ago it was. You never know when someone will pop loose a screw."

"Whatever." Reno hesitated as if he wanted to say more, but he simply added before he hung up, "Let me know if there's anything else you need."

"Okay."

****

Lindsey used the rhythm of her work to keep herself distracted from the situation, still resisting the idea that someone she knew was out to harm her. She was on edge waiting for the next shoe to drop, and she tried to block that from her mind. She finished the Marquez sketches and met with them, put the final touches on two other projects, and met with two new prospective clients. She was hardly in the mood to deal with new people, but the discipline would be good for her.

But at night, with all the alarms set, security outside in place and everyone else gone, she and Nick could relax with each other and explore their growing relationship. They shared childhood stories, likes and dislikes, even argued over television programs. It made Lindsey realize exactly how shallow her previous relationships had been.

They learned each other's bodies as well as their

minds and personalities. Certain touches or caresses could ignite the heat that flowed constantly between them. He was far more experienced than she, and he taught her all the tricks of exquisite pleasure, driving both of them to greater and greater orgasms. She was an eager student, quick to learn. Before long, she was able to torment him as he did her, driving his body crazy while preventing him from that final release until he begged for mercy.

"I've never been like this with another woman," he confessed one night as they lay in each other's arms, depleted. "Making love with you is unbelievable."

"Really, now. What about all these other women I've heard about?" she teased. "Quinn said—"

"Quinn needs to mind his own damn fucking business," Nick growled. He turned her face toward him and kissed her so deeply she thought he'd reached her soul. "This is different," he told her when he could catch his breath. "Much, much different. More than merely giving in to sexual attraction. And don't you dare forget it."

Still, Lindsey had no idea where this thing between them was going. The stalker still dominated their lives, creating an artificial situation What if this all fell apart when the stalker was caught and their lives went back to normal? Somehow, she had to prepare herself for that. She'd learned long ago not to put too much trust in anything men told her.

And despite his protestations, when Nick had a chance to think about the whole children thing, it was very possible he'd realize that could be a deal-breaker. That he really wanted children with his own DNA.

On Friday, Nick decided to leave two men to keep

an eye on the building front and back, and one in her apartment to give the appearance they were still there.

"Just in case," he told her as they finished breakfast. "I think we need to change our routine, and I want to install an alarm at the ranch."

She raised her eyebrows. "You think that's necessary?"

"I do. In Ruben's and Mary's place and the barn, too. We'll set them up so each has its own keypad, but the main controls will be in your house. Also, I want a panic button in your bedroom."

"Is that in case I need someone to save me from you?" She gave him a wicked grin.

"No, it's in case I'm the one who needs saving." He smiled back at her and covered her hand with his, giving it a light squeeze. "The less exposure you have out there the better I feel."

"Well, we'll have to do some tall talking." She got up to clear away their dishes. "I know how Ruben will react."

"We have to tell him about the bus incident," Nick insisted. "If he's aware that there's real danger, he'll want to take every precaution possible. We'll just say it's to back him up. I sure don't want that man to feel I don't think he can take care of you."

"You really believe whoever this is will follow me out to the ranch?" Lindsey felt her good humor slip away. "That seems a little farfetched."

"Nothing about a stalker is farfetched, honey. The only predictable thing about them is their unpredictability."

"All right. I'll call Mary and tell her she'd better have plenty of food to feed you." She turned toward the sink.

She sensed Nick move up behind her. In a moment, he wrapped his arms around her and kissed the side of her neck. "Good. I need to keep up my strength."

They'd been eating lunch in every day, just as a simple precaution, Nick sending someone on the team for takeout. They ate in the apartment, enjoying the quiet break in the day together. But Lindsey was beginning to get claustrophobic.

"How about going out for lunch today?" she suggested. "I haven't been outside these rooms in three days."

"Lindsey," he began.

"You'll be right beside me," she pointed out. "Just for a change, please? I'm going nuts. We'll even take extra bodyguards if you insist."

"I insist. But I just want you to know I'm not too happy about it."

Craving Mexican food, she decided on La Fonda, just off Loop 410. Nick was agreeable, but when they went to the underground garage, plans for lunch disappeared.

Someone had maliciously attacked Nick's SUV, which was parked in its usual spot near the stairs. The windshield and side windows were smashed, and the side view mirrors completely ripped off. The tires were slashed, and the body had been viciously keyed. Looking at Nick's face, Lindsey was stunned by the visceral rage she saw.

"Stay right here," he commanded in a tight voice.

With a visible Herculean effort, Nick managed to get himself under control and walked around the vehicle to fully assess the damage.

"There's something inside here," he said, looking in the driver's side. He pulled his handkerchief from his pocket and reached in and lifted out a piece of paper.

I'm watching you, too. Beware the eyes. They are all around you. You cannot save her.

If it hadn't been evidence, Nick would have crushed it into a tiny ball. "So they want me, too? Well, bring it on. I'll be ready for them."

He took out his Nextel cell phone/walkie talkie and spoke into it quietly. In seconds, a young man in a gray suit came jogging down through the garage.

"I'm sorry I didn't see any one, Mr. Vanetta." He stopped next to Nick. "I thought I heard something at the other end of this floor and went to check it out. They must have created a diversion to draw me away."

"Ya think?" Nick snorted. "From now on you stay with the vehicle. And keep your eyes open from wherever it's parked."

"Yes, sir. This won't happen again."

"Damn straight it won't."

Nick speed dialed his office and got Reno on the horn, relating what happened to him. His partner received the information with a quiet that belied his fury.

"You watch your ass," he told Nick. "This is getting very ugly."

"No worry on that score. But I may need to tighten up the security arrangements."

"Whatever you need, just let me know. I don't take kindly to someone threatening my partner. Have Tony pull the tapes from the security cameras, although I'd guess whoever this is would have made sure to conceal his face."

When Nick walked back to Lindsey, she was standing near the damaged vehicle, looking both scared and angry. He cradled her cheeks in his hands and scanned her face. "Are you okay, honey?"

She sighed. "I'm fine. What did the note say?"

"Nothing you need to see. Believe me."

She jerked her head away and curled her hands into fists. "Don't bullshit me. I'm not some hothouse flower. Tell me exactly what it said."

He swallowed a smile. His little spitfire wasn't going to be cowed by anything. Good for her. He watched the anger flash in her eyes as she listened to him.

"So he's after you, too. This is too much." She shoved her hands in her pockets. "Now you'll be in danger, all because of me."

"Lindsey, I'm paid to be in danger, remember? And we still don't know what this is really about."

"Except it sounds very specific." She pointed toward his vehicle. "This isn't just collateral fallout from the job. This is very personal."

"Only because it centers around you," he told her. "It isn't the first time I've had this happen with a client, and it won't be the last. "

"I don't want you hurt because of this."

He could see that, despite the anger, she was fighting to hold herself together. Heat surged through him that had nothing to do with sexual awareness. It was the first time since he was an adult that he could remember anyone except his parents caring about him this way. Damn! Maybe something good was coming out of this after all.

"I can take care of myself. Promise." He walked

her back to the elevator and nodded at one of the gray suits waiting for him. "This is Angelo. I want you to go upstairs with him. Go into your apartment and wait for me. You can fix us a couple of sandwiches, since our lunch trip is out for today. I have some things to take care of, and then I'll be up."

"I think I've lost my appetite." She moved into the elevator, leaning on the door to keep it open.

"You have to eat. We both do. No time to get sick." He put his hands on her shoulders and forced her to look at him. "We're leaving for the ranch right after I get done. Tell Brianna you have some personal business to take care of that came up suddenly and get her to change any afternoon appointments you have. I didn't see much on your calendar, anyway."

"Only one appointment, and she can move it. Oh, Nick. When will this end?"

"Soon, sweetheart. Believe me. Now go on with Angelo."

****

To Lindsey, it seemed to take forever until Nick was back upstairs. Angelo lounged unobtrusively in the background, eyes ever alert, listening through the ear bud comm, obviously monitoring what was going on with the other members of the team. She cleaned up the files on her desk and arranged her sketches on her worktable for Monday. Then she buzzed for Brianna.

"You're leaving early?" The woman tilted her head, a questioning look in her eyes.

Lindsey nodded and gave her the story she and Nick had concocted. "Before we could leave for lunch, I got a call on my cell. I have to take care of some personal business with the ranch. Cancel my three o'clock, and tell Mark I'll meet with him on Monday."

"Everything okay, Lindsey?" Bri's sharp eyes took inventory of her face.

"Yes, fine. Everything's fine." She hoped her voice sounded calmer than she felt.

"Okay. I've got plenty to keep me busy. Don't worry about that."

"You and Mark can cut out early, too, if you want," Lindsey told her. "It's been a tense week for everyone. Go have a drink someplace."

"Thank you. We'll see." Brianna stood up and gave her a brief hug. "You just take care, okay? See you Monday morning."

Lindsey locked up the drawers of her desk before going into her apartment. She changed into shorts and a loose shirt. She had no idea what Nick planned to do, since there weren't any casual clothes for him here, and he wouldn't do too well at the ranch in a suit. Finally, she scrounged around in her kitchen and fixed peanut butter sandwiches and milk. She offered food to Angelo, too, a watchful figure in the background, but he shook his head.

"I'll catch something later," he told her.

"I hope you like childhood comfort food." She smiled at Nick when he finally came upstairs.

He took the plate and glass and laughed out loud. "Are you kidding? The only thing I can't live without is peanut butter. My mother thinks it's a staple of every diet."

He wolfed down the sandwich and milk, put his plate and dish in the dishwasher, then threw toiletries into his shaving kit. The only clothing he took was his dirty laundry.

"We'll stop by my house so I can pick up some more clothes and ditch this stuff," he told her. "Let's go. I hope you said your goodbyes in the office because I want to leave from the apartment."

"Any special reason?"

"Yup. The door from your apartment opens into an opposite hallway leading to the back elevator, right? So it's hard for anyone to tell if you've left. Angelo's going to hang around and see if anything catches his eye." He took her arm. "Let's get out of here."

He triple checked the alarm before hustling her out to the elevator. When they got to the garage and he walked to his parking spot, she stopped, speechless.

"What exactly is that?" She pointed.

The shiny SUV had been replaced by a dark green pickup truck, dusty and with its share of dents.

"That, sweetheart, is our new transportation. I'll fit right in at the ranch, don't you think?" His eyes were twinkling.

"You have got to be kidding."

"Nope. It's part of the company fleet. They towed the SUV and sent it out for repair. This one would be very hard to damage. Also," his voice dropped conspiratorially, "don't let its looks deceive you. The doors are reinforced steel and the windows are all bulletproof glass. I'm not taking any more chances."

"Unbelievable." She couldn't take her eyes off the truck. "Nick, how did this person know that was your vehicle, and what you're doing here?"

"He's obviously been paying closer attention than we realized. I briefed the team staying behind on what to look for while we're at the ranch. We'll see if they come up with anything."

Nick threw their small cases in the space behind the seats, then helped her climb up into the truck. "We're going to take a little scenic tour on the way to the house. I've got someone riding tail behind me to see if we draw anyone's interest. My phone number is unlisted so they'd have a hell of a time finding out where I live. I don't want to make it easy for them by leading them there."

Lindsey's head was spinning. So much had happened in such a short time, but she was impressed by the speed with which Guardian operated and their firm grasp of the situation.

She was actually glad they were going to the ranch. Maybe she could get Nick to go through those boxes with her, the ones she'd already opened as well as the ones still shut tight. With his investigator's mind, he might spot things she had missed. Or know the questions to ask. Tomorrow. Tomorrow she'd approach the subject with him. Maybe drag him up to the attic with her.

Nick muscled the truck expertly through the traffic, cruising around the streets downtown, then heading East on I-35, exiting and doubling back. They had passed El Mercado, the Mexican Marketplace, and driven west for a few exits on I-10 when Nick's little communicator beeped.

He pressed the walkie/talkie button. "Yeah? Good enough. Thanks." He disconnected the phone and laid it on the seat next to him. "We're clear," he told Lindsey. "We'll run by my house and then head on out."

The house smelled of lemon and mint and something else indefinable but pleasant. As before, it was immaculate.

"Have you been sneaking out during the day and cleaning your house?" she asked.

Nick laughed. "I have a housekeeper who comes in three days a week, four if I need it. Sometimes, when I'm on a job, I don't see my house for weeks or even months. I'd never leave it unattended that long, and I also don't have a lot of time for housework. She does my laundry, too, in case that was your next question. And shuttles my suits back and forth to the cleaners."

"She sounds like a gem. I hope you pay her well."

"You can bet on it." He was on his way upstairs. "Come on and keep me company. We'll be just a few minutes."

His bedroom was exactly as she'd imagined after seeing the rest of the house. Large, floor-to-ceiling windows added plenty of light to the room; the wood flooring was brightened with colorful scatter rugs. The king-sized bed, with its chocolate comforter and abundance of pillows, dominated the room. Rows of photographs completely filled a small table next to a big easy chair.

Lindsey was startled when a muscular arm slid around her waist.

"You didn't get to see the bedroom last time," he whispered. "Today isn't the time, but we're going to initiate that bed pretty soon."

"I'll bet that's been the scene of some pretty hectic acrobatics," she teased.

Nick looked at her with a tight expression on his face. "Just so you know, I've never brought a woman into this house before. You're the first one who's ever been here. I never wanted anyone here before. This is the part of me that's private. You're the first woman

I've wanted to share it with."

She swallowed hard, and her voice dropped to a whisper. "Thank you for saying that."

He touched his lips lightly to hers before setting her away from him with determination. "If we keep doing that, we'll never get out of here. Just sit over there like a good girl, and I'll make this quick."

She wandered over to his dresser, drawn by a framed photograph of a large group of people. "Who are all the people in these pictures?"

He had yanked a suitcase from the closet and was stuffing clothes into it. "My family. My sisters and brothers and their respective spouses and children."

"Are you the only single one left?" she asked inquisitively.

"That's me. I think my mother's given up on me, although my sisters haven't."

"I'm curious. You have to know Quinn gave me the rundown on your reputation. Why haven't you ever married?"

"Never found a woman I wanted to wake up with in the morning. Every morning." He was beside her again, giving her another quick kiss. "Until now. Okay. I'm ready."

She stared at him, trying to figure out what his words really meant.

Don't make too much of it.

"What?" He frowned. "Come on, sugar, we have to move."

He'd changed into jeans and a T-shirt, exchanging his polished boots for jogging shoes. He carried a large duffel bag in one hand and a thick aluminum briefcase in the other, using the briefcase to urge her into motion.

Before they left, he checked his alarm system, making sure everything was set.

"That's a pretty complex system," Lindsey commented, watching him.

"I'm away a lot," he told her, "so I installed a high-powered system that I'm pretty sure no one can figure a way to bypass. Only my housekeeper and the agency have the code."

Despite all the twisting and turning they'd done on the way to his house, Nick still kept checking the rearview and side-view mirrors, sometimes even doubling back around a block just to check the traffic. When he was satisfied they were clear, he finally headed toward the Interstate.

"Did you call Mary and tell her we were coming out?" he asked.

"Sure did." Lindsey swallowed a grin. "I think she started cooking right away."

Nick laughed. "Whatever else happens, I'll be well fed by the time this is over."

"Is that all?" she asked, suddenly shy.

Nick reached over and captured her hand, linking his fingers with hers and placing their hands on his thigh. "No, sugar, that is far from all. Believe me."

Please make it so. Please don't let this be just another fast ride with a bumpy end.

She hated to realize how much of that, just like the stalker, was really out of her control.

"By the way," he said, "I've got someone working on the nursing home angle. I figured if we went in there and started asking questions, everyone would clam up the way they did with you."

"So what are you doing?"

"They had an opening for an orderly, and one of the guys on our staff was a medic in the military. Reno pulled a few strings, and he got the job. Now he's busy making friends and sucking up gossip."

"I just know there's something no one's telling me," she told him. "My mother was almost ready to come home when this happened."

"If there is, we'll find out about it. You can count on that."

Ruben was on the porch, leaning against the railing, watching them as they drove up. When they got out of the truck, he came down to meet them. "About time you remembered where you live, little one."

"Just had a really busy week, Ruben. That's all." She stepped into his hug. "Everything's okay. Honestly."

His eyes searched her face at length, looked over her head at Nick, then he shook his head. "We'll see. Best you get yourselves a cold drink, and we'll sit out here for a while. You can tell me what's put that terrible look in your eyes."

Nick lifted his duffel and Lindsey's small case out from behind the seats.

Ruben took them out of his hands. "I'll take these upstairs. You folks go get some of that lemonade in the fridge, and we'll have us a nice little chat. And I want the truth, *niña*. You hear?"

As casually as she could, Lindsey said, "You can put both of those bags in my room."

Ruben looked at her, his face totally impassive. He nodded and headed back to the house, but not before Lindsey saw a faint smile twist his lips.

Damn.

Am I making a mistake? This whole thing seems to have happened so quickly. So easily. Am I just another notch on his bedpost, despite what he keeps saying? I'm vulnerable and he knows it. Is he just taking advantage of that fact?

Lindsey shook herself mentally. She was going crazy with all these questions, and she had no answers to any of them.

Suck it up and enjoy it. Just enjoy it.

Mary fussed over them in the kitchen, hugging Lindsey and even Nick. Then she fixed a tray of cold drinks and cookies and insisted on taking it out to the porch herself.

By that time, Ruben was back outside leaning against the porch rail, a hard look on his face. He waited until Lindsey and Nick sat down with their drinks and Mary was back in the house before speaking. "Okay. Give. What's happened?"

Lindsey let Nick do most of the talking since he could deliver it more concisely and in greater detail. She sipped at the lemonade while Nick gave him all the information he had.

"I wish I had more to tell you," he said. "We've covered everything and interviewed dozens of people, and we still don't know any more than we did in the beginning."

Ruben nodded his head. "All right. What's up next?"

"I want to install a full security system here at the ranch," Nick told him.

Ruben arched one eyebrow. "You think whoever this is will try to get to her here?"

Nick shook his head. "Not necessarily. It's a lot

harder out here. I just don't want to leave any base uncovered."

"Barns, too?" Ruben asked.

"Everything." He studied Ruben's face. "Including your house. It only makes sense," he insisted, as Ruben began to object. "Someone who takes the time to learn this setup could sneak into your place, knock out the two of you, and then get to Lindsey."

Ruben grudgingly admitted Nick was right. "But I want to be with your men when they come out so I can learn exactly how it's done."

"Absolutely," he assured the other man. "They'll be here first thing in the morning. And I mean first thing. They like to start their day early, and this will be a time-consuming job."

"I'll be waiting for them." Ruben's face and tone said he'd be ready for anyone trying to hurt his *niña*, too.

"One other thing," Nick said. "I'm hoping you and Mary can help us with this. We've pretty thoroughly checked out everyone Lindsey has come into contact with since she opened her office and even some of the people she knew in Austin. So far it looks like a dead end, but we'll keep looking. That leaves only her past, which she seems to have no information on."

Lindsey twisted her hands together in her lap. Her past had always been a mystery to her, too. Her parents had avoided all her questions about other relatives, where they had come from, why they had settled here. She hadn't pushed them, since they seemed so determined to focus only on the present. But now they were both gone and she was facing a crisis in her life.

She gave Ruben a hard look. "We've been through

this before, Ruben. I want answers to my questions."

"It's hard to have much of a past in Cibolo." Ruben danced around the question. "When you sneeze, everyone knows you've got a cold."

"I understand that. But somewhere, somehow, there's something we need to find out. Things people in Cibolo probably know nothing about. Any little clue you can think of will help. You have to know something." She hated the desperation n her voice, but since her mother's death, her past had become an obsession.

The front screen door slammed, making Lindsey jump. Mary was back on the porch, wiping her hands on a towel and fixing her gaze on all of them, Ruben included. Lindsey had to press her lips together to keep from laughing. When she got going, Mary was a real virago, a force to be reckoned with.

"Nobody gets dinner until I know what's going on," she told them. "I know something's up, and I don't intend to be left out of it. So let's have it."

Lindsey swallowed a laugh and looked at Nick. "Better do what she says or you'll starve to death."

"No problem. I'll talk all night as long as it gets me Mary's cooking."

Lindsey listened quietly, watching Mary's reaction as Nick went through it again, repeating everything he'd told Ruben, answering Mary's questions as best he could.

"We've checked everyone on the list Lindsey gave us," he repeated, "but we've hit a blank wall. We even sent people to Austin to check out her connections there and came up empty. Like I told Ruben, I'm beginning to think this has to do with Lindsey's past. It's very strange that there are no relatives out there. *Everyone* has family somewhere. And what about personal history? How come there's no trace of the family before they bought this ranch?"

When Ruben and Mary exchanged glances, Nick caught the signal that passed between them.

"What is it? Something? Anything?" He studied each of them. "You have an idea, don't you?"

Ruben shook his head. "Lindsey, baby, maybe it's time for you to go through all those boxes upstairs. The ones you've been avoiding. The ones your mama refused to deal with. She and your daddy are both gone now. Whatever secrets you find can't hurt them anymore."

"You think there are secrets up there?" She stared at Ruben.

"I think you need to look at what's in those boxes," he said, his voice firm.

"What boxes?" Nick asked.

"There are some old cartons up in the attic," Lindsey told him. "My mother would never open them. She kept saying it was old junk and to forget about it. In fact, if I remember"—She wrinkled her forehead.—"one of the things she said when she had her heart attack was, if something happened to her, take everything and burn it."

"Didn't you think that was strange?" Nick asked. "What if there might be something in them you'd want to see? Like old photos? Or family information? You said you didn't know anything about your family history. Maybe there's something in there for you to find."

She chewed on her bottom lip. "I don't know. I

guess I figured if there was anything important in the boxes, Mom would show it to me. And what could there possibly be in my family's past that would make someone come after me like this?"

"Not to be crass," he pointed out, "but what about your trust fund? Anything there? Anyone who might think they deserved it more?"

She shook her head. "I'm an only child. My folks didn't have any siblings that I know of. Quinn manages the trust for me, and I don't think *he's* trying to bump me off or whatever."

"Okay." Nick stood up. "Let's have dinner and leave all this for tonight. I think it would do us both good to turn in early. Tomorrow, the techno twins will be here with a crew. I'll have some work to do with them, but after lunch, we should get those boxes down."

"All right." Lindsey sighed. "If you think we'll find anything. I guess I've just been putting it off for too long, anyway."

"Do this, Lindsey," Ruben said again. "It's past time."

Mary shooed them out of the kitchen when dinner was over, and Lindsey started up the stairs. When she looked over her shoulder, Nick wasn't behind her. "Coming?"

"I'll be up in a minute."

She guessed he was planning to tour the perimeter with Ruben, making sure everything was as secure as possible until the alarm system was in. Probably even afterward.

In the bedroom, she turned back the spread, folding it neatly at the foot of the bed. She put Nick's suitcase on the valet stand in the closet, stripped off her clothes, and headed for the bathroom. When the water in the shower was good and hot, she stepped inside and began to lather herself with the soap. She closed her eyes, letting the water cascade over her. Her knee was still a little sore, and she was wound as tight as a drum from the day's episodes.

The door slid open, and the bar of soap was lifted from her hand.

"I think this is my job," Nick said in a low tone. "You just relax."

For a moment, Lindsey was tempted to tell him to back away, that she wanted to shower by herself. Again, that anxious feeling that this was too much, too fast, and too smooth raced through her. Deliberately, she swallowed her misgiving, convincing herself if it all crashed, at least she'd be happy with the memories.

She leaned forward, bracing her arms against the shower wall. Very gently and very slowly, he began to lather her back, tracing light circles on her shoulders and down her spine and making her shiver. Carefully he soaped her buttocks, letting his hand roam easily over her curves.

Her inner pulse began to thrum, and she tried to turn toward him, but he murmured in her ear. "Don't move."

He slid his hands down her legs and farther down to her feet with the same circular motion, then he used his fingers like feathers, tracing the insides of her calves and thighs. She had never thought her body had so many erogenous zones, but with Nick, each inch of her body came alive. Suddenly, his hand, slick with the soap, slid into the cleft of her buttocks, slowly rubbing, teasing. The walls of her sex flexed and contracted as need spread through her.

Then he turned her to face him and began the same process in the front, massaging her breasts and the tight pink nipples with his soapy fingers. Then down to her navel where the tip of one finger circled it. His fingers moved with the barest of touches into that soft area of her folds, his soap-slicked thumb finding her sensitive nub while two fingers easily penetrated her.

Her body felt liquid, formless, and the throbbing deep inside her intensified. She could hardly stand and had to clutch Nick's shoulders for support.

"Now your turn," he whispered, handing her the soap.

Lindsey didn't think she could function, as weak as she was from his ministrations, but Nick clasped his hand over hers and placed it on his chest. She took a deep breath to steady herself and began soaping his chest, running her fingers through the dark mat of curls as she lathered them. She smiled at the hiss of his breath that escaped as her fingernails grazed his nipples, spreading soap on them and brushing it away.

She paused at his navel to trace the indentation, the tip of her finger fitting into it exactly, then following the fine hair of his groin until she reached the darker tangle and then… His erection was so huge and enormous that she could barely grasp it with her slippery hands.

Creating more lather, she spread it on him slowly, gently teasing him with her fingernail. His whole body shuddered at her touch. When she placed one hand on his chest, she felt the heavy beating of his heart.

Shaking from desire, she thought she would burst out of her skin. She didn't know how much longer she could do this. Just the feel of his skin beneath her hands made her hotter than a pistol.

Without warning, a low growl burst from his throat. "Enough."

He rinsed them both quickly before helping her out of the shower and drying them with big towels. Then he lifted her and carried her to the bed. The minute their bodies hit the cool smoothness of the sheets, they were on each other like wild animals, touching, teasing, and twisting together. Every time he touched her skin, tiny flames licked at it, searing it. His eyes, when she looked in them, glittered with desire.

His lips came down on hers, and his tongue thrust past her lips and teeth into her willing mouth, licking at the soft skin. She reveled in the feel of his big body covering hers, surrounding her, and she rubbed her breasts against the thick hair on his hard-muscled chest. When he eased one nipple between the knuckles of two fingers and squeezed gently, heat speared all the way to her hungry sex.

His hot, wet mouth pressed a kiss between her breasts, then he trailed the tip of his tongue along the length of her abdomen, tasting the tiny drops of water that still nestled in her navel and clung to the dark, golden hair covering the entrance to her sexual heat. Groaning with desire, he nudged her thighs apart and laid his palm over her mound, feeling her dampness, stroking the fold, sliding his fingers into her wetness, and stimulating her inner walls.

She was hot, so aroused she could barely breathe.

"Your skin is so soft, so sweet, and your body so hot. I'd like to fuck you forever, bury myself in you, fill you so your muscles are clenched tight around my cock." He nipped the lobe of one ear. "Want to kiss that sweet ass of yours, run my hands over it, squeeze it. Drive my cock into it and fuck you there until you scream."

His words made her burn as desire rose fast and furiously. With Nick she'd reached a level of sensuality that was totally unexpected, and she reveled in it. She moved restlessly against him, wanting him to fill her, to give the kind of satisfaction no other man had ever been able to elicit.

She moaned as the need built higher.

Pressing her against the mattress, he levered her knees apart, and she arched upward, her body silently begging.

"Now," she pleaded. "Please, Nick. Please now."

His strong fingers tilted her hips to give him deeper penetration, and he entered her with a long, slow push. She was wild, wrapping her legs around him, hooking her feet onto his back to lift herself and move with him to the rhythm. She stretched to accept him, pulsing around his thickness, a wave of pure lust sweeping over her so strong it consumed her.

The only sounds in the room were the point and counterpoint of their breathing and the slide of skin against the cotton fabric of the sheets. When their climax hit, it grabbed them both at the same time, shaking their bodies, creating a dark whirlpool that sucked at them.

They lay for a long time afterward, holding each other until their breathing slowed and eased. Finally, Nick slid to one side, still holding her cradled in his arms, pulled the covers over them, and settled her more comfortably against his body.

"I will always take care of you, Lindsey." His voice covered her like melted chocolate. "Do you believe me?"

She hesitated only a second. "Yes. I do."

At least I want to. But what about love? Is that in there anywhere? Never mind. I'll enjoy what we have.

She sighed and relaxed against him.

He kissed her forehead and her cheeks, and still holding each other, they fell asleep.

****

Where are you? How did you slip away?

I want to make sure you know I'm always, always watching.

Do you lie awake at night, filled with fear? Is your mind racing to figure out who I am? You cannot imagine the degree of suffering I wish on you. Can you feel the hate?

I will reveal myself sooner or later, but not until you are crazed with terror. Shall I cut you with my knife, hundreds of tiny cuts so you bleed slowly? Or shoot you in your arms and legs so you can't move while I do whatever I want to increase your pain.

What you have now will be nothing. Your money can't save you, and neither can that asshole who thinks he's protecting you. I have eyes on you both. You think you're so smart. Just wait. Soon you'll know. Then I'll have the upper hand.

Bitch!

Chapter Eleven

Nick was on the porch at seven the next morning sipping his coffee when the white panel van with no markings drove down the road from the highway and parked next to his truck. He walked over to greet the four men in jeans and T-shirts who piled out and began hauling out equipment cases.

Beside the barn, Ruben was coiling rope and eyeing everyone, so Nick walked the crew over and introduced them. He couldn't ignore the traces of reservation lingering in the man's eyes.

"I know you don't have much faith in all this electronic gear," he half-joked. "I just want you to know I really appreciate you going along with the program.

"Whatever protects the *niña*," he said. "Want me to show your men around?"

"Please." He leaned closer to Ruben. "But I just want you to know my Sig Sauer is tucked away at the small of my back."

Ruben's lips twitched as he suppressed a grin. As he walked away, he flipped up the tail of his shirt and Nick saw the Kimber resting in a similar place.

Good. One way or another, we'll be ready for trouble.

Lindsey came out of the house while two of the men were carrying equipment into the barn. Nick looked up from his conversation with the head of the crew and smiled at her.

She smiled back, and as she came down the steps, she punched him lightly on the arm, as if she knew what he was thinking. She had tied her thick, dark, silky fall of hair back in a ponytail, and instead of her regular glasses, she wore wide sunglasses. Memories of last night flashed in his mind.

"I'm going riding," she told him. "My horse needs some exercise. Don't suppose you'd care to join me." She arched an eyebrow in amusement.

"Uh, not at this moment." He chuckled. "Thanks anyway."

"Chicken. I'll get you yet. You can't be on a ranch and not ride."

"We'll table that for the moment. Okay, if I can't talk you out of this ride, someone will be going with you." He motioned to Ruben, who nodded.

"What's going on?" She planted her hands on her hips and glared at them. "I'm safer here than any place else."

Nick waved a hand at the landscape. "Lindsey, this place is surrounded by hills covered with juniper and oak trees that make good hiding places. I'm not taking any chances with your safety."

While she was still fuming, Ruben came out of the barn leading Jingo. Beside him, already in the saddle, was one of the hands Nick had met that morning, a no-nonsense man named Sanchez.

Lindsey's eyes widened at the gun that rode low on Sanchez's hip, and the shotgun strapped to the saddle. A pair of binoculars hung around his neck.

"Wait a minute," she began.

Nick held up his hand. "Ruben says Sanchez is the best shot on the ranch besides him. We knew you'd want to go riding first thing. You insist on going; we insist he goes with you. Take it or leave it."

"He is right, little one," Ruben pointed out. "We think we're protected here, but we don't know who this is or what they're liable to do. He's managed to get private information about you. He could just as easily find a way onto the ranch, and it's pretty open country out there. You'd be a prime target."

"Fine." She threw up her hands. "Just…fine." Blowing out a breath of frustration, she stomped off to her horse.

Nick swallowed a grin as she swung gracefully into the saddle. She waved and then she was off across the fields, Sanchez beside her. Just looking at her sitting so easily on the horse, like one unit running free, made his heart catch a little. Yup, he was in big trouble. But it strengthened his resolve to keep her safe, no matter how angry his efforts might make her.

He'd been working with his team for more than thirty minutes, supervising the prep for the alarm system, when he heard hooves thundering and looked up to see Lindsey and Sanchez riding hell bent for leather toward the ranch. Alarm bells clanging in his head, he walked over to the barn to meet them. Sanchez's face looked like a thundercloud, and Lindsey was clutching the reins of her horse, trembling.

"What?" Nick asked as he jogged up to them, trying to beat back the rising panic. They were both still alive and unbloodied so what the hell had happened?

"Bastard," Sanchez growled.

"Who?" Nick snapped. "What are you talking

about?"

"We got to the big hill near the north pasture when I saw something glinting in the sun. Before I could get the binoculars on it, I heard the rifle shot. If I hadn't started Lindsey toward the trees, she'd be lying dead back there, or at least badly wounded."

Nick swallowed the sour taste of acid in his mouth. He'd had a bad feeling about this. Letting her go on the ride had been a big mistake. "Did you get a look at who it was?"

Sanchez shook his head. "I heard the engine of an ATV. Whoever was riding it was over the hill and gone before I could get a glimpse." He swung down from the saddle. "I'll take care of the horses. You'd better see to Lindsey before she faints."

Nick was aware that Lindsey hadn't said a word. She was still trembling, her face pale, clinging to the pommel of her saddle. Nick reached up, and she collapsed forward into his arms.

"I'm sorry," she said in a low voice. "I should have listened to you, but I thought for sure…"

"That you'd be safe on your own property," Nick finished for her, holding her tightly against him. "Yeah, whoever this is, they're doing their homework."

"I don't feel safe anywhere anymore." Her voice was muffled against his chest. "God, Nick. I thought I was so strong, that I could handle anything. But I seem to keep falling apart."

"Listen to me." Nick cupped her chin and lifted her face to him. "Stronger people than you have been smart enough to be afraid when someone comes after them like this. Don't put yourself down. You can bet I'm going to glue myself to your side. No one—and I mean *no one*—is going to get to you until this is over."

She wrapped her arms around him, holding tightly. He felt something turn over in his heart, something completely unfamiliar. Something he didn't want to analyze right now.

Lindsey sighed and moved out of the circle of his arms, glancing around the yard. "Ruben looks like the sentinel on duty, keeping out the Philistines," she joked.

The older man was working on ranch equipment and quietly keeping an eye on the strangers.

"Ruben and I have come to an understanding. He'll let me put any kind of gadget I want around here as long he can still shoot first and ask questions later."

Lindsey threw back her head and laughed, albeit somewhat shakily. "That is so Ruben. Good for him."

"Come on," Nick told her, taking her by the hand. "I'll show you what we've done so far."

****

They had just finished lunch when Nick's cell phone rang. He looked at the readout and headed toward the patio. "I'll take this outside. I won't be long."

As he slid the patio door open, Lindsey heard him say, "Hi, Stacy. What's going on?"

His voice had a softness that wasn't there when he spoke to his office or his men, and a wide grin split his face.

Lindsey fought the urge to eavesdrop on the conversation while at the same time chiding herself for acting like an idiot. Of course women would call him. Did she think that, just because he told her they had something special, he was cutting himself off from everyone else? But the way he said this woman's name and the look on his face indicated she was something special, too, and the knife of jealousy twisted in her gut. She hated thinking about him with other women.

No! He's mine! You can't have him!

Well, that was pretty damn stupid. He certainly wasn't hers. Despite everything he'd said, there was still nothing binding Nick Vanetta to her except this job and great sex. Probably the best sex she'd ever have. But maybe it was time to rein that in. Protect herself. Forget about that tiny piece of hope she'd been nurturing.

"Everything okay?" she asked when he came back inside. She was proud of the casual tone in her voice. "No problems at work?"

"No, this wasn't work-related and everything's fine. Ready to hit the attic?"

Lindsey bit back the urge to ask him who'd called and just nodded. She wished he would wipe that stupid grin off his face. With an effort, she tamped down her irritation. "Yes. All set. Let's do it."

They pulled down the stairs that led up to the attic, really not much more than a crawl space, and climbed up to find the boxes. There were six file storage cartons, dusty and beginning to rot in some places. They obviously hadn't been touched in ages.

"Take them to my bedroom," Lindsey said. "I have that big desk in there, and we'll have room to spread stuff out."

And keep them out of Mary's and Ruben's eyesight until I look for myself.

It didn't take them all that long to move the stuff from the attic to her room. Nick stacked the boxes on the floor and lifted the first one to her desk.

"I guess you're mother really didn't want you opening these." Nick was working to open one with the scissors he found in the desk, slicing through layers of masking tape.

"I can't imagine what's in them." Lindsey pulled at the tape as it finally came loose. "All our family pictures are in albums downstairs. My mother was very meticulous about doing that."

Nick shrugged. "Maybe this is from before you were born, which is what I'm hoping. There's got to be something in here, somewhere, that will help us find answers."

Finally, the box was open, and Lindsey yanked the lid off. "What on earth?"

The box was filled with loose photographs, thrown in helter-skelter. Many of them had the sepia tone of very old pictures, the rest were black and white. She began taking them out, looking at them carefully in amazement. "I have no idea who any of these people are. Here." She dug both hands into the box. "Help me take them all out and see if there's writing on the back of any of them."

Many of the pictures had water in the background, the people in the photos dressed in bathing suits or shorts.

"This is an ocean," Nick said, pointing to one of the pictures. "You can tell by the breakers coming in. Is there anything that tells us where? This country has a lot of coastline."

Help me! Help me!

Water closed over her, choking her, filling her nose and her throat.

Help me! Please!

Lindsey dropped the pictures and clutched at her throat, gagging as she fought for air.

“Lindsey?” Nick pushed everything aside and grabbed her.

“Can’t…breathe.” The words were dragged from her throat.

“Come on, honey.” Nick shook her. “What is it? What’s wrong, sugar?”

Lindsey pushed at the hands gripping her, trying to shove whoever it was away. And then, as suddenly as it started, the episode was gone, leaving her trembling.

Nick wrapped his arms around her and hugged her to his chest, his big, warm hands stroking the length of her spine. “Darlin’? Are you okay?”

Her throat was still so tight she couldn’t speak. When her pulse rate finally slowed, she managed to nod. “I’m sorry.” Her words felt as if they’d been scraped from somewhere deep inside her.

“Sorry? For what?” Nick’s voice had a slight tremor to it. “You scared me half to death. What just happened here?”

She shook her head. “Could you get me a glass of water, please?”

He brought her one from the bathroom, along with two aspirin. “Take these. No arguments.”

She leaned into him while she swallowed the tablets and drank the water. The heat from his body warmed her, and after a few minutes, the chill that gripped her dissipated.

He tightened his arm around her. “Are you ready to tell me about this, Lindsey?”

She looked up at him. “Yes, but later. Okay? Let’s go through the rest of this stuff.”

"I'm not sure that's such a good idea." He was still holding her, his lips brushing her hair. "Maybe I should get Mary up here."

"No, I'm fine now." She drew in a long breath and slowly let it out. "Really. Okay? Please don't get Mary involved. Whatever it was is gone. Please? I swear I'll tell you all about it. Later."

He'll think I'm crazy. And maybe I am.

Nick hesitated a moment, his gaze moving from her face to her eyes and down to her trembling hands. Then he nodded. "This is against my better judgment, but okay."

"Thank you."

She managed to pull herself together, although inside, she was still shaking like a field of prairie grass in the wind. The blood in her veins felt ice cold. How could the nightmare intrude on her during the day when she was awake? Was there a clue here in all these pictures with the ocean in them? Was that what this was all about? But why? And who were these people?

Steeling herself, she picked up another photo and handed it to Nick. "Here. This says 'Nina and me at the cottage.' But no geographic designation, and I have no idea who Nina is."

"All right. Let's see what else is in here."

They went through every photo, trying to match people and make separate piles. The name Nina was written on the back of several other pictures, always with the same inscription. At least a dozen shots had a teenage boy sitting on the sand holding a baby. These all had the same identification: George holding baby Marie Elizabeth.

"Elizabeth was my mother's name." Lindsey said.

"I wonder if there's any connection. I have no idea who George is or who wrote this stuff. It looks like my mother's handwriting, but I can't be sure. And why would she hide it from me?"

"Let's try another box," Nick suggested.

They worked through most of the afternoon, digging their way through three of the boxes. The tech crew interrupted them briefly to set up the alarm in the bedroom, and twice Nick left to check on their progress in other areas. The rest of the time, they spent trying to find a pattern to the pictures.

Although a few of the names were repeated over and over, none of them were familiar to Lindsey. And there was nothing else in the boxes except the photos. Nothing to explain who the people were or where the pictures were taken, and nothing to tell them what they had to do with Lindsey or her parents.

It wasn't until they began dividing the shots from the third box into piles that the first landmark appeared. A huge house loomed in the background, two-storied with a big front porch and a glassed-in sun porch.

"This kind of house wasn't usually built anywhere except in the New England states," Lindsey said, "and almost always by the water. I took a class in northeastern architecture at the university. A lot of wealthy people had large summer homes at the ocean that looked like this. But New England's a big place, and this doesn't give us much information."

"Well, you know your parents were solid financially," Nick pointed out. "You told me they paid cash for this place, and your trust fund is of substantial size. Maybe they were part of the upper class wherever this is."

"So what does this mean? They came from wealth? Whose family had it? And is this their house? Was my mother just visiting?"

"Hold it, hold it." Nick held his hands out in a stopping motion, laughing. "One question at a time."

She rubbed her forehead. "I don't even know where they lived before they came to Texas. It's odd to think we never discussed it, but our lives were so full…"

"I'm not sure we have answers yet for anything you want to know."

"But they have to be in here somewhere. Nick, I need to find out who all these people are. Maybe they're relatives of mine." Frantically, she grabbed the scissors and began slashing at the tape securing another box.

Nick grabbed her hand and took the scissors from her. "Let me have this before you slice your hand open. Settle down." He slit the tape efficiently and pulled the cover off.

Lindsey's eyes widened, and she dove in with both hands. "Look, Nick, papers. Here are all kinds of papers. Oh, help me get them out. We have to go through them." She would have swept all the pictures in their carefully sorted piles off the desk, but Nick caught her hands.

"Stop. Let's move aside these stacks that we spent so much time putting together so carefully. Then we'll look at this other stuff." He laid each of the piles neatly on the bed and took two fistfuls of material from the newly-opened box, handing one pile to Lindsey. "Here. I'll look at this batch, and you can go through these others. Let's see what we can find."

Many of the papers were old letters, dated in the 1930s and 1940s. From the words she read, some of them were obviously love letters, to and from people she'd never heard of. No return addresses were to be found nor any clues to their destination. She and Nick sat side by side on the floor, reading silently for more than an hour.

Lindsey was reading another letter when shock made her hands shake and her heart stutter. She reached out and touched his arm. "Nick. Listen to this. It's a letter, and much more current. Look at the date. It's thirty years ago."

Carrie,

I have just come from visiting Brent and Marie. Little Barbara is now four years old, and I don't know how Marie does it. The child is a terror. She teases the animals viciously, kicks at the nanny, and has the most awful temper tantrums. Marie thinks she is pregnant again, and I worry about the new baby. I tried talking to Brent, but I think you would have more luck with him than I, since he is, after all, your son. Something must be done. This is not a good situation. I await your reply anxiously.

Affectionately,

Renee.

Lindsey wrinkled her forehead. "What on earth do you suppose this is about? Who is Marie, and who is this Barbara who was so awful?"

"Here's another one." Nick held it out to her. "Apparently written a couple of months later. Whoever Renee is, she sounds desperate. She wants Carrie to persuade Brent to take Marie and the baby away after the birth. This kid Barbara must have been some little devil."

"So it seems." Lindsey unfolded another sheet. "Here's another one written in March. Renee says the baby is due in July. Brent is planning on taking Marie and the child to Grey Rocks, wherever that is. Carrie wants them to leave Barbara in town, and Brent just ignores her."

"Okay." Nick handed over one he'd opened. "This one's from Carrie to Renee. Now Carrie's beginning to get distressed. She's spoken to her son and gotten no further than Renee. The two women are trying to figure out what to do. Lindsey, this sounds like something out of an English mystery."

"I know, I know." She leaned back, pushing the hair away from her face and shoving her glasses back up on her nose. Her eyes were dry with fatigue.

Nick studied her face. "Linds, I'm not too happy with the lines of strain around your eyes, or your obvious exhaustion which you keep trying to hide. Come on." He stood up and held out his hand to her. "We've been at this all afternoon. We both need a break. Up out of the chair."

"But..."

"No buts. We're going outside for some fresh air. I need to see how close the guys are to finishing, anyway."

Lindsey allowed herself to be led downstairs and out of the house. Some of the horses had been turned out to the near pasture and were idly grazing. The last golden rays of the sun cast a warm glow over the landscape.

She stood up on the fence rail and whistled to Jingo, who came trotting over obediently. She'd grabbed a carrot on her way out of the kitchen. She took it out of her pocket and held out her hand to the horse, palm open.

Nick came up behind her as the horse was chomping his last bite.

"You weren't formally introduced the other day." She laughed. "Nick, meet Jingo. Jingo, this is Nick. Be nice to him. He's a very important person in my life. He's keeping me safe."

"And maybe a little more than that." His hard muscled arm slid around her waist, his lips close to her ear.

She didn't say anything in response, the memory of the phone call striking at her. Words were, after all, only words easily said.

"I can see you need a refresher course."

Tilting her face up, he kissed her so hard she could feel the entire shape of his lips. His tongue twined with hers, then scorched the inside of her mouth. Despite her intentions she wrapped her arms around his neck, pulling him even closer.

A sound at her elbow broke their concentration, and she turned her head to see Ruben standing there.

"You two want to save that for later?"

Lindsey blushed and Nick chuckled, but he dropped his hands.

Ruben grinned. "It's okay. I figured when you had me put both suitcases in one room that you weren't up there playing cards. I just came to fetch you for supper."

"Thanks, Ruben. We'll wash up and be right there." Nick kissed Lindsey lightly on the nose before leading her back to the house.

Over the meal, Nick gave them a progress report on the security installation. Then they discussed the results of their afternoon research with Ruben and Mary. Neither of the Medanas said much, just kept nodding their heads impassively.

"But don't you think this is something?" Lindsey asked anxiously. "Maybe if I can track some of these people down, it will give me a clue to who's stalking me. Nick said it's a good bet the answer is somewhere in my past."

"Those boxes are not *your* past, little one," Ruben said. "They're someone else's past. You need to keep that in mind while you're digging around in that stuff."

"Did Mom or Dad ever mention any of these people?" She rattled off the names they had come up with, even though all they had were first names. "Do you recognize any of these names?"

"I think you should just keep looking," Mary said, starting to clear the plates. "Just remember, whatever you find, that's about other people. It isn't your past there in all those papers."

"I get the feeling you're hiding a secret," Nick said, looking from one to the other. "Something you want Lindsey to find out for herself. Or maybe not at all."

"Just keep looking," Mary said.

"If there's something there to find," Ruben added, "you'll know it when you see it."

After a while, Lindsey and Nick gave up trying to pry information out of them and went out to the porch, hoping to sort out the jumble of information running through their brains. Sitting in the rockers, they hashed over what they'd discovered so far, trying to make some sense of it.

Then Nick changed the subject.

"Are you ready to tell me about that little episode you had before?" he asked, his voice quiet.

"It was nothing." Lindsey kept her eyes on her lap, wondering how she'd even explain what happened. "Really, Nick. It was just some kind of spasm. Can we drop it, please?"

He was silent for a moment. "For now. But it's not off the table." He stood up and pulled her with him. "Tomorrow's another day. We need fresh eyes, so let's go to bed and get some rest."

But when they climbed into bed, Nick reached for Lindsey, but the memory of the phone call washed over her and she turned away.

"I'm really tired tonight," she told him. "Exhausted."

"Want to tell me what's wrong?" he asked after a long moment.

"Nothing." Her voice was muffled by her pillow. "I'm just really beat."

Another long moment, then he leaned over and brushed a kiss against her cheek. "Whatever you say. We probably need all the sleep we can get, anyway."

But he pulled her against him, molding her to his body and refusing to let her go. His heat burned against her, and she had to force herself not to turn around. After a long while, her taut muscles relaxed and she drifted off into an uneasy sleep.

****

Help me! Help me! I can't breathe!

Lindsey swam as hard as she could, fighting the current but losing ground. The voice grew fainter, more desperate.

Please! Help me!

Her lungs were burning as she fought for breath and her body began to tire.

No! No! I can't stop.

"Lindsey. Lindsey, wake up."

Someone was shaking her, calling her name.

"Come on, Lindsey. Open your eyes."

Fingers gripped her.

"No," she screamed. "Let me go. I'm almost there." She flailed out with her hands, pushing at whatever was restraining her.

"Breathe, Lindsey. Come on, honey."

The words finally pierced her brain, and the water in her nightmare began to recede. She gasped for breath, sucking in great gulps of air. Her heart hammered so loudly she could feel it pounding in her eardrums, and she shook all over.

"That's it, sugar. Big breaths. Come on."

With great effort, she forced open eyes that felt as if they'd been frosted with cement. An image swam in the mist that seemed to hang in the air. *Was she still under water?* She blinked her eyes, and a face came into focus. "N-Nick?"

"You got it." His arms wrapped around her, rocking her back and forth. "Just relax. Lean against me."

Great sobs burst from her as terror gripped her. She shook with them, pressing against Nick who held her against his firm body and murmured soothingly to her. Gradually, the edges of the nightmare faded until, exhausted, she lifted her head from his shoulder and looked at him with eyes still not quite focused. She was drenched with sweat, and her lungs burned with the effort to breathe.

"Better?" Nick's eyes were heavy with concern.

"I think." She drew a long shuddering breath and let it out.

"I'm taking you in the shower, then putting you in a clean nightshirt and getting you some brandy. And then, whether you want to or not, you'll tell me what the hell made you scream so loud every hair on my body stood up."

"No water." She pushed at him, her eyes still wild. "I don't want water."

"Shh," he crooned, pulling her back into his arms and gently rubbing her back. "I'll be holding you the whole time, darlin'. You're safe with me. I won't even let your head get wet."

His touch and voice eased her enough to let him bathe her, standing her in the shower so the spray was directed only at her back. Finally, she began to relax under his hands.

The hot water helped ease the tension in her muscles. Nick soaped her body with tenderness, rinsed her off carefully, and dried her with a fluffy towel. Then he pulled a sleep shirt from one of the dresser drawers and slid it over her head.

"Don't move," he commanded, putting her back in bed and propping her up on the pillows. He yanked on his boxers. "I'll be right back."

She closed her eyes, trying to shake the memory of the nightmare from her brain.

Then Nick was back, pressing a glass into her hand. "Take a big slug first, then sip on it."

She did as he told her, coughing at the first swallow when the liquor burned a trail down her raw throat.

"Little sips now," Nick murmured, stroking her hair.

When she drank slowly, it went down better, steadying her. She could hardly look at the man sitting beside her.

"Uh-uh, no hiding." He put his hand gently under her chin and tilted her face toward him. "No more ducking this, Lindsey. I want to know what this is and how long it's been going on."

She was so exhausted from dealing with the nightmares herself, and Nick's strength was the only thing propping her up. She needed to tell him, to let someone share this burden with her. Maybe he could figure it out.

Putting the glass down on the night stand, she curled into him and told him about the nightmares. When they started, how long between episodes…everything. When she finished, she felt as if every bit of energy had been drained from her body. "A lot more than you bargained for, right?"

"I can't believe you've been going through this and didn't bother to tell me." He tipped up her face again and forced her to look at him. "Listen, sugar, I come from generations of Italians who believe the world revolves around superstitions and omens. Something's going on here, and we have to find out what it is."

"You're sure you don't want to take back your contract?" Her voice was so low it was almost a whisper.

"I think I'll pretend I didn't hear that." He shifted position so he was lying next to her, his body curved around hers. "Tonight you need to sleep, and I'll be right here holding you. But tomorrow, Lindsey, we're talking about this nightmare business. And that's an order."

"All right." It felt so good to know she didn't have to do this alone anymore. She snuggled into the safety of his arms, but it was still a long time before she dared to fall asleep again.

Chapter Twelve

They slept later than usual Sunday morning. Lindsey's face still showed signs of strain that concerned Nick. He tried to talk her into breakfast in bed, but she was having none of it. Something was bothering her, and he was damn sure going to get it out of her. For some reason last night, she'd pulled away from him. He could almost see the distance. If she hadn't had the nightmare, would she even have let him touch her?

He scoured his brain, trying to think of anything he might have said or done, but he came up empty. Finally, he left her to dress while he went downstairs to check on his crew, who'd arrived early again to finish up the security job. But he wasn't done with this. One way or another, he'd get it out of her.

"The alarm system is nearly set to go," he announced when he joined Lindsey at the kitchen table. He bent to brush his lips against hers, but she turned her head giving him her cheek. He stared at her for a moment before he sat down. Okay, this was going to stop, just as soon as he got her alone.

Mary served them enough food for an army, having already fed the men from Guardian as well as the ranch hands.

"How much longer until they're finished?" Lindsey asked.

"They've got about another hour's work ahead of them, and then they'll be done. Before the guys leave, we'll go through it and make sure everyone knows how the system works in every building. I'll feel a little better when it's finally turned on."

Ruben, who was drinking a cup of coffee, grunted and automatically reached for the gun at his back. Nick smothered a smile, because it was the same thing he was tempted to do. He was determined to keep everyone as safe as possible, and the alarm system gave them an edge they didn't have before.

He was pleased at how quickly Mary and Ruben, for all their protests, picked up the procedure. With each test he ran, Nick checked at the office to make sure everything was working perfectly. Finally, he was satisfied and sent the crew on its way.

"Come on." Lindsey tugged on his hand. "Now that we're electronically safe, can we get back to the boxes?"

Mary followed them upstairs with a pitcher of iced tea and two glasses. "Thirsty work," was all she said before clumping away.

"Let's talk a minute first." Nick dropped into the big armchair by her bed. He tried pulling her into his lap, but she tugged her hand away and sat on the edge of the bed.

"Okay." Lindsey folded her hands primly in her lap and stared at him. He could badger her all he wanted, but she was going to put space between them. He could have Stacy and leave her alone. "Talk."

Nick stared right back at her, a muscle in his jaw twitching. "Fine, if that's the way you want it. Problem one. Your stalker and your nightmare. My inner alarm system is telling me the two might be connected."

Lindsey frowned. "But how? I don't even know what the nightmares mean, except someone's drowning and wants me to save them. I've never lived near water in my life or swum in anything larger than a small lake. And that was when I was a lot younger."

And since the dreams started, swimming has definitely not been on my agenda. Taking a shower is all I can manage without freaking out.

"But there's water in some of the photos," he reminded her. "That means it plays some role in your life. There's a reason your mother had this stuff taped up and hidden away." He rubbed his chin. "I just wish I knew what kept her from destroying everything. My grandmother would say a message is trying to get through to you." He grinned. "My grandmother hasn't been wrong too often. Tomorrow, I'm going to get the office started on trying to trace some of these people."

"All right," she agreed. "What's the second thing?"

He studied her for so long a feeling of unease pulled at her. "What? Is it worse than the stalker?"

"I'm trying to figure out what's changed between us since yesterday morning. One minute we're fine, the next I feel like I'm in a deep freeze zone."

Lindsey dropped her gaze to her hands, unable to bring herself to look at him. "I told you last night. I think everything's happened too fast. For me, anyway. I'm not used to this. I need to take a step back."

She could feel his eyes boring holes in her.

Finally, he pushed himself out of the chair. "Fine. Let's drop it for now and get back to work here."

She felt a mixture of relief and regret. Why didn't he push harder? Why didn't he ask if something happened? But he wouldn't and she knew it. If she was truthful with herself, he was probably relieved.

They followed the same procedure with the contents of the boxes as the day before. Pull out photos, try to match them to others in the carefully arranged piles, look for inscriptions on the back. An hour had passed when they found the first clue to any identification.

"Nick, look." Lindsey tried to keep the excitement from her voice. "Here's a picture that was taken at the same beach, with a bunch of people, and there's a lighthouse in the background. See? It's pretty clear." She handed over the photo.

He looked at it carefully. "Good. This isn't much, but it's something. When we get done, I'm going to scan it and email it to the office so someone can start looking for a match. No sense waiting until tomorrow."

"Today? But it's Sunday."

"Lindsey, Guardian runs twenty-four/seven. Problems don't confine themselves to business hours. And I don't really want to wait on this stuff."

Under the careless piles of photos in the remaining boxes, they found more correspondence between Carrie and Renee. As in the previous letters, the women were mostly concerned with the little girl, Barbara, and the coming baby. They were frustrated in their attempts to get Marie and Brent to take the situation more seriously but didn't go into further explanation of exactly what that situation was.

"These are obviously the grandmothers," Nick told her. "And they're very good friends."

"Do you think they could be *my* grandmothers?" Lindsey stared at one of the letters she was holding.

"Anything is possible, Lindsey." He turned over another letter. "But right now, we're only speculating."

"Oh, here it says the baby was finally born." Lindsey read from the page in her hand. "It's a boy. Charles. Marie and Brent are very excited. Carrie is panicky, though. She's still worried about Barbara."

"Here's another letter," Nick said, pulling a thin sheet of notepaper from the pile. "It's dated much later than the one you're reading. Carrie wants Renee to convince Brent to take Marie and Charles to the cottage and leave Barbara at home with the nanny. The little boy's first birthday is coming, and she has an uneasy feeling."

Lindsey studied the photo she'd picked up. "I wonder if they listened to Renee."

"Apparently not, because here's a picture of the happy family—mother, father, daughter, and son." Nick handed the photo to her. "I guess they made it to the beach together. Recognize anyone?"

Lindsey took the photo from him and nearly passed out. Her hands began to shake.

"Lindsey?" Nick reached out and put his hands on her arms. He tried to take the photo from her, but she had a death grip on it. "What is it? What do you see? You look like you're going to faint."

"Oh, Nick. Oh, my God." She pulled away from him and thrust the photo at him. "These people? They're my mother and father."

"What? Are you sure? Maybe you should take another look."

"I don't have to. I recognize them." She took the photo back and stared at it again. "They're a lot younger, but it's definitely them. Here, I'll show you."

She grabbed two small, framed photos from the table next to the chair and put them down beside the one from the box. "See? It's the same people."

Nick looked at them closely. "You're right. There's no mistaking it. That man and woman are your parents."

"But their names were different," she burst out. "Their names were Andrew and Elizabeth, not Brent and Marie like it says here. Nick, what's going on? What is this about? And who are the children? They can't be my sister and brother. I was an only child."

"Take it easy." When Nick tried to pull her into his arms, she stiffened and tried to push him away. She even turned her face away from his attempt at a reassuring caress on her cheek. "Let's keep this picture separate and see what else we can find."

"Open the last box," she demanded. "Open it now, Nick."

He barely had the tape cut away and the lid removed before she was digging into it furiously. She pulled out two handfuls of documents and began to scan through them rapidly. Suddenly, she yanked one out of the pile.

"Here. This is another letter between the grandmothers. From Renee to Carrie." Lindsey's hands were shaking. "She says the tragedy is destroying her. She can't eat or sleep. She doesn't know how she will cope with it. She says she prays for Marie and Brent and the children, that they will find peace in heaven. My God, did they die?" She shook her head in frustration. "But it doesn't make sense. My parents were alive for a long time after this. I don't understand."

"Okay." Nick plucked another sheet from the pile in his hand. "Here's one from Carrie to Renee, the same kind of stuff. Looks like an answer to the letter you're holding."

"What does she say?"

"Just that she feels the same, she doesn't know how to deal with the tragedy. She wishes Brent and Marie had listened and maybe this could have been averted. She doesn't think so, though. She says this was a heartbreak waiting to happen. She is so distraught she doesn't know what to do."

"We have to find out who these people are," Lindsey said, raking her fingers through her hair. "And *where* they are. Something is terribly wrong here, Nick."

"Here's another piece of the puzzle, although a very small one." He studied the scrap of paper in his hand. "At least it's something else I can track down."

"What? What is it?"

He held out the paper. "It's part of a newspaper clipping, but most of it's been torn away. See? You can read the name, *The Beach Recorder,* and a part of the headline, but that's all."

"What does it say?" she demanded, trying to reach for it.

"All that's left is the first part of the headline *Tragedy Strikes Young...* That's all." Nick put it to the side. "It gives us a starting point, though. I'll scan this with the pictures and shoot them to the office. I need to find out who's monitoring email traffic today and tell them what I want them to do."

Nick pulled his laptop out of the big metal case he carried everywhere and booted it up. He got the network name and password from Lindsey then scanned the documents into his cell phone and sent them to Guardian. Lindsey tried to sit patiently while he called his office and tracked down the person he needed.

"Start right away," he ordered, after telling him what he wanted. "This is a priority. Call someone else in if you have to, but I want something back by the time I call tomorrow morning."

Finished, he closed the laptop and set it aside.

"I'm going to pack everything away in some sort of order," he told Lindsey. "That way we can find something quickly if we have to. I want you to lie down and rest before supper."

She wanted to tell him he didn't have to keep pretending such concern for her but just shook her head instead. "I can't rest. I'm too wound up. My head is spinning. Let me check my messages on my cell phone and then walk down to see the horses. That always makes me feel better."

"Okay," he agreed. "We'll just turn in early tonight, then and get some sleep."

He better understand that sleep is all we'll be getting.

To distract herself, she clicked through her cell messages. Unprepared for one that jumped out at her, she dropping the phone and bit off a scream. She barely heard Nick pick up the phone from where she dropped it or the curse he muttered under his breath. All she could think of was the message.

I'm still watching you. You can't get away.

Nick barely caught her as she crumpled in his arms.

****

She was floating, suspended somewhere, weightless. If she kept her eyes closed, she was sure she could stay this way forever.

"Lindsey?"

The voice sounded far away, familiar, warm. She reached for it, but it was so elusive. "Lindsey, honey, can you hear me?"

She felt something wet and cold on her head and hands rubbing at her wrists. The same voice was shouting, "Mary? Mary, can you come up here?"

Lindsey stirred at that, the floating feeling dissipating, and forced her eyes open. She turned her head and realized she was lying on her bed. "Nick?"

"Right here, honey."

Then Mary's voice. "Ruben, go downstairs and get me the phone number for the doctor."

Lindsey looked over Nick's shoulder to see both Ruben and Mary standing behind him. "No doctor. Please. I'm okay." She tried to sit up.

"Uh-uh." Nick pushed her back onto the pillows. "No getting up for you right now."

"No doctor, Mary," she repeated. She closed her eyes again, and then pushed them open. "I just feel really stupid. I never faint."

"I never should have told you to go through all that old stuff." Mary wrung her hands. "It's too much for you, *niña*. Better burned and forgotten."

"No, you're wrong," Lindsey told her. The memory of the text message swept into her brain, and her pulse skipped. "And it wasn't the boxes we were going through that did this. I got a message on my cell phone from the stalker, and it startled me."

"I'd say startled is not the word, little one," Ruben said. "You fainted, and you look like hell."

"Gee, thanks, Ruben." She tried to grin. "Compliments always make me feel better."

"Hold on a minute, Lindsey." Nick stood up from where he sat on the edge of the bed. "I need to make a call."

He moved to a corner of the room, and Lindsey heard him punch in a number. He spoke quietly for a few minutes, then hung up and came back to sit beside her.

Mary had gone into the bathroom to wet the cloth again and now hovered nervously beside the bed.

"She'll be okay," Nick told the older woman. "I'll get her into bed. But maybe you could make her some strong tea?"

"Strong tea with a shot of whiskey," Mary agreed. "She needs to get some color back."

"That'll be good. Just yell when it's ready, and I'll come get it."

Nick shooed everyone out of the room, then lifted Lindsey off the bed and stripped off her clothes. She wanted to protest but couldn't find the strength. He found her sleep shirt from the previous night and pulled it gently over her head. "I'll go check on that tea and bring it right up to you. And I want you to drink it all."

"All right." She bit her lip, uncomfortable at what she was about to ask him. She didn't want to send him mixed signals. She sure didn't want to seem so needy. But more than that, at this moment, she didn't want to be alone. "Will you stay up here with me?"

"Sure." He kissed her forehead. "Count on it."

He sat with her while she drank the tea laced with

whiskey, then made her lie down, stretching out beside her. At first she thought about pushing him away. The problem was, she also wanted him next to her. Wanted his warmth and the safety of his body. Wanted to feel what he made her feel.

Okay, I'm a fool and a sucker, but right now I don't care.

Nick began to stroke her, his hand caressing first her shoulders, then her arm. Light, feathery touches. Then, pausing only a moment as if waiting for her to stop him, he eased up the nightshirt and cupped one breast. She loved the warm, rough feel of his hands and the brush of his thumb over her nipple. Right now, in spite of her inner conflict, she needed this to take away the fear she couldn't seem to push away. She nestled her head into him and gave herself over to the sensations cascading through her.

Nick nipped the lobe of one ear, then stroked it with his tongue. He paused a moment, as if waiting for her to stop him, but when she arched herself against him, he continued exploring her body. Pressed against him, she could feel the heavy thickness of his cock even through the fabric of his jeans. Without thinking, she eased her hand out from beneath the covers, released the snap on his pants and drew down the zipper. His grip on her tightened when she slid her hand inside his boxers and closed her fingers around his shaft.

The moment she tightened her grip and began to stroke her fingers up and down, he sucked in a breath. "You'd better mean business, darlin', or else you can stop now."

"I mean it," she assured hm. *At least the need for physical satisfaction. And for something to take away the terror of my nightmares.*

"Then let's give you better access."

He drew back the covers, and before she could organize her brain, he had stripped both of them and tossed their clothing to the side. Then, as if desperate to tear down the barrier she was throwing up between them, he rolled her onto her back, spread her legs wide, and slowly began to lick every inch of her hungry, pulsing sex. He stroked her wet flesh with his tongue, teased her clit with light nips of his teeth, and placed a row of sucking kisses on the lips of her sex.

Immediately, heat surged through her and her pulse accelerated. Her need for him shot into high gear. When he thrust his tongue inside her, she nearly jackknifed, the sensation was so erotic.

"Yes," she hissed as she pressed her feet to the mattress and tried to lift herself to him. But then she nearly lost her mind when he coated one finger with her juices and painted the tight pucker of her rear opening.

"One of these nights, I'm going to fuck you here," he told her in a gravelly voice. "Then you'll really belong to me."

"Yes. Whatever." She tossed her head back and forth, so aroused, so on the edge, she would have let him do anything. She tried to twist her body and reach for his shaft, but he kept her pinned in place.

"No. This is for you. For us."

Then, abruptly, he slid his hands beneath her buttocks, lifted her, and drove inside her.

"Oh, god," she cried and locked her ankles at the small of his back.

There was no further buildup, no slow strokes and hot kisses as he pounded into her. This was hot, hard sex as he drove into her again and again.

Sliding one hand between them, he found her clit and tugged on it until she screamed with need. At the moment she thought she would lose her mind if he didn't at last bring her to orgasm, he thrust once, twice, three times, hard and fast, and they exploded together. The spasms shook them so hard she was afraid her bones would crack, but she hung on tightly and rode out the storm with him, consumed by the shattering climax.

As the last shudders subsided, she lowered her legs, and Nick eased himself from her body. He pulled her against him, curling his hot, hard frame around her, not saying a word, just holding her.

Finally, he kissed her on the cheek then eased the covers over her. "I'm going downstairs to take care of some things. I want to make some more calls and not disturb you while I do it." He kissed her again. "Try to sleep a little, okay?"

She wanted to ask him if he was going to call Stacy, but she didn't want to know. Instead, she lay there, still trying to catch her breath and slow her racing heart. Thinking about the frantic almost desperate coupling that had just happened and wondering what was driving them. Surely it was a mistake on her part when another woman hovered in the background, yet she'd needed that intense connection. The locking together of their bodies.

But what had driven Nick? And what message had it sent to either of them.

Her head hurt from thinking so she closed her eyes, trying to shut out everything, and actually slept for a long dreamless time. She awoke when she felt the mattress dip beside her.

"Better?" Nick was leaning over her, his arms braced on either side of her.

Her immediate reaction was to push him away, but she was too exhausted, despite the nap, to get into a discussion of what was going on.

"No dreams. That's always good." She pushed herself up and shoved her hair back from her face. "What time is it?"

"Almost six. Think you could eat some supper? Mary made her famous enchiladas."

Lindsey forced a smile. "I'm always hungry for those."

He made no mention of the explosive sex they'd had. Instead, he studied her face, as if searching for answers there.

"How about if I bring a tray up here for both of us?" he asked at last.

"Absolutely not." She swung her legs over the side of the bed. "I'm not an invalid. I had a little fainting spell is all, and I'm fine. Let me wash my face and throw on some clothes."

She was surprised to discover she was ravenous. The aftermath of shock, Nick pointed out.

"No more photos tonight," he decreed. "Tomorrow is plenty of time to get back to them, and you need a clear head to do it."

"The message on my cell," she began.

"I've got the guys working on it," he told her. "I've got the phone so you won't have to even look at it until tomorrow. Then we'll get you a new one."

"A new phone? But how will I get my messages?"

"You can always call the office or use a code to tap into the answering machine. So let's call it a day."

After dinner, Nick made sure she got into bed again, then left her long enough to take a last turn around the outside with Ruben, checking to make sure all the alarm panels were set. Lindsey left the bedside lamp on and was staring at the ceiling, trying to sort out the jumbled thoughts in her mind, when he came back into the room.

"Give me a minute to shower, okay?"

"Yes. Of course."

He frowned at her, then shrugged and headed for the bathroom.

She would have had his things moved to another room, but that would bring too many questions from too many people that she didn't want to answer right now. When he slid into bed next to her, he smelled of soap and toothpaste and his own musky scent.

For a moment, she was tempted to nestle against him, but the memory of that phone call was still too fresh. The sex earlier she could chalk up to therapeutic, a cure for the nightmares. She just couldn't do it again, not with this between them.

He started to say something but shook his head and picked up the television remote.

They spent the evening watching an old movie on television. Finally, Nick turned off the television and reached for her.

"I'm very tired tonight, Nick. Today exhausted me."

He spooned against her, one arm circling her, and brushed a kiss against her cheek.

"Lindsey, whatever's bothering you will have to come out. If tonight's not the right time, okay. For now, let's just get a good night's sleep."

She tried to relax, but long after Nick fell asleep, she lay in the dark, the moonlight shining through the window illuminating the two photos of her parents, the old and the new. A terrible dread settled over her as she thought about the Pandora's Box they were about to open…and what could fly out.

Chapter Thirteen

Nick was already up, showered and dressed, and drinking coffee when Lindsey made it downstairs in the morning. She was glad she'd had the space to herself to dress and get her scrambled brain working after the highly charged emotion of the previous day. Not to mention the frantic, desperate sex.

"You sure you want to go into the office today?" he asked.

"Of course." She lifted her chin. "It's Monday, and I have work to do."

A half hour later, Nick piloted the truck through Interstate traffic as they drove to the office. "I'm hoping my techs found something in the documents I emailed them. They scanned in each of the photos we emailed them. We've got some pretty sophisticated recognition software, so if these faces ever showed up anywhere, we can find them."

Lindsey fidgeted with the clasp on her seat belt. "One minute I want to find the answers," she told him, "and the next I'm almost afraid to."

He reached over and touched her hand. "Whatever we find, don't you think it's better than not knowing? Especially if there's a chance it leads us to your stalker and we get that monkey off your back."

"This is all so hard for me to absorb. First I didn't have a past. Now it's possible someone from it is out to get me." She shivered. "What did you find out about the text message?"

"Bad news. It was sent from a throwaway cell phone. Completely untraceable. Whoever is doing this is smart and covers his tracks well. The phone is a dead end, just as this person knew it would be."

"What will you be doing today?" she wanted to know.

"Sticking to you like glue." He slid a glance at her. "You don't leave my sight."

Which could prove uncomfortable rather than reassuring, considering the current state of her emotions where this man was concerned.

The office was humming when they got there. Brianna was on the phone talking while typing on the computer. Through the open door to the workroom, Lindsey could see Mark bent over the drafting table, furiously intent on what he was doing. There was a stack of messages for her on the corner of Bri's desk that she picked up and leafed through as she walked into her office.

"I'll be in the apartment," Nick told her. "I have calls to make, and I want to boot up my laptop."

"Fine." She turned away with her messages still in her hand, ordering herself to focus on work.

Thirty minutes later, Nick was back at her desk. "Okay, you need to make some changes here. For the moment, no new clients."

"Wait a minute," she protested.

"Just for the here and now," he added. "The office is still checking everything, including what we found in those boxes. But we don't know who's coming out of the woodwork, and your stalker could easily pose as a new client to get closer to you."

Lindsey felt the blood leave her face. "You're kidding, right?"

Nick shook his head. "Not one bit. The guys at Guardian are still running those photos, but there are a lot of databases to go through. Then, if they get a hit, we have to use a computer aging process to see what that person or persons would look like today. Until we can do that, I don't want any strangers having access to you."

"Oh." Lindsey put down her pen and leaned back in her chair, rubbing her forehead. "I see what you mean. That makes sense."

"You're busy with ongoing work anyway, right?"

She nodded. "Yes, and I can use the time to finish that."

Nick rested a hip on one corner of the desk. "As a matter of fact, I'm thinking you should plan to take a little time off."

"Time off?" Startled, she waved her hands at the files on her desk. "But—"

"Not much. But when we get a lead on where those photos were taken, I'll want to go there and check things out myself." He grinned. "And I know for damn sure you'll want to go with me."

"Yes, you're right." She tried to give him an answering smile, but her mouth couldn't quite manage it. "Although I'm still terrified of what we might find."

He leaned forward and reached for her chin, tilting her face up. "Whatever we find, I'd be right there with you, okay?"

As casually as possible, she took his wrist and moved his hand away, trying to ignore the confused look on his face. "Okay."

He opened his mouth to say something else, shook his head, and walked back into the apartment. At noon, he came to fetch her for lunch. "I ordered a pizza. Again, I don't want anyone to know your lunch plans, so Tony is going to pick it up on the way over. He's bringing me some information."

"Oh, Nick." A thread of excitement wiggled through her. "Do you think he's got something?"

"Looks like it. But let's wait until he gets here and we check it out."

Following Nick's instruction, she was deliberately vague with Brianna and Mark about her lunch plans. She locked the office as soon as they'd left and headed into the apartment. Tony had just arrived with the pizza.

"You must be the most expensive delivery man around," Lindsey kidded him.

"No joke." He grinned. "You should see my hourly rates."

"Have you got something for us?" Her voice was eager as she pulled plates and glasses out of the cupboards.

"I do, but let's not let the pizza get cold. We can talk while we eat." When they were settled at the table, he opened his briefcase and took out a folder. "Let's look at the newspaper first, the one the clipping was from. That was a little easier."

"You mean that was a real publication?" Lindsey tried to tamp down her excitement.

Tony nodded. "*The Beach Recorder* was—-repeat *was*—-a weekly newspaper that served all the oceanside communities on about a twenty mile stretch of Route 1A in Maine. Bar Harbor was the central point, and the coverage spread out from there in both directions. They covered mostly society stuff, local activities, things like that."

Lindsey pushed her glasses back up on her nose and tucked her hair behind one ear. "I can hardly believe I have a connection to anything in Maine. That's like the other end of the earth from here."

"Maine explains the presence of the water," Nick pointed out. "And if there's something your parents wanted hidden from you, they picked a place to settle about as far away as they could get."

Tony nodded and flipped over a page. "I agree. It might explain why you have no relatives to speak of. They've all been buried in another life."

"So what about the newspaper?" Nick prompted.

"It stopped publishing about twenty years ago," Tony said. "The man who owned it died, his wife didn't want to keep it going, and no one was in a hurry to buy it. By then, everyone was getting their news from the dailies and even the advertisers weren't interested in retaining their contracts. So the widow just closed up the doors, sold off the equipment, and that was that."

"But isn't there some way to find the rest of that article?" Lindsey tried to swallow her anxiety and frustration. "I can't believe there aren't old copies somewhere."

"Actually, there are." Tony flipped another page. "But not on microfiche or anything we might be able to access remotely. You have to go the physical location. Which you may want to do when I tell you the rest of this."

Nick helped himself to another slice of pizza. "And where would that be?"

"The Bangor Public Library has archived all the copies of the paper for the entire forty years it was in print. Bangor's less than an hour's drive from the coast. It's a lot of tiresome work to go through all the issues, but I'm sure you'll find what you're looking for there."

"Forty years worth of newspapers?" Nick shook his head. "Let's hope we won't have to go through every one."

"There's more," Tony went on. "We were able to identify the lighthouse in the picture you emailed. It's called Howard's Lighthouse after the people who ran it for years. It's not far from Indian Island, about ten miles from Bar Harbor. The houses on the island are a mixture of large summer homes and smaller cottages. All owned by the rich or famous, however."

Lindsey put down the slice of pizza. "Nick, we have to go there. And I mean right away. I have to have answers, and I have such a strong feeling some of them are there. Maybe all of them."

"Slow down, Lindsey. I already told you we'd take a trip as soon as we had some information." He looked at Tony. "What about the rest of the pictures I sent over? Anything there?"

"We're still working on them. I marked this whole project a priority so I hope to have something soon." Tony chewed and swallowed a piece of pizza.

"And the cell phone?" Nick prodded.

"Not much there. Like I told you this morning, it was purchased at an electronics store in the big mall downtown. I'm going over there myself after lunch. I don't like the runaround they gave the guy we sent out so I'll give it a try myself. Just don't expect me to come back with anything" He closed the folder and helped himself to another piece of pizza. "So, what's the drill now?"

Nick pulled out a tablet from his briefcase lying on the counter and began making notes. "Tomorrow, Lindsey and I will fly up to Maine. Not today," he added quickly, as Lindsey opened her mouth to object. "We have a lot of arrangements to make first." He pulled out his cell phone and punched in a number. "Sarah? I called Reno's private number, but it rolled over to you so I'm guessing he's not around." He listened for a moment. "No, no big deal. I just wanted to let him know I'm flying to Maine in the morning. I'd like to use the Gulfstream if it's not otherwise booked." He nodded. "Yeah, I can do that. We'll send it back, and I'll call when we need to be picked up. Yes, the Ferrell case." He nodded again. "Right. Pass me along to Janet, will you?"

Lindsey listened while he gave his secretary instructions to arrange for the company plane, their landing at the Bangor airport and a rental car.

"An SUV, whatever model they've got available. Also a motel room in Bangor for one night, then reservations in Bar Harbor."

"Two rooms, please," Lindsey interrupted.

I will not mention the phone call. Let him think whatever he wants. He can have all the women in the world. Just not me.

A sharp pain stabbed at her heart as the memory of that phone call popped up, and she forced herself to take a deep breath.

Nick studied her face, then nodded while Tony stared from one to the other. "Two rooms, Janet." He glared at Lindsey. "But make sure they're connecting.

Uh-huh. Thanks."

He hung up, put down the phone, and concentrated on his pizza, not looking at either Lindsey or Tony.

Finally, Tony broke the uncomfortable silence. "You want to fly down to Bar Harbor?" he asked. "You'd be closer to the center of these activities."

"Not if we want to go to the library in Bangor. I'd rather go through the old newspapers first so we're armed with a little more information."

Tony left, and Lindsey cleared away the debris from lunch while Nick finished making notes.

Finally, he put the tablet down, leaned back in his chair, and beckoned for her to sit down again. "It's possible we could be gone as much as a week. Can Brianna hold down the office that long for you?"

"Of course. She's got plenty to keep her busy. She can take the meetings with the builders and bring any changes back to Mark. I'll go over all the projects with him today so he's familiar with what he needs to do. Besides, I'll take my laptop with me and my cell so it's not as if she won't be able to communicate with me."

"Don't tell them where we're going," he cautioned. "Just say you need a little time off with everything that's going on."

Lindsey raised an eyebrow. "Surely you don't still think either of them could be involved?"

"I don't know, but I'm not taking any chances. Do you need to get any clothes from the ranch? I can go by my house to pick up my stuff."

"If I need something, I'll just go out and buy it." She turned on the dishwasher. "Let me go meet with Mark and Bri. They should be back from lunch by now. After that, I can pack."

When she told Mark and Brianna she'd be going away for a while, they both stared at her.

"All this business is really stressing me out," she explained. "I need this break."

"Why don't you just go to the ranch?" Bri asked.

"Nick—Mr. Vanetta—believes I'll be safer if I'm someplace unknown to the stalker." Lindsey tried to make her tone as casual as possible. "But I'll have my cell on all the time if you need to reach me. So let's go over each project and see what needs to be done."

She was glad for the chance to avoid Nick for a while. The atmosphere between them had been even more strained after her room arrangement request. She knew sometime during the long trip he'd want answers, and she needed to figure out exactly what she wanted to say.

"Have a good time, wherever you're going," Brianna told her when they'd finished. "Is the hunk going with you?"

Lindsey laughed. "Don't I wish!" Nick had been specific that no one know the details about the trip, including the fact he'd be with her. "But someone will have bodyguard duty."

She spent the next two hours going over things with her staff, then sent both Mark and Brianna home. "You'll both be carrying a heavy load while I'm gone. Enjoy a few extra hours of free time while you can get it."

Back in her apartment, she packed quickly, grabbing things from her closet and drawers. Nick was a silent presence, hovering near the entire time. Zipping the suitcase shut, she turned to him. "Since we're not leaving until tomorrow, where are we sleeping tonight?"

"Guardian has a condo we keep for visiting clients." He narrowed his gaze. "And before you say anything, it has three bedrooms. You can take any one you want."

Before she could comment, his cell phone rang and he stepped out of hearing range.

"We're set for tomorrow," he told her when he hung up. "The plane will be ready for us at the airport about ten o'clock. I didn't want to make it too early. Janet arranged for someone to meet us in Bangor with our rental and our reservations and any other information we'll need."

"Great. Let me get my briefcase with all the photos and things. I had it next to my desk." When Nick started ahead of her, she put a hand on his arm. "I'll only be a second, okay? Don't worry. Everyone's already left for the day."

She had just bent down to pick up her briefcase when she heard a sharp *crack!* and the sound of breaking glass.

Chapter Fourteen

Rifle shot!

Nick was through the apartment and into the office in seconds. Lindsey stood at her desk, ghost white and shaking uncontrollably. Behind her and to her left, cracks spread out from a hole in the glass like a large spider web.

"Down!" he shouted at her. "Now."

He grabbed her and threw her to the floor, not stopping to be gentle, and crouched down next to her. Yanking his phone from his pocket, he speed dialed a number.

"Tony? Someone just shot at Lindsey from outside. Check with everyone out there, then get your ass over to the hotel next door and see if you can spot anyone carrying something that would conceal a rifle. See if they'll let you look at their security tapes, too. I'm calling the police. This will definitely get their attention."

"Rifle? Did you say rifle? What's happening?"

"Someone's using this office for target practice," he told her. "Just stay down."

"My God, Nick! He tried to shoot me. He's really trying to kill me."

Nick lifted his head slightly and peered over the desk. "No, I don't think so. He carefully aimed wide of where you were standing. He wanted to frighten you and let you know he was still watching. I'd say he accomplished his objective." He rose a little more and looked around. "I think we're okay now. Whoever did this had no intention of hanging around."

He lifted Lindsey up and sat her in her desk chair. She still trembled so hard she had to clutch the arms of the chair.

"Are you okay for a minute?" He ran his eyes over her. She was pale, her lips almost bloodless, and her hair was in disarray, but she was obviously trying to pull herself together.

Good girl.

"Yes." She nodded. "Do whatever you have to."

"I want to make another call and then let some people in." His voice was tight with anger and tension. "I'll be right back."

McCune was in his office when Nick reached him, but said he'd be on his way at once. Nick disarmed the alarm panel in the front office and opened the door just as Tony came pounding down the hall.

"What the hell is going on?" Tony asked. "What's this about a rifle? Who's got a rifle?"

Nick took him into the office and pointed to the bullet hole. "I don't think he wanted to hit her. He aimed wide of the mark, and I think it was deliberate. He just wanted to scare her. And did a damned good job, I might say."

He wanted to kick his own ass. He'd made a promise to stick to her like glue, then let her go into the office alone even for a few moments. He should fire himself.

"I sent Scott and Dutton over to the hotel," Tony said. "I'm sure whoever did this is long gone. Maybe the security tapes will tell us something, but I'm not hopeful. This is one smart dude."

"We need a team here to check out everything," Nick told him.

"Already taken care of. I called the office myself." Tony glanced at Lindsey. "Listen, you need to get her out of here. And I mean right now. Let us do our stuff here. Do you want me to call the cops?"

Nick shook his head. "Already done, but they won't find anything more than you will. Can you get the window fixed before tomorrow? I don't want her staff showing up to work with a bullet hole in the window. They'll freak out."

"Yes. I'll call you when I'm finished here. You take the lady and get her wherever you're going."

"The condo. It's the safest place I can think of. But we need to use a little razzle dazzle here. If you'd get her suitcase from the apartment, I'll get Lindsey. We can talk on the way down to the garage."

At that moment, the bell rang on the fax machine in the office and a sheet of paper began printing out. Nick grabbed it before Lindsey could and swore loudly when he pulled it out.

"What?" Tony asked.

"Look at this. That son of a bitch."

It was a picture, taken from a distance, of the window with the bullet hole in it. This time there was no writing on it.

"He had to have taken this immediately after the shot," Nick said. "It was sent from the business center at the hotel. Look at the header on it."

"What is it, Nick?" Lindsey tried to grab the fax from him. "What's on the fax?"

"Nothing you need to see."

The ringing of Tony's cell interrupted them as Nick jerked the paper out of Lindsey's reach.

"On my way," Tony said quietly and headed for the front door of the office.

"What's going on?" Lindsey demanded, twisting her hands together so tightly the knuckles were white. "Somebody tell me something. Please."

"I think you'd better give that message to me." The voice was deep and low.

Nick jerked his head around at the sound to see Reno walk through the door Tony had just opened. He had thunder in his eyes and his face was lined with rage.

"What are you doing here?" Nick asked.

Reno reached for the sheet of paper. "I take it very seriously when someone tries to kill one of our clients, and my partner and my brother are both in the line of fire." He stared at the photo. "Shit."

"My sentiments exactly," Nick echoed.

"Is anyone ever going to tell me what's going on?" Lindsey asked, drawing Nick's attention from the paper.

"Let me introduce you to someone. Lindsey Ferrell, meet Reno Sullivan. The brains behind Guardian."

"Nick's far too modest." Reno reached out to take one of Lindsey's trembling hands. "We all pull our weight. In any event, it's a pleasure to meet you. I only wish it were under different circumstances." He looked at Nick. "I asked Sarah to get the entire file and put it on my desk. You and Lindsey get out of here. I brought the team Tony requested to work the scene and see what we can find."

"Nothing, most likely," Nick told him. "It's been the same each time."

"No more." Reno shook his head. "It's time for us to get the upper hand. Where are you two staying tonight?"

"The condo if it's empty."

Reno nodded. "It is. You've got a key, so go on. Get out of here, then."

"The cops are on the way," Nick pointed out. "We've got to talk to them first."

"I'll handle it. And cover your tail." He turned to his brother. "Tony? The usual game of tag, all right?"

Tony nodded.

The men all shook hands. Nick took the suitcase and led Lindsey out to the elevator. Tony got in with them. Nick studied her face, trying to assess her mental state.

"I'm fine," Lindsey said, in reply to his unasked question.

"No, you're not, but you're a damn fine trouper."

He clamped a lid on his frustration. He was itching to reach for her, but she'd erected this invisible wall between them and he didn't have a clue in hell as to why. He settled for taking one of her hands.

"We're going to play a little game when we get in the car," he told her. "Just trust me and everything will be okay."

"All right." But he could tell she wasn't very happy about it.

"I don't think the shooter is still out there. He did what he wanted to, although he absolutely could still be lurking somewhere around. He hung around long enough to take that picture and fax it to you minutes after he fired. I intend to keep you out of harm's way, and that means making sure no one sees where we're going. I want whoever it is to lose track of you."

In the parking garage, Tony took Lindsey's arm and gently tugged her in his direction.

"What's going on?" She looked at Nick. Everything was coming at her too fast.

"Tony will take care of you, okay?" Nick assured her. "Just go with him."

"We're doing a little bait and switch here, love," Tony said. "Just stick with me. Whatever I tell you, just do it, all right?"

She nodded wordlessly, but her mind was going a hundred miles a minute. Who was doing this? How did they always know exactly where she'd be standing? What had she ever done to anyone to earn this kind of campaign of terror?

Tony hustled her to yet another a black SUV parked next to the outer wall of the elevator. He helped her into the back and told her to lie down on the seat. "Don't look up for any reason until I say you can."

Lindsey nodded, then curled up and wrapped her arms around herself as Tony threw a blanket over her. She had no idea of time as they drove or even where they went. She sensed when they left the surface streets and entered the Interstate, and then when they exited, but that was all. Twice, she heard Tony on his cell speaking in low tones. Finally, he pulled to a stop and told her she could sit up.

She threw the blanket off. "Where are we?"

"The garage at my condo." He opened the door for her. "Come on. Just slide across. Nick's right here."

She scrambled out of the vehicle and Tony helped her into the truck.

"All clear as far as we can tell," he said. "We had two cars tailing you. They didn't spot anything, and I kept a good eye on my own rearview mirror. Also, I came in by the back entrance, so if anyone was on my ass, I'd have seen them. Get going."

"Okay." Nick looked at Lindsey. "One more time, get down as low as you can."

Lindsey crouched on the floor, not even daring to breathe as they raced through the city. Finally, they were at another underground garage. Nick parked, helped her out, and led her to the elevator.

The condo was as basic as a place could be, totally without personality. Even in the stress of the situation, she itched to bring in some color, rearrange furniture, give the place some personality.

"Sit," Nick told her, leading her to the couch. In seconds, he was handing her a glass with some liquid. "Here. Drink this. No argument."

She frowned. "What is it?"

"Brandy. Just like the other night." He wrapped her fingers around the tumbler. "Remember, don't chug it. One big swallow, then sips, but you have to finish it. That's an order. I'm going to get your stuff." She heard him moving around for a while, and then he was beside her again, taking the glass from her hands. "Good girl. You drank it all."

She couldn't deny the fiery liquid had warmed her blood a little, although it hadn't reached the knot of cold fear that lay inside her like a huge boulder. More than anything, she wanted to lean against Nick's solid chest, but her fears and the memory of that phone call wouldn't let her.

"Shower first, then dinner," he said. "Then an early night. How does that sound?"

"Nick, why does someone want to kill me?" She couldn't get that terrifying thought out of her mind.

"I don't know, Lindsey. Maybe they only want to scare you, but we'll for sure find out who and why. That's a promise. This trip should give us some of the answers."

He led her to one of the bedrooms where he'd put her suitcase and then through another door into the private bath.

"Towels, soap, whatever you need. If you can't find it, just yell." He took her cold hands in his warm ones and squeezed them. "You can't keep up this wall forever, darlin'. Sooner or later—and I'd like it sooner—you'll have to tell me what the hell is going on. Now go shower."

She stood under the water for a long time, hoping its heat would melt the cold inside her, but nothing seemed to affect it. Rummaging in her suitcase that Nick left at the foot of the bed, she pulled out a pair of sweats she'd tossed in without really thinking about it. Now she was glad to have the comfort of their warmth and softness.

In the kitchen, she found Nick just turning steaks on a countertop grill. Potatoes were counting down in the microwave.

"I'll have everything on the table in a few minutes," he told her and inclined his head toward the counter behind him. "How about pouring us some wine?"

"First the brandy, now the wine." She had to

swallow the urge to laugh. "Are you trying to get me drunk?"

He turned his head, and the look he gave her was so intense she had to tear her gaze away from him.

"Sure, if I thought it would work." Then he looked back at the grill. "Just drink what you want."

She couldn't have said whether the food or wine tasted good, but she ate and drank because she knew she needed to. By the time she finished, the terror gripping her had been reduced to a manageable size.

That disappeared, though, when Nick's cell rang. He looked at the Caller ID and stood up. "I need to take this in the other room."

"If it's about me, I should know about it," she protested.

"If it's important, I promise I'll tell you. No sense stirring anything up if we don't need to."

But her curiosity drove her to move around to where she could overhear the conversation. And the cold feeling came back icier than ever.

"No, everything's still okay. I told you I'd make it and I will. We should have this wrapped up before then. After that, it will be my top priority."

Was it the same woman who'd called him the other night? His next sentence confirmed her suspicion.

"Stacy, when I make a promise, I keep it. Quit worrying, sugar. You know you can count on me."

Sugar! He called her sugar. Did he toss the word around like a used penny? Well, she'd told herself to expect this, despite his oblique promises of a future. She'd been right to call a halt to what was going on between them. The problem was Nick Vanetta was in her blood and getting over him wouldn't be the easiest thing to do. Especially when they were about to spend the next few days together. Maybe she should just tell him to put someone else on the case and go to Stacy, whoever and wherever she was.

She tiptoed quietly to the bedroom he'd given her, stripped off her clothes, and crawled into bed. At last, the terror and fatigue of the day caught up with her and she fell into a dreamless sleep.

****

I'm watching you and laughing. Did you like my little trick with the rifle? That was a blast, if you'll pardon the pun. A little farther to the left...

But no, it's not time yet. When we get to the end, I want to savor the moment to enjoy every minute of your pain. To watch you bleeding out and know that no one will help you.

You think you've lost me again, bitch? Not likely. I don't care where you go to ground. I'll find you. I know how to find you. I've done my homework well.

I'm patient, you know, and the prize is worth the wait. Pretend you're secure. You'll let your guard down, and I'll be right there.

We're almost at the end of the game.

Soon, very soon.

Bitch!

Chapter Fifteen

Lindsey was filled with nervous energy when Nick hustled them out of the condo early the next morning.

"I called the pilot and told him we'd be there an hour earlier," he told her.

"Did something happen overnight?" Oh, god. Now what? She wasn't sure she wanted to hear the answer.

"No." He shook his head. "I just want us out of the city in case the stalker somehow catches up with us."

"Down on the floor again, right?" She forced a smile.

"Gotta do it, Lindsey. I refuse to take chances."

She crouched down under the dashboard but kept her face tilted up so she could still talk to Nick. "I'm really nervous about what we'll find in Maine."

"I understand. But it's the only place we're going to get the answers you need. And hopefully get a lock on your stalker."

"You're right." She tried to adjust her cramped position, closing her eyes as the truck sped along the streets. "Do we have to change vehicles again?"

"No. We're good to go in this one."

Finally, when they hit Interstate 10, he told her she could sit up.

"I need to be two feet shorter if we're going to do this very often," she grumbled.

"Sorry about that." He reached a hand over and

helped her up onto the seat.

At the airport he drove to a private hangar in the charter service area. A sleek Gulfstream Five stood glistening in the sun, the Guardian logo painted discreetly in navy blue on the white surface. A man in a pilot's uniform came out of the building next to it and walked over to Nick.

"Nice to see you again, Mr. Vanetta. It's usually Mr. Sullivan who flies with us."

"We decided he shouldn't have all the fun." Nick grinned. He turned to Lindsey. "Miss Ferrell is our client on this trip. Let's be sure we take good care of her."

"Absolutely." The pilot shook Lindsey's hand. "Nice to meet you."

A second man, also in uniform, retrieved their luggage from the car and carried it onto the plane.

Lindsey gaped when they finally climbed the stairs into the cabin. The interior was beyond anything she was used to. She and her parents had never traveled outside of Texas, preferring to take their vacations in the many spots the state had to offer. At least that's what they had always planned. When she found it necessary to fly for whatever reason, she always felt like a sardine packed in a can.

But this…this was unbelievable. The cabin was outfitted with six lounge chairs, each with a table bolted to the floor next to it that could be swung over to use for work or dining. There were two couches and an overhead television that the chairs could be swiveled to face. To the left as they entered the jet, she glimpsed a small kitchen completely outfitted.

"There's a bedroom and bathroom through there,"

Nick pointed, "if you want to freshen up or anything." He chuckled at the look on her face. "Not bad for a poor bodyguard, right?"

"Maybe I'm paying you too much," she joked.

"Actually, I think you're only paying for one of the chairs." He buckled into the seat next to her. "We didn't take time to eat this morning because I wanted to get going. I don't know about you, but I'm starved. Ed will serve us breakfast once we're off the ground. "

The flight was pleasant and comfortable. Except for the understated hum and vibration, Lindsey felt as if she were sitting in a living room. The breakfast could have come from a gourmet restaurant and was served with a minimum of fuss.

If only she wasn't so tied up in knots.

She had to get her feelings for Nick under control. She didn't own him, after all. Quinn had been specific about Nick's wanderlust where women were concerned so why was she surprised when he was talking to other women while supposedly discussing a future with her? She figured all the things he'd said to her were just part of his usual treatment of whatever woman he was with.

Wait! He told you he'd never had another woman in his house.

True, but that just meant he stayed in the house of whoever he was seeing.

Sex with him had almost become addictive. Now she had to keep remembering his sweet words were just that—sweet words. Making love. No, scratch that. Better not personalize it too much. *Having sex* with Nick had given her an unbelievable sense of well-being. But then, the overheard telephone calls wiped away that euphoria, leaving her with a cold dose of reality.

She resented Nick playing her the way he was, making her feel something that obviously didn't exist. When this was over, she still had to keep the pieces of her life together. Nick would no doubt go back to his normal, uncommitted life. Selfishly, she hoped he'd carry some of the memories with him, but there was no guarantee of that, either.

Well, she couldn't say she hadn't been warned. She'd have to look at it as a onetime gift to herself.

Despite all that, she trusted him completely to keep her safe. Today, he seemed totally relaxed, even in the face of the growing tension of the situation.

"More coffee, Miss Ferrell?"

She jumped at the sound of Ed's voice. "No. Thank you."

She tipped her chair back and tried to read the book she'd shoved into her purse, but after fifteen minutes, she realized she was still on the same page. Nick had taken his laptop out of his briefcase as soon as he finished eating and worked steadily until they made a brief landing at about one o'clock.

"We're just dropping something off for Reno," he told her. "We'll probably top off the tanks and be wheels up again in a few minutes."

When they were back in the air, Ed served them a lunch of club sandwiches and cold drinks. While they ate, Nick asked her again about life in Cibolo when she was growing up.

"Maybe there's something hidden away in your mind that might give us a clue," he pointed out.

"I doubt it." Nervously, she tucked a strand of hair behind one ear. "My life was very normal. Almost boring you might say."

She told him stories about Ruben and Mary and talked about how she and Quinn met at school one day and instantly became friends.

"You know," she said, wrinkling her forehead, "I remember an air of sadness that always hung over my parents. We never had relatives we visited or even had any contact with, and my parents had very few close friends. Quinn's parents were probably the closest thing we had to an extended family."

Nick listened attentively, and she could tell he was processing everything she said. Talking about herself and her parents took Lindsey out of the conflict raging inside her, and she began to feel the knots unravel. By the time they reached Bangor, however, the photos and the stalker were front and center in her mind again, and the knots in her stomach were retying themselves.

When she walked off the plane at the Bangor airport, she felt as if she was stepping off a precipice with a great cavern yawning before her.

It will be all right.

She had to keep telling herself that, even though no one could promise her it would be so.

A stocky man in jeans and a plaid shirt was waiting for them at the aviation office. He greeted Nick as they came off the plane. "Dan Gregory."

"Nick Vanetta." They shook hands. "I think you usually work with Reno."

Dan nodded. "He called and explained what you needed. The vehicle's over there. The dark blue one." He pointed. "Here are the keys, and your confirmation for tonight at the Fairfield Inn right near here. You'll also find a map of Bangor and one of Maine in the glove box."

"Thanks." Nick took the keys from him.

"I was able to take care of the situation on Indian Island, too." He handed over an envelope. "All the information's in here."

Nick introduced Lindsey and thanked Dan for his work. After telling the pilot they'd be calling the Guardian office when they were ready for pickup, he helped Lindsey into the SUV. "The motel's only about five minutes from here. Let's check in and get our bearings. I want to call the office and see if they've come up with anything else."

Lindsey held her breath when Nick registered for them at the hotel, then breathed more easily when the clerk handed them two keys. He handed Lindsey hers, his eyes full of questions, then picked up their luggage and headed toward their rooms.

"I have some calls to make," he told her, unlocking her door. "After that, I think we should go over the maps Dan left for us. Would you rather do it in my room or yours?"

"Yours is fine. I'm just going to unpack enough for tonight so I won't be a minute."

"Good." After making sure she was settled in her room and there were no surprises waiting for them, he unlocked the connecting door and walked into his room without another word.

His feelings couldn't be clearer if he slammed it. But I can't change things. In the end, I'll be the one who gets hurt.

****

Nick ended the last of his calls and tossed the cell phone onto the table. He unfolded the maps Dan had given him but found himself unable to concentrate.

What the hell was wrong with Lindsey? The way she had shut herself off from him he might as well have had the measles. He racked his brain, trying to think of anything he'd done or said that could have kicked this off but nothing clicked.

He didn't ever remember a woman affecting him this way, slamming into him with the force of a freight train. The feelings and emotions were strange to him, but they also told him this was something special. Something he'd better take care of. For the first time in his life, he no longer had the urge to sample everything he was offered. He had a one-item menu and planned to stick to it.

If he could get Lindsey to open up to him.

Okay, so maybe this had started out with the suddenness of an explosion, but she'd been as affected as he was. He knew it. So what had made her put the brakes on? No, not just jam on the brakes but withdraw from him in all but the most polite ways? This wasn't the time to push her, but as soon as they wrapped this up, he was damn sure going to find out.

Damn it all, anyway.

Rolling up his sleeves, he tried to turn his attention back to the maps.

****

When Lindsey walked into his room, Nick was poring over the maps spread out on the round table by the window.

"Anything?" she asked, sitting down opposite him.

"I think so, but I want to wait until we get some dinner and relax before I go over it with you. Dan marked the library on the map of Bangor and highlighted the route to Bar Harbor, so we shouldn't have any trouble with directions."

"What did he mean, he took care of Indian Island?"

"I wanted to be able to stay there, if possible," he explained. "You know, blend in a little and engage people in conversation. Only there are no motels or inns on the island itself. However, Dan has a small firm here that provides security for a lot of the people on the island. One of his clients has a cottage he's happy to let us use while we're here."

Lindsey cocked an eyebrow. "Is there any place where you *don't* have connections?"

"I hope not." He winked. "We'd be in big trouble if there was."

The wink made her heart stutter, and she turned away so he wouldn't see its effect on her.

They spent what was left of the afternoon reviewing the notes they'd made. To Lindsey it was almost as if he were making sure he had all the players organized in his mind before taking the next step. He probably saw resolution. She saw a yawning precipice and had to swallow the nausea climbing up in her throat.

They chose a restaurant near the motel for dinner. As soon as they were seated, Nick ordered drinks for them—whiskey and water. When Lindsey countered with a request for wine, Nick shook his head.

"Bourbon's better. You'll need something stronger."

"You haven't said a word about what you learned from your office. Is the news you have so bad you have to get me drunk to tell me?"

"No. I just want you fortified to absorb it." His voice was matter-of-fact as he explained what he'd been told. "The couple in the picture is, in fact, your parents. That's definite. The guys at the office compared the photos we found with the ones you had using facial recognition software."

"But that's impossible." Lindsey felt as if she'd landed on another planet. "That just can't be true. My parents never left Texas."

"Not after you were born," Nick reminded her. "Their names before that were Marie Elizabeth and Brent Andrew Dolman. They owned a large summer home on Indian Island, a place that had been in Brent's family for years. Marie's family also had a home there. The boy in the pictures was her older brother, George."

Lindsey's head was reeling, and she felt dizzy. How was all this possible? "You mean I have an uncle out there somewhere? One I've never even heard of, let alone met?"

"So it seems. I have people checking to see if he's still alive and, if so, where he lives."

She took a swallow of her drink, hoping the alcohol would steady her, grateful now for Nick's insistence on the whiskey.

"What on earth could have happened to make them change their lives so drastically and hide away in Texas?" She shook her head in bewilderment. "Why did they feel the need to start their lives over using new identities? They left family behind and everything."

Nick took one of her hands in his and rubbed her knuckles with his thumb. "That's as much as the office has been able to piece together so far. I'm hoping we'll find more in the library tomorrow."

Sparks raced through Lindsey at the physical contact with him. She looked at Nick, realized he'd felt the same thing, and pulled her hand back. Surely that wasn't hurt on his face? Probably just wounded pride.

"This is all so…mind-boggling." She wasn't sure how much shocking news she could take. "Nick, if this is all true, then what happened to those two children—my sister and brother—and why did my parents change their names?" She swallowed against the sudden tightness in her throat. "I don't understand anything."

"I want to ask you to do something." He started to reach for her hand again, then stopped and instead fiddled with his drink. "You may not want to, but I think it's very necessary, and now is the time for it."

"What do you want that's so awful? Wait. If it's that bad, maybe I should finish my drink first." She swallowed a large gulp and sputtered, wiping tears from her eyes.

"Easy," Nick cautioned. "Sip, remember?"

She quickly drank some water. "I forgot this is bourbon." She set her water glass down carefully. "Okay. Let's have it."

"I want you to call Mary and tell her Reno would like to come out and talk to her and Ruben. Tell her what you've found out so far. Give her permission to tell him whatever it is that you and I both know they aren't telling you."

"Oh, Nick." She shook her head. "I don't know if they'll do it. I can hardly get them to talk to *me*. And Reno would go himself? What's that all about?"

"This is too sensitive to send one of our agents," he explained. "It's obvious they know at least pieces of the story. I want whatever information they have before we go to Indian Island, if possible. Will you do it?"

Lindsey chewed on her thumbnail. "I guess so. But

my asking doesn't mean they'll say yes."

"I know, but at least it will open the door."

"All right." She took another drink of water. "I'll do it when we get back to the motel."

They ordered their dinner, although Lindsey wasn't sure if she'd be able to keep anything in her stomach. Everything she'd learned was too unsettling. She could hardly get her mind around the fact that her whole life had been a lie.

Back in her room, she tamped down her reservations and put the call through to the ranch. Nick stood beside her, waiting. When she told Mary what they had found so far and what she wanted her and Ruben to do, there was a long silence on the other end.

Then Ruben came on the line. "When we suggested you look in those boxes, we didn't think you'd carry it quite this far, little one." His voice was somber. "But I guess it's your right to know. You finish what you're doing and come back here. Then we'll talk. Only to you, though. And maybe that guy you're playing footsie with. I guess he should know, too."

Only there's no more footsie.

"They won't do it." She sighed, hanging up. "Ruben said only to me, after we get back." She raked her hands through her hair, then pushed her glasses back up on her nose. "But we aren't going to get anything out of them until we get back to the ranch, so we might just as well keep plunging ahead."

"Then I think we should go to sleep," Nick said. "I want us to be fresh for the morning."

"Fine. I'll see you then."

Lindsey thought about locking the connecting door, except what if she needed him in the middle of the night? What if, God forbid, she had another nightmare? She shuddered but left the inner door unlocked. She suddenly realized how tired she was. Sleep sounded very good. She showered quickly and climbed into in the unfamiliar bed, closing her eyes.

Help me! Help me!

Her lungs were starved for air, but she kept pushing through the water. She *tried to open her eyes, but her lids felt glued shut.*

Hurry! Help me!

She was so tired she didn't think she could take one more stroke, but the tiny voice kept ringing in her ears.

Hurry! Hurry!

"Lindsey. Wake up, sugar. Come on, Lindsey, snap out of it."

There was a hand over her mouth, and she tried to pull away from it. A scream tried to push its way out of her throat.

"Lindsey, it's me, Nick. Open your eyes for me." The voice was insistent, penetrating the fog.

As if she was pushing boulders from her eyelids, she opened them very slowly. Nick's face swam into her blurred vision.

"Nick?" she mumbled against the fingers on her lips.

"It's me." His eyes were heavy with concern. "Are you okay? Can I take my hand away?"

She nodded and opened her mouth to draw air into her lungs. When her racing heart slowed, she looked at him. "What happened?"

"You screamed so loud I expected someone to call the police. It's a good thing you left your side of the door unlocked."

“I screamed?” she repeated.

“I thought I’d have to suffocate you to keep you from waking up the entire motel.”

“I had the nightmare again.” She shuddered.

“Sure seems that way.” He brushed her hair back from her face. “Lindsey, I don’t know what’s going on with you, but I don’t think you should be alone for the rest of the night. Will you let me sleep here with you, hold you, if I don’t make any moves?”

Certain she was making a mistake but knowing she’d be better off with him in here, she nodded and moved over to make room for him. The sight of his muscular body clad only in boxers almost made her change her mind about their relationship. But he was good as his word. He just wrapped his arms around her and pulled her against him in a comforting embrace.

“I hate this,” she said, her voice soft. “Hate it, hate it, hate it.”

“I know.” He tightened his arms around her. “Do you want me to get you some hot tea or something? There’s a coffee maker here that I can heat water in.”

“No.” She shook her head, burrowing against his chest. “Just hold me.”

Despite the comfort of his big, warm body, Lindsey lay awake for a long time, her mind a jumble of thoughts. Who was she really? What would they find out tomorrow? And where did the nightmare fit into all of this?

Chapter Sixteen

"I think this building has been here since the colonies were founded," Lindsey whispered as they climbed the broad steps of the Bangor Public Library. She was trying to ease the bad attack of nerves she'd woken up with.

"So has the librarian," Nick whispered back, pointing to the woman behind the checkout desk.

Lindsey elbowed him to be quiet, then waited while he explained to the woman what they were looking for.

"Oh, yes, we have those," the woman assured him. "But they're down in the basement. No one ever asks for them." She made a slight tsking sound. "I'm sorry, but I'm afraid it's very dusty down there."

"That's all right. We're dust proof," Nick told her.

Lindsey jabbed him again.

"Follow me, then." She marched down the stairs ahead of them, her soft rubber soles barely making a sound. Throwing open the door to a long, narrow room, she pointed out the boxes of newspapers on the shelves. "If you could get those down, sir, it would be a great help. You can spread them out on that table over there. Those chairs are none too comfortable, I guess, but it's better than standing up."

"We'll do just fine," Nick assured her.

"Well, all right. My name is Grace if you need any

further help."

"Thank you." He urged Grace back upstairs, then scanned the labels on the boxes. "Let's see if we can make this a little easier," he told Lindsey. "According to the letters, the baby must have been born in 1970. He looks to be at least a year old in those pictures, so they had to be taken the following year. Let's start with 1971 and work forward."

He took down the appropriate boxes, pulled out the issues they wanted, and gave half to Lindsey. The process was tedious. *The Beach Recorder* may have only published weekly, but each issue was at least fifty pages.

"Who would ever believe there was so much news in these teeny little communities," Lindsey commented, stopping a moment to stretch her arms and rotate her head. "Of course, most of the paper is a bloated society column. I can't believe some of the stuff that's in here."

"Everyone wants their fifteen minutes of fame." Nick grinned. "And some people, it seems, want it more than once."

A picture of a crowd at a party caught her attention and she sat forward, excitement skittering through her veins. "Nick, look at this. Here's a picture of my—the Dolmans at somebody's event. See?" She pointed to a page. "They're standing with a bunch of political bigwigs. I guess they really did move in high society."

"That means they spent some significant time around here." He turned another page. "Let's keep looking. Maybe there are more pictures of them."

They found six more shots of Brent and Marie at social functions with a group of the island's elite. After that, they searched each page carefully, looking not only for the headline but for any mention of the couple or their family. A picture began to emerge of a wealthy, successful attorney, his socially important wife, and their place in island society.

According to the newspaper write-ups, Brent Dolman practiced corporate law in Boston and sat on the boards of many of the corporations he represented. He may have come from old money, but he apparently hadn't rested on the family's reputation and fortunes. Lindsey was stunned by the picture of her parents that emerged from the articles and society columns.

"I've got the article."

Her head jerked up at Nick's words. She reached across to take the paper from him. "Let me see."

He held onto it firmly. "Let me read it to you, Lindsey. Please. Just listen to what it says."

"Why? Will I hate it?" Her pulse skipped, and her hands curled into fists.

"No, but it will be a shock," he said. "And it opens other doors we need to go through. Just sit and listen. Please."

In a calm, even voice, he read the story of the tragedy that hit a prominent young family summering on Indian Island. According to the newspaper, Brent and Marie Dolman and their two children, Barbara Ann, six years old, and the toddler, Charlie had gone out for an afternoon sail. Marie was pregnant with their third child, which made the trip even more curious. They were caught in a sudden storm, and everyone was washed overboard. The children's nanny called the Coast Guard when they didn't return. The boat was found floating several miles away on the ocean, but three days of searching had not turned up any survivors.

She blinked. “That’s it? No other details?”

“I haven’t read any further. But that’s all it says here.”

“And Marie was pregnant?” Lindsey placed her hand over her own stomach. “B-But if that’s really them, they can’t be dead because they lived in Texas.” She was suddenly finding it hard to breathe. “And this means I had a sister. And a brother.”

“So it would seem.”

“I don’t understand any of this, Nick. Not one bit.” Nausea crept up into her throat, and she forced it back. “Let’s keep reading. There’s bound to be some follow-up.”

In the next week’s issue, the paper reported divers were no longer searching for the remains of the Dolman family. A memorial service was held, organized by their families, and memorial markers were set in the Dolman family plot in Boston. A tiny notice the following year announced the summer home previously owned by Brent and Marie Dolman had been sold to a family from New York.

“What about the nanny?” Lindsey’s mouth was dry, and her heart thudded against her ribs. “Does it say anything about her? Who she was? Where she went to?”

“Wait. This isn’t all. It’s continued.” Nick flipped through several pages. “Yes. Here. Now it talks about the estate. Boy, this paper really prints everything. The estate was probated by one of Dolman’s law partners. Most of it went to a judge who was a former law professor of Brent’s.”

“A law professor? What a strange bequest.”

“Norma and Howard Littman, the nanny and the

caretaker, received a million dollars. Jesus, Lindsey." He looked up from his reading. "That's a lot of money to leave the household help. Something doesn't add up here."

Her head was spinning. "Nick, we have to find out what happened. Someone must know. Maybe we'll find someone on the island who does. Maybe the people who bought the house can put us in touch with Carrie and Renee, if they're even still alive. Maybe someone can track down the Littmans."

"That's a lot of maybes."

"Come on." She was up and pulling at him. "Let's go. I want to try and find out."

"Hold on." He picked up the papers with the articles in them. "First let's see if Grace can make copies of this stuff for us. They must have a machine here someplace. Then I'm going to call the office. They're better equipped to search than we are here. Besides, Reno may have to use a little muscle to do some of the digging."

"What do you mean?"

"I want to get a copy of the probate papers," he explained, "and I want someone to talk to the partners at the law firm. At least one of them must still be practicing. Then we'll go over to the island and reconnoiter. Slowly and casually."

Grace was happy to make copies for them, carefully collecting a quarter for each one. She insisted on giving them a receipt, taking what Lindsey thought was forever to write it out.

Finally, they were back in the car and on the highway.

"Do you really think—I'm not sure I even want to

ask this—that my nightmares have anything to do with this?" Lindsey twisted her hands together in her lap.

Nick stole a quick look at her. "I told you I have a grandmother who believes in things like this. She'd say someone is trying to send you a message about what happened. That their soul was wandering and can't rest until the truth comes out. Or maybe someone else who died that night."

"God, Nick, it seems so…otherworldly."

"Stranger things have happened."

She rubbed her forehead. "But that would explain the water and the drowning voice, wouldn't it?"

He reached over and squeezed her hands. "You said the nightmares started when your father died. Then they disappeared and came back when your mother passed away. Right?"

"Yes."

"So my grandmother would say, each time a soul went to heaven, someone was trying to get a message through to you."

Lindsey leaned her head back. "I feel like I'm in a nightmare again, only this time I'm awake."

"But now I'm right here with you."

Yes, you certainly are. And that's good and bad. Damn.

"Lindsey, don't make yourself sick over this. We're going to find all the answers, and then you'll finally have some peace."

"Lord." She rubbed her eyes. "I certainly hope so."

The drive from Bangor to Bar Harbor took less than an hour. Dan Gregory had given them good directions to the ferry they needed, and by early afternoon they were chugging across the short distance to Indian Island.

The first thing Lindsey noticed was the abundance of pine trees that covered much of the island. They obscured most of the homes, although rooftops peeked out here and there. Docks protruded from the beach like so many extended wooden fingers, with boats anchored at their moorings. Here and there, a sailboat lazily skimmed the waves. April weather in Maine was still on the chilly side, but a few hardy souls had opened their homes early.

"It seems almost too cold for this now." Lindsey shivered, pulling the edges of her coat together.

"It is, although my guess is a few early birds always arrive on the island. But that's why we're able to use this cottage. The owner won't be here for another month."

They drove along a road that wound into the interior of the island, past high brick walls and thick privacy barriers formed by the pines. Occasionally, a smaller, less protected house stood out, but Lindsey guessed even those people demanded their privacy. Trying to talk to anyone might be a real challenge.

The road curved back on itself like a switchback, and soon she caught a faint glimpse of the water again through the trees. Eventually, Nick turned off the road and bumped down a gravel driveway that ended in a wide clearing. A garage big enough to hold four cars stood at an angle to the two-story white house. The dormer windows and glass-enclosed sun porches reflected the afternoon sunlight. A side view showed a wide expanse of green lawn dotted with flagstones stretching to a narrow strip of beach.

"This is a cottage?" She stared, open-mouthed. "I

wonder how big it has to be before they call it a house. Lord, Nick. I'd love to come here on a real vacation. Are you telling me we have this whole place to ourselves?"

"You bet." He fished a key ring from his pocket along with a folded piece of paper. "Let's go in, turn on the heat, and scope the place out. Then I'll get the luggage."

Every room was large, part of an open, spacious design. An open-hearth fireplace dominated the living room. A sun porch like the one they'd entered held a dining room table and chairs as well as comfortable lounge furniture. The master suite located just off the living room had the same magnificent view of the water as the living room.

"Wow." Lindsey moved from room to room, studying the design. "I love houses like this. I had to draw one as a class project, and I always wanted to do one for real."

"Maybe you'll get the opportunity when we wrap this up," Nick encouraged her.

They sorted out the sleeping arrangements without too much discomfort. Nick seemed willing to give her the space she needed, at least for now. While she unpacked and put her things away, Nick sat on the couch in the living room making calls. She hoped Guardian had more to tell him. Her impatience to find answers was growing thin.

"Anything?" she asked, walking back into the living room.

"Yes and no."

"That's your favorite answer, isn't it?" She pushed her hair nervously behind her ear.

"Sometimes, that's all I've got. Anyway, the office is working a trace on the Littmans. If they were paid staff employees, it means they have Social Security numbers, which I hope will help us find them. I also asked for a search of other articles on the drowning and on the Dolmans."

"What about the estate?" she prodded. "You said maybe someone could find out about the beneficiaries and go from there."

"That's Reno's department." He circled something on his tablet. "He's setting a meeting with one of the partners in Dolman's old firm. Two of them are still practicing, believe it or not."

"He's going to Boston? Just for that?" She was amazed at what this firm could and would do for its clients.

"He wants to see the probate file and find out about the balance of the estate." He tossed the electronic device on the coffee table. "Something stinks here, Lindsey, and Reno's got the best nose for rooting out stuff like that. He'll call back when he has a day and time set up."

His cell rang, and he tapped the icon to answer it. "Yeah? Yeah? Okay, just a sec." He reached for the tablet again and picked up his stylus. "Okay, go. Uh-huh. Uh-huh. Yup. Got it. Thanks." He stood up and reached for her hand. "Get your jacket. We're going out again."

"Where to?"

"When I called earlier, I asked the office to find out who bought the Dolman place," he explained. "There has to be a recorded deed, and Guardian can search it out better online than we can begging at city hall. And more quickly. They did, so now we're going to see if anyone's in residence."

The house was back on the other side of the island, surrounded by a high stone wall almost obscured by tall bushes. An iron gate barred the driveway, but a small speaker box sat just to the left.

Nick pushed the Call button.

"Yes? Who is it, please?" a disembodied voice asked.

Nick introduced himself, told whoever it was that he had identification and explained they were trying to trace the previous owners. After a long minute, the gate swung open and they drove through.

"I guess now I know what they call a house," Lindsey mused.

Three stories of New England architecture rose before them, clapboards weathered by storms and age. A pitched roof swept up to the sky and tendrils of smoke curled from a chimney. Mullioned windows sparkled in the sun. No porch on this side, just a wide stoop leading up to double doors. One of them swung open as Nick and Lindsey pulled into the circle in front.

A woman somewhere between fifty and seventy, dressed in a navy dress and sensible shoes, stepped out to wait for them.

"I'm Mrs. Hutchins," she told them. "The housekeeper. The Reynolds family isn't in residence at the moment. I'll try to help you, but I don't know if I can tell you anything."

After checking Nick's credentials thoroughly and acknowledging Lindsey, she led them inside and took them all the way through to the kitchen. Lindsey tried not to gawk as they passed the rooms. Her architect's antenna was vibrating, noting all the fine details of workmanship, the excellent placement of rooms and windows. She'd like to come back some time and really take a good look.

"Would you like some tea? I was just about to fix some."

Nick and Lindsey both nodded, and they waited while Mrs. Hutchins fussed with cups and saucers and a plate of cookies.

She sat across from them, stirring sugar into her tea, her eyes bright and questioning. "If you'll tell me what you want to know, I'll try to answer your questions. As long as it doesn't violate anyone's privacy," she amended. "The Reynolds family guards its privacy very tightly."

"I represent clients who are searching for long lost relatives," Nick told her. "The information we've uncovered led us here. Feel free to check on my agency before you answer any questions if that will make you feel better."

Mrs. Hutchins studied the business card Nick had given her, then rose from her chair. "If you don't mind. I'll be just a moment."

Lindsey sipped her tea nervously, her body filled with tension, as they waited for the woman to come back. When she did, her face was hard to read.

"So are you willing to help us?" Lindsey burst out, unable to sit quietly any longer.

Mrs. Hutchins nodded. "Yes. I called Mr. Reynolds at his office, and he gave me permission to answer general questions." She took a sip of her tea and set the cup down, placing it precisely on the saucer. "The Reynolds family purchased this place more than thirty years ago. Ownership has since passed to the younger Mr. and Mrs. I've been working for them for ten years, and before that I lived in Portland. I'm sure I've never heard any of them mention people named Dolman."

"Then you never knew anything about the people who owned this house before?" Lindsey was growing impatient. The more walls she met, the more dead ends, the more impatient she became to find answers. Somewhere in her past was someone who wanted to kill her and this was their best chance so far to find out who that might be.

"Not really."

Not even Nick's careful questioning could extract further information from the housekeeper. The only thing she knew about the Dolmans was they'd owned this house at one time.

"Well, thank you for your time," he said at last, his tone polite. "We're staying on the island for a few more days at the Burton place." He pointed to the business card. "My cell phone number is on there on the bottom if you should happen to think of anything."

Maybe it was the mention of the Burtons or the fact that the Burtons thought enough of them to have them as guests on the island. Whatever the trigger, something had unexpectedly made them acceptable. And Mrs. Hutchins had a sudden memory recovery. "Actually, now that you've jogged my brain, it seems I do know some of the story. Such a tragedy."

"Anything you can remember would be helpful," Nick assured her.

"Well, it isn't much, really." She pursed her lips. "I heard Brent and Marie Dolman were a nice young couple. Both of their families had homes on the island for years. Mr. Brent Dolman brought his wife and children here to this place after they were married. They were all very well thought of. When Mr. and Mrs. Reynolds bought this house, people were quick to tell them the story."

Lindsey almost rolled her eyes. *I'll just bet.*

"The residents were shocked by the tragedy," Mrs. Hutchins continued. "Mr. Dolman was an excellent sailor, they said, and could handle a boat in any situation. Still, the mystery was why they would do something as foolish as going out with a storm coming in."

"What about the Littmans?" Nick asked. "I understand they worked for Brent and Marie. Are they still around?"

The housekeeper clicked her tongue. "I heard they were destroyed by the whole thing and moved away somewhere." She narrowed her eyes. "You know they inherited quite a large sum from the Dolmans."

And no less than they deserved, her tone implied.

What was behind that?

"Do you have any idea where they might have gone?" Nick prodded. "Or what happened to the senior Dolmans? Or Mrs. Dolman's parents?"

Mrs. Hutchins shook her head. "I'm sorry, but I don't." Her attitude indicated she'd given them all she was going to.

They thanked her and went out to the car, heading back down the driveway. As they approached the gate, it swung open to let them exit the grounds.

"Something is weird here." Nick's thumb tapped the steering wheel as they drove back along the road. "One of the stories in the paper mentioned the storm forecast, too, and Brent Dolman's sailing experience. This whole story just doesn't ring true."

At that moment, his cell phone buzzed and he answered the call impatiently. "Vanetta. Yeah. Uh-huh. Great. Can you text it to me along with directions? Good. Thanks again."

He pulled over to the curb while he retrieved the text message. He left the message on the screen as he made a U-turn and started back the way they'd just come.

Lindsey tried to quiet the nervous energy running through her. "Where are we going now? What was that call about?"

"That was the office," he said. "They found the address of the place where Marie's parents lived. It's been sold also, but I thought I'd see if we could learn anything from the new owners. I just hope the house is open and someone's there."

Luck wasn't with them this time, however. The house was obviously still battened down for the winter, and no one had come to open it yet for the season.

"This was a long shot." Nick sighed. "But it was worth a try."

Lindsey chewed her bottom lip. "So what's next? We can't just sit around and do nothing."

Nick opened the folder from Dan Gregory and glanced through one page of notes.

"Okay, we're going to stop at the tiny little market right near the ferry landing. Dan says it's a good place to pick up supplies. Then I'm going to call Guardian again and see what else they've come up with."

****

I found you, you spoiled brat. Did you think I

wouldn't?

You surprised me, figuring things out. I had to make some quick adjustments to my plan. Can't torture you much longer. At least not the way I have. But when I get hold of you...

Last night, I stabbed the Barbie doll forty times. It should have been you. I wanted to see your blood everywhere. But soon it will be your turn. Very soon.

Now I have to move fast. I knew the cat would be out of the bag soon. Maybe it's time. Yes, it's definitely time. The game is almost over.

You had it all, didn't you? Well, you won't have it anymore.

Now I get what's mine. What should always have been mine. And you can't stop me.

Bitch!

Chapter Seventeen

The wind had picked up by the time they got back to the house, and Lindsey was happy to get inside. Nick hauled wood in from the stack by the back door and lit a fire in the fireplace. While Lindsey stood in front of it warming herself, he pulled a bottle of wine from one of the grocery sacks, found two wine glasses in one of the cupboards, and carried everything into the living room.

Balancing the filled wine glasses, Nick stretched out on the floor in front of the fire, leaning back against the couch and patting the floor next to him.

"Come sit beside me, Lindsey. You're wound tight as a drum. I'll make my call to the office, then we can try to relax."

"I don't think I know the meaning of that word anymore." She nibbled at her bottom lip. "And I'm fine on the couch. Thanks."

He turned his head, his eyes studying her face as she sat primly on the edge of the furniture.

"Lindsey, I don't plan to rip your clothes off if that's what's worrying you. I don't know what the hell is suddenly going on with us, but I thought it would be nice to sit here together and try to unwind. Is that such a bad thing?"

She wanted to ask him if she was just a substitute for Stacy. If being handy put her at the top of the list.

"I have no idea what wild ass idea is running

around in that brain of yours," he continued, "or what set it off. Whatever it is, we'll deal with it later. Meanwhile, just come sit by my side. We'll have some wine and watch the fire."

Realizing she could precipitate an argument she wasn't yet ready for, Lindsey lowered to the floor beside him and gratefully accepted the wine. She sipped it slowly while Nick spoke to his office. The conversation was long, although his side consisted mostly of "Yeah" and "Uh-huh" and "Good, very good."

"Tell me what that was about," Lindsey demanded as soon as he disconnected. "Have they learned anything else?"

"I'd say we're making progress." He took a swallow of his own wine. "Reno has an appointment in Boston tomorrow at Brent Dolman's former law firm. One of the partners has agreed to meet with him."

Lindsey jerked upright, almost spilling her wine. "So my father actually was an attorney? A partner in a big firm?"

"Looks that way. The article in the paper was as factual as it could be. Reno's going to tell them about your stalker. Hopefully, that will prod them to give him a look at the probate file and find out about the weird bequests. He'll call us as soon as he's done and let us know how it went."

"Those nightmares I had." She fiddled with her hair, doing the thing where she tucked it behind her ear. Damn, she needed to break herself of that. "I know this will sound weird to you, but it's as if the past was reaching out to tell me to save myself. To find the answers to a puzzle I didn't even know existed. My mother was pregnant with me when this happened, so in essence I *was* in the water. And could have drowned."

"My grandmother would tell you it's not weird at all," Nick disagreed. "Whatever energy reached out to you when your father died, it tried to prod you into looking for answers. And when your mother died, they came back stronger than ever. In a way, you actually might have been in the water and could have drowned."

"But I didn't, thank God. I just wish my mother had told me all this a long time ago." She stared at the fire. "Speaking of my mother, any word from the nursing home?"

"Our man is still working there, and he's been able to pick up bits and pieces of conversation from the other employees. I guess the break room is a good place for gossip, and he's a master at ferreting it out. He's convinced that someone was there that day, someone who got past the nurses' station, and no one wants to talk about it. Liability and all that."

"Right now, I just want answers," she told him. "Liability's the last thing on my mind. What about the Littmans? Have they found any trace of them?"

He nodded. "But it's not all good. They relocated to a small town in upstate New York, using part of their windfall to buy a small business and a house for them and their daughter."

"Daughter?" Lindsey frowned. "There was no mention of a daughter in any of the articles. Nothing indicated the housekeeper and her husband had any children at all. Where did a daughter come from all of a sudden?"

"It's possible someone else was caring for the child while they worked for the Dolmans. That happened often in those days. Domestic help was not encouraged to bring along their families."

"How weird," Lindsey commented. "To leave your own kids and go off to care for someone else's."

If I could have children, I'd never leave them for someone else to raise.

Nick snorted. "You wouldn't believe some of the strange things I've seen in this business. Anyway, I've got someone on it, but it will be tomorrow before they get back to us with any results. I did get more on the photos, though."

"You mean they know who the rest of those people are?" she asked, clutching her wine.

"As we thought, Marie Dolman had a brother named George, and we're trying to find out what happened to him. Also, it appears that Brent Dolman had two brothers we're trying to track down. We're also checking for siblings of all the grandparents. That's it so far."

"But that's more than we had before." She leaned back against the couch. "I just wish everything didn't take so long. The only comfort is at least the stalker can't get to me here."

Nick built up the fire, and they sat quietly watching the dancing flames and feeling the warmth wrap around them. Lindsey's mind was working overtime, trying to absorb all the information while forcing back the constant dread that crept over her.

"I can't shake the idea that something horrible is hovering over us," she told Nick.

"I can't promise you what we find will be pleasant, but at least we'll finally have the answers you need. And hopefully, we'll catch your stalker at the same time."

"If only." She sighed.

Nick was as good as his word. He allowed her to keep a minimal distance between them and didn't try to touch her at all. She could feel the repressed sexual tension radiating from his body. Not that hers was much better. But she couldn't afford to let down her guard until she knew the real score with him, and other things took priority right now.

Eventually, lulled by the warmth and the wine, they both dozed off. They were still asleep when Nick's cell phone rang and woke them. He looked at his watch as he grabbed for the phone.

"My God, it's nine o'clock. Holy shit." He tapped the phone to accept the call. "Vanetta."

Lindsey could tell from his side of the conversation that it was his office, and the length of the call told her they had more information for him. She fidgeted waiting for him to finish. Finally, he hung up, but he took a long moment before he turned to her.

"Did they find out anything more?" Her voice was taut with apprehension.

Nick flopped back against the pillows. "We seem to be getting someplace, but I'm not sure where. The Littmans died two years ago in a house fire while they were asleep. Arson was suspected, but no one could prove anything. The daughter, who was thirty-seven at the time and had been in and out of their lives for years, apparently just disappeared."

"You mean, as in gone?"

"Uh-huh. Someone thought they'd seen her about a week before the fire, but they weren't sure." He shifted so he was leaning on one elbow, looking at Lindsey.

"And that's another wrinkle. Something's not right there, either."

"What?" Lindsey sat up abruptly. "What do you mean?"

"From what we can tell, the Littmans took their million bucks and tried to set up a new life. Guardian managed to track Mrs. Littman through the domestic agency that sent her to the Dolmans. The agency knew about the husband because he was part of the package she presented, but they were pretty sure the two of them never had any children. Yet, all of a sudden, they showed up in this little town in the middle of nowhere with a daughter. I think that daughter is the key, somehow."

"But how will we find her?" Lindsey worried her bottom lip. "If Guardian can't find her, probably no one can."

"We have a lot of resources at our disposal, Lindsey. It'll happen, believe me. If she's alive anywhere, my staff will find her. And tomorrow, Reno will call us from Boston with a report on his visit there."

"I can't just sit around and wait," she told him. "I'm too antsy."

He nodded. "I understand, but at the moment, we don't have much choice. Let's fix something to eat, and tomorrow, we can hang out at that little convenience store and see if we can pick up any old gossip."

They cleaned up silently after dinner and went to their rooms early. Alone in her bed, Lindsey slept fitfully, afraid to let herself go and become prey to the dream. And she was still bothered by the situation with Nick. Her head and her heart didn't quite seem to be in agreement. And her body ached for his. But she wasn't about to let herself in for another round of heartbreak.

When she woke in the morning, she was anything but rested.

****

Nick was up shortly after dawn, his sleep disturbed by dreams of Lindsey and the uneasy feeling that something was going on with her she didn't intend to share with him. He had lain awake a long time the night before, going over in his mind almost every minute of every day and night since he'd first walked into her office. He replayed conversations, actions, even their lovemaking until it made him so hard it was almost painful.

He supposed Quinn could have called and warned her about him again, but that wasn't exactly Quinn's style. He'd have called Nick first, checked what was going on, and made it known Lindsey was completely off limits. And he hadn't done that.

So what was the problem?

He wanted this woman in ways he'd never wanted another in his life. He wanted to make love with her, laugh with her, grow old with her. The baby thing didn't bother him at all. He knew people who'd adopted kids very successfully.

He could feel the edges of the case coming together. And after they did, he and Lindsey Ferrell were going to sit down and have a long talk. Meanwhile, he needed a pot of strong coffee to get him through the day. He broke the uneasy silence at breakfast by telling Lindsey stories of growing up and his fights with his sisters and brothers.

"I really envy you a large noisy family," she said, a

wistful note in her voice. “Maybe when we find the answers to this puzzle, I’ll turn out to have relatives, too.”

“That would be nice. Families are great. And I’m really close to mine.”

“I know.” She sighed. “Well, whatever happens, happens. I just hope some of it turns out to be good.”

After they cleaned up the kitchen, they drove around the island, checking the Ormond house again in case someone had shown up since yesterday. Eventually, they landed at the little convenience store. Lindsey browsed aisles tightly packed with every kind of merchandise while Nick chatted with the owner and his wife.

The couple was in their sixties and had lived on Indian Island all their lives. Even more important, when Nick worked the conversation around to the drowning as casually as he could, they remembered the tragedy vividly. They were happy, with little prodding, to recount what they knew.

“That storm did it,” the man said. “I never knew why they went out on the water with the weather closing in. No one did. They were experienced sailors, so I guess young Dolman just thought he could beat it to shore in plenty of time.” He shook his head. “They were getting ready to go home to Boston for the winter. I guess they just wanted one more sail before they left.”

“Everyone was so upset about it,” his wife added. “They were such nice young people, with everything going for them.”

“What about their families?” Nick asked. “Are any of them still around here?”

“Oh, no.” She twisted her lips in dismay. “Their

parents were just destroyed with grief. Those two grandmothers were close friends. They hung onto each other, waiting for the rescue boats to come in, crying like I'd never seen. What a mess."

"The marine patrol dived for three days," the old man continued. "When they didn't find anything, the parents hired a private crew and kept them looking for a long time. They didn't find anything, either."

"After a while everyone just gave up," the woman sighed. "They sold them big houses and left the island. Don't think any of them have been back since. Couldn't bear to see the spot again, I guess."

"They had a couple working for them, didn't they?" Nick arranged his features in an innocent expression. "I heard one of them looked after the children."

The old man gave a bitter chuckle. "That little girl was a handful, that's for sure. No one could stand to be around her. I don't know how that nanny ever put up with her. Lordy. When she had a temper tantrum, you could hear her clean to Boston. Scream and carry on like the devil himself was after her."

"One time when she was in the store," his wife put in, "we had to ask them to take her out. Her poor daddy was trying to buy her some candy, and she was kicking everything in sight. It's a wonder she didn't break up the whole store. I sure did feel sorry for them."

"Do you think anyone else around here might remember what happened to that older couple?" Nick asked.

"Don't think so. They wasn't real friendly to begin with. And when this all happened, they didn't even stay around for the search. Just packed their things and up and left."

"Thank you for your time," Nick told them and urged Lindsey out to their vehicle.

"Why are we leaving?" she asked. "We don't have all our answers."

"I think I got everything from them we can. Let's go back to the cottage and see what we can piece together from what they said. And how it fits in with everything else we found out."

Once inside, Nick stoked up the fire until it produced a nice blaze. Then, determined to see if he could breach that barrier Lindsey had erected, he pulled the big soda cushions in front of the fire. He lay down with his head on one and patted the other.

"Come get warm." He smiled. "It's cold outside, and I'm lonely."

He watched conflicting emotions chase themselves across her face, her teeth worrying her bottom lip.

"Come on, Linds," he urged. "Just a little relaxation and conversation."

When she finally lay down beside him, he waited a few moments before taking her hand. He held it like that, listening to the flames crackle, until he felt her body relax a little. Then, slowly, he brought her hand to his lips and pressed a kiss on it. When he traced her knuckles with his tongue, she tried to pull away, but he tightened his hold, kept teasing with his tongue and in a moment she relaxed again.

So far so good.

He went slowly, taking his time, not wanting to spook her. But moments later, he rolled to his side and brushed light kisses over her lips, her jaw, and her neck. She jerked her head away and moved as if to get up, but he pulled her back.

"Just a kiss, Lindsey. Today has been tough for you. Let me help you relax."

Whatever battle she was waging with herself, she apparently needed to try and forget it for a while because her body relaxed and she accepted his kisses again. He paid careful attention to every inch of her mouth, then nuzzled that sensitive place behind her ear. A little moan drifted from her.

Okay, a little further now.

Before long, he slipped his hand beneath her sweater, smoothing it across her abdomen and sliding up to cup one breast. At the same time, he blew in her ear and nibbled on the lobe. He knew exactly what turned her on.

She tensed beneath his touch, resistance stiffening her, but then he inched his hand beneath the waistband of her slacks, all the time kissing her, nibbling and licking. She hadn't pushed him away yet so he pushed his luck.

He took his time, stroking and licking and touching all those places he'd learned aroused her and turned her on. He knew the moment he had her, when his fingers slid between the wet lips of her sex, over her clit, and down toward her opening. She made a token resistance, but he knew just how to stroke and touch, how to use his fingers in all her most sensitive places.

When he went to work on her clit, she moaned and opened her legs for him. He slid his mouth over to hers, brushing her lips with his before sliding his tongue into her mouth and tasting her everywhere. He never took his hand from between her legs, knowing just how to touch and tease, feeling her growing more liquid, hotter, ready for him.

He chanced removing his hand but only for the time it took to rid her of her slacks and panties. Then he went at her in earnest. He didn't care if he came or not, just that he gave Lindsey an incredible orgasm and that she understood it happened only with him. He kissed her until neither of them could breathe anymore, sucking her tongue and scraping it with his teeth, all the while rubbing and stroking her clit.

When she was close to the edge, he knelt between her thighs and stroked every inch of her sex with his tongue. He squeezed the cheeks of her buttocks and traced the damp tip of his finger around her rear opening. Everything seemed to drive her higher toward a climb.

The release, when it came, shook every inch of her body and every muscle clenched and spasmed. Just as she came, he slid three fingers inside her and felt her inner muscles clench hard around them. She shuddered over and over again, slamming her thighs together around his arm, trapping his hand inside her. When the last little shiver died away, he slid his fingers from her and, making sure she watched, licked each of them clean.

"Better than anything I've ever tasted." He transferred her taste to her lips with his tongue.

"Listen, Nick," she began.

He touched his fingers to her lips. "Don't say it, whatever it is. Just relax in the pleasure of it."

"You didn't—"

He shook his head. "This wasn't for me. I wanted to take the edge off for you. I—"

At that moment, his phone rang.

Lindsey tensed as he rolled over to answer it and listened without saying a word. When he disconnected the call, she sat up beside him.

"What was that about? I know it's something. And probably bad, right?"

"Maybe, maybe not." He stood up and reached out a hand to her, which she took with some reluctance. "Let's make some coffee, and I'll tell you. But first, I need some information from you."

The coffee didn't take long to brew, and they carried mugs of it to the kitchen table.

"Tell me," she demanded. "Right now."

"All right." He took a sip of the hot liquid. "Lindsey, who is Judge Harold Webster? Do you know him? Or of him?"

"Why are you asking?" She pushed her glasses up on her nose. "Harold Webster was a very old friend of my father's. He's dead now, but I have faint memories of him from when I was a kid. My folks apparently knew him from…someplace." She frowned. "Funny, I don't recall how they knew him. I don't think either of them ever said. He's the only person I remember coming to visit them, and that only happened a few times. Why?"

"He's also the man who inherited the balance of your parents' estate, about five million dollars."

Her pulse ratcheted up, pounding everywhere in her body. Could this be the breakthrough they'd been hunting for? "How on earth did Reno get him to give up that information?"

"As your parents' sole heir you have certain rights. Quinn, who has your power of attorney, has the authority to act on your behalf. He's the one who convinced the law firm to have a confidential conversation with Reno."

"And?" she prodded.

"After some complicated financial maneuvers, the money eventually ended up in the bank in Cibolo."

Lindsey couldn't breathe.

"Lindsey?" Nick's look was intense. "Do you understand what I'm saying?"

"I can't believe it. Any of it. It's just so unbelievable." She made herself sip some of the coffee to moisten her dry mouth, her hands holding the mug trembling slightly. "What is it all about, Nick?"

When Nick reached for her hand, she jerked it away. She didn't want him to touch her, not now.

"As far as we can figure, it appears when your folks came to Cibolo, the judge turned the money back over to them. Your dad bought the ranch and breeding stock with cash and invested the rest of the money very, very well."

She freed her hands from his and wrapped them around her coffee mug, clutching it with a death grip. "This is so unbelievable."

Nick nodded. "Yes, it is. Anyway, the judge was also the one who recommended Ruben and Mary. They were newlyweds then, and somehow he knew of them. And you know that's worked out great." He shifted in the chair and leaned forward. "But there's still a big gap between the supposed drowning and the appearance of your parents in Cibolo.

"Like, where are my brother and sister?" she asked. "Are they alive somewhere? If my parents moved to Cibolo, why didn't they take the other children with them? What the hell happened all those years ago?

Nick, I think I'm more afraid now than I was when we stated this."

"We need to go back to the ranch so you can sit down with Ruben and force him to tell you what he knows. My guess is it's a lot. I think he knows the whole story."

"I feel like this is happening to someone else." She ran the tip of one finger around and around the rim of her mug, as if an answer would rub off on her.

Nick got up to pour more coffee. "I've been in this business a long time, and I'd bet the farm this whole situation with the stalker will all boil down somehow to money. It usually does."

"Nick, if my parents owed money to someone, I'd be happy to pay them. But who would they owe? Especially if they had so much?"

"I think we'll find out it's a little more complicated than that," he told her. "I asked Reno to beep our pilot and tell him to be ready for takeoff about noon tomorrow. We'll pick up Reno on the way back. Then we'll go directly to the ranch and try to bring this to a head."

Lindsey scanned his face, trying to read his eyes. "You already have a pretty good idea who we're looking for, don't you?"

He nodded. "But it's only an idea."

"Then tell me," she cried. "I have a right to know."

"From what Reno has been able to learn, we think the Littmans received a large sum because they took your sister, Barbara Jean, with them. The money was to assure her care and—"

"And what?"

"Keep her away from you."

"What?" Lindsey nearly choke on the word.

"Lindsey, we're gathering the final proof to show you, but it seems Barbara Jean had a nasty vicious temper and liked to hurt animals and people. She wanted to be the center of attention and hurt anyone who stole that from her."

"Like my brother, who seems to have disappeared?"

"Like him. And you. Your parents wanted her gone before you were born." He blew out a breath. "You won't like this, either, but Reno traced her to San Antonio."

Her heart almost stopped. "So you think she's the one who…"

"I do." He nodded. "He's got people on her case, looking for her. So let's just get through tonight, and tomorrow, we'll head for home. I think by then we'll be able to find all our answers."

"Won't you even give me a hint?" she pleaded. "It's my life, you know."

"And I plan to take damn good care of it." His voice had a dangerous edge to it. "So please don't give me a hard time, okay?"

"Nick." She wet her lips. "What happened before—"

"Was good," he finished. "Don't lie and tell me it wasn't. Lindsey, I don't know what happened to make you retreat behind that wall again, but I'm not giving up. And you can take that to the bank. Just as soon as we have your stalker put away, you and I are going to have a long talk."

She swallowed the rest of her objections and nodded her agreement. "I just wish it was over now."

"Amen to that."

Did he mean he was glad because now he could walk away from her with a clear conscience? That he'd done his job, and he could go back to his other life?

I can handle it. I'm strong. He'll never know how I feel.

****

Lindsey spent the rest of the afternoon curled up on the sun porch, staring out at the water and trying to sort out the jumble her well-ordered life had become. Nick pretty much left her alone except to bring her tea twice and ask if she needed anything. She was grateful for the space he gave her, on a number of levels.

At six, he made soup and sandwiches and coaxed her to the table. They were still sitting there when Lindsey's new cell phone rang. She looked up at Nick.

"Who could this be? No one has the number but the Medanas and my office, and I already checked in with them earlier. Besides, it's a text ring and none of them like to text."

"Look at it," he ordered, "but be prepared for anything."

She tapped the Message icon and waited for the text to appear. When it did, her heart nearly stopped beating.

I found you, bitch. Now you're dead.

She stared at the message, afraid for a moment she would faint. Panic gripped her, and she looked wildly around, as if the person was standing right there.

Nick grabbed the phone, read the message, and cursed loudly. Then he stood up and cleared their plates. "Okay. I think time just ran out on us."

"How did she find us? I thought you said Reno had

people on her."

"I said they were looking for her. This woman has a history of being able to disappear. This remote island is probably not safe any longer. We're getting out of here tonight." He pulled her up from the chair. "Come on. Let's pack and spend the night in Bangor. If we hurry, we can catch the last ferry to the mainland."

"I…I…"

"Come on, Lindsey." His voice was soft and coaxing. "It's okay."

"I…can't…I…don't…" She couldn't seem to make herself say anything that made sense.

Nick eased her back down in the chair, then brushed a kiss over her lips. She didn't even try to turn away from him.

"No problem. Just wait here. I'll do the packing and call the ferry office to make sure they don't leave without us."

"How did she find us, Nick?" Oh, God. This was as bad as her nightmares. Worse, even. "How did she know where we were? We were so careful."

"We don't know that she did. This call could be coming from anywhere, designed to make you think exactly what you did. Right now, I just want us to get out of here. I'm going to call Reno and update him, then get our things. Wait right here for me."

Nick was still in the bedroom when Lindsey thought she heard the crunching of tires on the gravel outside. Who could be coming here? Surely not *her.* Not here. She went to the back door and peered through a slit in the curtains but couldn't see anything outside.

Stay away from the door. You don't know who it is. Get Nick.

She hurried back into the kitchen where she could hear Nick moving around in other parts of the house, shuffling their bags, checking the fireplace. "Nick? Where are you?"

A sudden scratching noise seemed to be just one more sound until she heard the back door open. An intruder burst in, dressed in heavy jacket and jeans with a scarf wound around her head. In seconds, she had the barrel of a gun pressed against Lindsey's head.

"Go ahead. Get him in here. We need to invite him to the party, anyway." She pressed the barrel harder. "Go on, bitch. Do it. Now."

Lindsey froze in place. Brianna James' familiar voice was the last thing she expected to hear. No, it had to be a mistake. This had to be wrong. Oh, God, was someone playing a horrible joke on her?

"Bri?" She could barely get the word out.

"Yes, it's me," Brianna sneered and yanked off the scarf. "Take a good look. I want you to know who I am. Who I *really* am. The child everyone wanted to get rid of."

Lindsey didn't think she could move. This had to be a nightmare. Any minute, she'd wake up.

Brianna took a small step backward, the gun still pointed directly at Lindsey's forehead. Her friendly, open expression was replaced by a vicious smirk. "Good, good. No more secrets. Now call for Nick to come out here. Right now."

No. She wasn't going to call him into danger. She needed to send him some kind of signal.

"You've got two seconds, bitch, before I start making little holes in you. Get him in here right now."

Lindsey drew a breath and tried to shout. "No. I

won't do it. If you're going to shoot me, go ahead. He'll just kill you."

"Oh, I don't think so." She wrapped her hands around Lindsey's hair and gave it a vicious yank.

Lindsey screamed in pain.

****

A chill ran down Nick's spine. Something was definitely wrong. Lindsey sounded scared out of her mind. Pulling his gun from his holster, he flattened against the wall and inched toward the kitchen.

"Lindsey?" He called out her name.

When he peered around the edge of the doorway to the kitchen, his blood turned to ice. He wasn't surprised to see Brianna James holding a gun to Lindsey's head. With the latest information, he'd been half-expecting her to be the stalker. And the look of hate on her face told him she wasn't about to be reasoned with.

"Come out, come out, wherever you are." Her sing-song voice had a vicious edge to it. "Come on out and play before I blow this bitch's head off."

Nick tucked his gun into the small of his back and moved through the open doorway into the kitchen. The look of stark terror on Lindsey's face cut straight to his heart. He'd promised to keep her safe. Instead, he'd left her right in harm's way. But he had no way of knowing they'd stayed there one day too long. The information had only now come to light.

"I'm here," he said as calmly as he could. "It's all right, Lindsey. Just do whatever she says."

"Good idea," Brianna said. "Smart thinking. Get your hands up. Up!" she repeated when he hesitated.

He opened his jacket to show her his holster was empty, hoping she'd fall for it. "No gun, Brianna."

"What do you want?" Lindsey's voice had a tremor in it.

Brianna spared a glance for Nick. "You know, don't you, Mr. Private Security? Yeah, you know all about it. Go ahead and tell her."

Lindsey's eyes darted toward him. "Nick? Is she really who you told me she was?"

He nodded. "Meet your sister. Barbara Jean Dolman."

If possible, Lindsey turned even whiter. "My…sister?"

"Yes, but we're not having old home week here, bitch. Too bad I didn't punch Mommy Dearest in the belly and make her lose you. Save me a lot of trouble."

"Guardian is good at digging up facts, no matter how deep they are buried."

He shifted on his feet, and Brianna sneered at him. "Go ahead. Make a move. I'd love it. I'll blow a hole in her head big enough to drive a car through."

"I'm not moving," he told her. "Just talking. I think your parents faked their deaths for a very specific reason. And I think it had to do with you and your baby brother. Maybe even something you did to him. We found letters your grandmothers wrote to each other in their distress and worry. It seems you weren't a very nice little girl, were you?"

She shrugged. "All speculation. Nothing more."

"I think they sent you off with the housekeeper and her husband," he went on, "and settled them financially to raise you, as long as you never had any contact with them. How am I doing so far?"

Hate glittered in her eyes. "That rotten little baby. He spoiled everything. I thought with him gone it would be just me. I'd be the special one."

"Didn't quite work out that way, did it?"

The woman let loose a string of curse words that made even Nick stare.

"They went off to a new life and left me with those weird old people. Do you know what they told me? That my parents were dead and they would take good care of me. That's a laugh. They even made me take their stupid name."

"I understand the Littmans were good people," Nick told her, wanting to keep her talking until he could make a move.

Lindsey, I'm going to save you. I hope you can hear what I'm thinking it. Feel it.

"Good for nothing," Brianna said in that same voice. "Never letting me do anything. Punishing me. And hating me. Oh yes, I knew how they hated me. The devil's child, they called me, when they didn't think I could hear them. They considered it their duty to chase the evil out of me. But I showed them. I had fun in spite of them. When I finally ran away, they didn't even try to find me. I'm sure they said good riddance. I wonder what my dear darling parents would have thought of that."

"I'm curious. How did you find out about Lindsey?"

She laughed, a sound tinged with a hint of madness. "I finally went home about two years ago, a little down on my luck and needing a new stake. When the Littmans weren't around, I snuck in their bedroom and dug around for money. I found a locked box in the closet. I picked the lock—one of my acquired skills—and guess what I found?"

"Information about the accident."

"Bingo. All the newspaper clippings as well as letters from Texas. Thanking the Littmans for helping them get away. Anguishing over that damned baby. Stupidly telling the Littmans where they were. Idiots, both of them." She laughed again. "What dummies they were. They even sent a picture of the ranch and this bitch, Lindsey. Dear mama was pregnant when everything happened, which was the reason for the entire charade."

"To save the baby from you." Nick's voice was soft, with a dangerous edge to it that Brianna didn't seem to notice. "So that's how you traced her, through their new name?"

"I did some research of my own. With the Internet, it's not too hard these days." She glared at Nick. "When I found out what the estate had been worth, I was determined to get it. All of it. It should have been mine to begin with. I had nothing, and the little princess got everything."

"Bad luck for Lindsey she ran the employment ad at exactly that time," Nick muttered.

"Bad luck for her, good luck for me. She was only too happy to hire me." She smirked. "And didn't I just play the role of the efficient assistant to the hilt?"

"Lindsey would have gladly shared with you," Nick said. "You didn't have to go after her the way you did."

"Didn't you hear me? I said I wanted it all." She raised her voice, nearly shouting now. "I deserved it. She had everything all those years."

"The Dolmans shelled out a million bucks for your care," Nick pointed out. "That's not peanuts."

"One million?" She snorted. "It's nothing compared to what they were really worth. Anyway, it wasn't for me, it was to bribe those two idiots to take me off their hands."

"I suppose stalking Lindsey was somehow part of your big plan?" *Keep her talking. Keep her distracted.*

"I thought it was a brilliant idea," she bragged. "I needed someone to blame her death on when I finally did away with her. You could be looking for the phantom stalker forever while I'd be home free with the money. Besides, I had fun with her."

"You sent all those faxes and photos and text messages."

"Yes." That nasty grin was back. "It was so easy to frighten her. I did everything on my lunch hour or right after I left at night. It's amazing what you can do without people asking any questions. Like renting a room in a hotel with no luggage."

"You're the one who insisted she call the police. Weren't you afraid they'd get onto you?"

"No way." She shook her head arrogantly. "I didn't leave any kind of a trail. I used public faxes in crowded places and disposable cell phones. And she may have become suspicious if I hadn't suggested it."

"Quite a plan. And then what? You figured you'd just step in with your birth certificate and all those other documents and claim everything as yours?"

"Of course. It would be easy." She flicked her hand in the air. "I got a copy of the will from the court. It states that when both parents are dead the estate is left in trust to the offspring of Andrew and Elizabeth Ferrell. Well, they can change their names, but they're still my parents. And I'm still their offspring. And I have the documents to prove it."

"What exactly happened with your baby brother all those years ago to put all this in motion? The one who seems to have disappeared?"

"You haven't figured that out yet? I thought those old bags had written it in their letters to each other. Why, I killed him, of course."

Nick tried to keep the shock from his face. "Killed?"

Brianna snorted. "Snuffed him out like a marshmallow. Just like I'm going to do with your girl here. Only I plan to have a little fun with her first."

"Wait." Lindsey held up a hand. "What happened to his body?"

"Buried in secret someplace. I think in Bangor. I heard the Littmans talk about it once. Lucky for me, they didn't call the police. They'd have turned me over to the asshole juvenile authorities and then where would I be?"

"You can't hold both of us with that gun," he pointed out.

"I only have to hold her. You make a move, and it's all over."

Nick stole a glance at Lindsey and saw tears rolling down her cheeks.

"You think I'm any happier about this than you are?" she demanded of Brianna. "I lost a brother I never knew, a sister I never got to know who might have been helped by the right doctors—"

"Doctors?" Brianna snorted. "You mean shrinks who would lock me up and throw away the key?"

"I mean who would have helped you. Our parents were wrong to do what they did."

"You mean selling me off to get me out of their hair?" She glared at Lindsey. "No shit. Too late for that now, though."

"It's never too late," Lindsey said. "I'll share with you All of it. Everything you should have had. Truly."

Good, Lindsey. Make her feel you sympathize with her. Distract her.

"You think I believe that?" Brianna's face turned red. "Not on your worthless life. Besides, this way, when you're dead, I can claim the whole thing. I've got all the birth documents."

Nick cleared his throat drawing her attention back to him. "How'd you find out we were coming to Maine?"

She shrugged. "I guessed. I knew you were getting close so it seemed obvious. I had done a complete search on Guardian and knew about the plane. After that, it was simple. I wasn't far behind you."

"So here you are." Nick stood calmly, hoping Lindsey would pick up on his signals not to freak or do anything to provoke this woman.

"Here I am," she drawled. "It's time the game was over anyway."

Her eyes burned with rage. She moved the gun slightly. With her hands still fisted in Lindsey's hair, she raked the gun barrel across her cheek, leaving a thin line of blood.

Lindsey gasped, her eyes wild with panic, her cheeks wet with tears.

Nick's gut tightened. "You don't need to do that," he said.

"Oh, but I do." The smile Brianna gave him came from the devil himself. "I want to make her suffer. To feel pain. Before I'm finished, I'm going to damage her in a hundred ways and let you watch her bleed and scream."

"Exactly what do you think that will accomplish?" Nick made his voice sound a lot calmer than he felt. This woman was really crazy.

"I had all those years of hell," she shouted. "Why should she get off scot free? And with all the damn money."

"You can have the money," Lindsey told her, blinking back tears. "You can have anything you want if you'll just let us go."

"Too late. Now I want the money *and* my pound of flesh." She raked the barrel of the gun down Lindsey's cheek again, new blood welling up to mingle with the other. "Getting your—*our*—mother wasn't near as much fun as I thought it would be."

"Getting *our* mother?" Lindsey had a wild look about her now. "What are you talking about?"

"I went to see her, you know. In the nursing home. I wanted to see the bitch that threw me away. I told her who I was and guess what? She had a heart attack! Right then and there." She threw her head back and laughed, a sound that was pure evil. "Too bad," she went on. "I wanted to cause her as much misery as she'd given me, but she died on me before I could do anything more."

Nick calculated how fast he could get his gun out and cursed the fact that he'd stuck it in the small of his back instead of his pocket. He looked at Lindsey, willing her to look at him.

When she did, he dropped his gaze to the floor, then back up again, hoping she'd get the signal. Brianna was busy concentrating on her gun. If Lindsey had just understood what he meant…

He let his arms hang loosely at his sides, shifting his weight to the balls of his feet. Brianna released the pressure of the gun slightly as she shifted it to a different position and that was all it took. Lindsey closed her eyes, went limp, and crumpled to the floor.

Nick dived for Brianna, grabbing for the gun, but she turned and fired before he could tackle her. He managed to grip her wrist and knock the gun out of her hand, then pressed her to the floor with his weight.

"You're done now," he told her, grasping both of her wrists. "We'll see exactly who's the bitch."

He could have killed her with his bare hands, but that would just put him on her level and that wasn't who he was. Besides, it was more important for her to pay for everything she'd done.

"Lindsey, honey, let me take care of this wild woman, and we'll check your cheek."

After flipping Brianna over and securing her with his belt, he looked around for Lindsey. When he saw her, his heart nearly stopped. She lay on the floor where she'd fallen, unconscious, a pool of blood spreading out on the floor around her body.

"Oh, Jesus God," he whispered under his breath.

Quickly binding Brianna's feet with his tie, he knelt beside Lindsey, checking the source of the bleeding. It welled in great bubbles from a nasty looking wound in her abdomen.

"Don't die, don't die, don't die," he prayed as he grabbed his cell and dialed 9-1-1.

The closest police were in Bar Harbor. They'd need to cross by boat to get to him, but maybe they also had access to a medivac chopper. Someone needed to get to Lindsey now. Assured that a chopper would leave immediately, Nick snapped his phone shut. Hands trembling, he did his best to stop the bleeding.

Chapter Eighteen

Time was a blur for Lindsey. People surrounded her, vague figures coming and going. Someone was screaming, but she didn't know who. Loud voices shouted to each other. And an unfamiliar sound intruded into her consciousness. Then she felt herself being lifted, moved around, placed on a hard flat surface, and a heavy bandage was pressed to her side.

She felt the prick of a needle and heard, "We've got the IV started."

"I know you hurt, Lindsey, but we can't give you anything until we get you to the hospital and you're evaluated," someone said, unfamiliar but soothing. "Can you hold on for a little bit? Here. Your boyfriend wants to hold your hand. I think he's going to shoot me unless I let him."

"I'm here, sugar. Squeeze my hand." Nick's voice, low, warm, comforting.

She felt whatever she was on lift off the ground and realized vaguely they were in some kind of helicopter. Probably a medical one, based on the equipment they were using on her. She clung to Nick's hand as they blazed through the night, her world tilting and turning. She was afraid she was going to vomit any minute, but Nick kept talking to her, begging her to hang on.

Nick, who she'd thought was only using her for

immediate amusement. Right now, she didn't care. He was her lifeline.

At the hospital in Bangor, more strangers waited for her, propelling her away on a gurney with wheels that bumped and caused pain with every movement. More hands on her. Incredible pain.

Finally, a new voice. Kind.

"Lindsey, I'm Dr. Robbins." She forced her eyes open to see him leaning over her. "Your vitals look decent despite the blood loss. We need to draw some blood for some tests, then we can give you something for the pain. In a minute, you'll start to feel better. Here goes."

"Nick?" she managed to croak.

"I don't know who Nick is, but if he's the man making all that noise, he's waiting right outside. Now just relax and let the medication do its work."

She drifted for a long time, in a state of semi-euphoria, the pain hovering in the background, images flashing across her mind. She couldn't wipe away that awful picture in the kitchen that kept replaying in slow motion. Brianna holding her at gunpoint, raking the gun down her cheek. Brianna with that awful story. Nick signaling her. Then the shot and the terrible burning pain in her side.

Bits of conversation penetrated her consciousness.

"I'd really like to take her back to San Antonio." Nick's voice, demanding, insistent.

"I don't think it's a good idea to move her until the bullet's removed." The doctor. She recognized his voice, too. Kind. "She's lost a lot of blood. The slightest jostling could move that bullet and start the bleeding again."

"I want her where I know the doctors." Nick again, sounding brutal.

"I assure you, we have an excellent staff here. We need to operate right away. Let us get the bullet removed and some repair work done. Then give us twenty-four hours in ICU, maybe another day or two after that and you can take her back on a Life Flight plane. Will that do?"

"Let them do their job, Nick." A voice she'd heard before but couldn't remember where. "They know what they're doing. Come on, let's get some coffee."

"If you go down to the surgical waiting room, I'll find you as soon as we're finished," the doctor told him. He cleared his throat. "One more thing. We'll have to give her a spinal and a very low dose of intravenous anesthetic so it may be a little rough for her. We can't take any chances with the baby."

Baby? What the hell was he talking about?

Lindsey tried to swim up through the fog in order to hear better.

"Baby?" Nick sounded stunned. "What do you mean, baby? That's impossible."

"Well, all I can tell you is, she's definitely pregnant. I'd say in the very early stages."

"She told me she couldn't get pregnant." Nick's voice became harsh, even angry. "Are you sure about this?"

"Absolutely. We always check in case we have to take precautions because of it."

"I don't understand how this happened," Nick was saying. He sounded cold, far away. "She said this couldn't happen. I don't understand any of this."

"Come on, Nick." The familiar stranger again.

"Let's go down the hall. They need to work on her."

A baby. The words echoed in her brain. Nick's baby. Unbelievable, but it seemed created by what she'd thought was their love. And which he, obviously, didn't want. A child would interfere with his plans.

A pain stabbed at Lindsey's heart, greater than any she felt from her wound. So everything had been a lie after all. She should have known this would be his reaction. By some miracle she'd conceived a child, and Nick, in his panic, was blaming her, resenting her. This was worse than being rejected because she couldn't conceive.

And who could she blame but herself? She'd let down her guard and ended up sucker punched. She tried to think what to do, but the medication was making her so groggy she couldn't focus.

Well, she might be losing Nick, but she would have his child, a child she'd thought was impossible. God had somehow chosen to bless her, and she would treasure this gift.

The doctor was back, explaining in that kind, soothing voice what was going to happen. "We'll keep you as comfortable as we can, but we can't depress the baby's heart rate. Okay? And you'll need to see your obstetrician as soon as we release you. Okay, then. If you understand all this, squeeze my hand."

She squeezed it as tight as she could. Then the stick of another needle, and she felt herself drifting again, sinking down into a very soft place.

****

The waiting room was a carbon copy of every one Nick had ever been in. Hard plastic chairs, a lumpy couch, out of date magazines. How come no one ever thought of the comfort of the people waiting, he wondered irritably. Of course, a comfortable chair wouldn't have mattered because he refused to sit down. Instead, he paced.

He had called Reno to tell him what happened, to come to Maine. His partner had messaged the pilot to pick him up in Boston at once. He came directly to the hospital the minute they landed and had been there for more than an hour with him.

"She'll be fine, Nick," Reno told him. "Will you sit down? You're driving me crazy."

"Yeah, right." Nick shoved his hands in his pockets. "I could have killed that damn woman with my bare hands. It's a good thing I had to take care of Lindsey or I would have."

"No, you wouldn't. Not deliberately like that."

"How the hell did this happen, anyway? I should have left the island yesterday. Or at least this morning." He looked at Reno. "She's pregnant. Did I tell you that?"

"I was right there with you when you got the news, remember?"

"That wasn't supposed to happen. She has a lot of scarring that the docs told her would prevent it."

"Nothing is absolute." Reno studied him. "Are you glad or mad?"

"Mad? Mad?" Nick raked his hands through his hair. "Hell, no, I'm not mad. I'm ecstatic."

"And what are your plans once all this is resolved?"

"I'm going to marry her, just as soon as I can get her out of a hospital bed. I'm going to be a father," he said with a note of wonderment. "A father! I can hardly believe it. God, this is wonderful. I'm going to take her home and settle down to being a satisfied husband and father."

"They'll put this on the front page of the paper," Reno joked, obviously trying to lighten the atmosphere.

Nick dropped into one of the plastic chairs. "You know, Ruben filled in a lot of the blanks about Lindsey's past when I called to tell him what happened." He replayed the conversation over and over in his head. "'I should have told you before,' the man kept saying. 'Maybe this wouldn't have happened.'"

Nothing Nick said could change Ruben's mind. Or Mary's either. And now Nick related it to Reno.

The story was one of the most devastating he'd ever heard. Two bright, beautiful young people, so much in love, blessed with everything—wealth, position, breeding, and good looks. The respected young attorney on a fast track in corporate law. The society beauty with brains as well as looks, a perfect complement to her husband. And they were genuinely nice on top of it. Their families were friends of long standing.

Then a child was born, the icing on the cake, it seemed. A blue-eyed doll with soft brown curls and dimpled cheeks, but a problem from day one. She was angry, temperamental, and given to violent tantrums. Marie and Brent were beside themselves.

The grandmothers, Carrie and Renee, saw something in the little girl neither of the young parents did, but they couldn't make the couple accept the truth. Even their pediatrician had no influence with them. When he urged them to get special treatment for the child, they fled his office and ignored his words.

This will pass, they'd said. She's just a high-spirited child, they told their families. But it only got worse as she got older. When Marie became pregnant again, the tantrums escalated. The child tore her mother's maternity clothes and defaced the nursery. Under great pressure, they agreed to try medication, and for a time, it seemed to work. She was calmer, more tractable and easier to be around. Then the baby was born, and the grandmothers sensed the growing danger.

But of all the things any of them could have predicted, the murder of the little boy was shockingly unexpected. Marie was destroyed. She cradled her dead baby for hours, unable to stop crying. She couldn't even look at little Barbara Jean. Take her away, she'd said. Get her out of my sight. Get her out of this house. She wanted to call the police and have her committed.

Brent couldn't bring himself to go that far, but Marie was pregnant again, and he couldn't put the new baby at risk, so they made a plan. They kept the body in the nursery with the door closed while they put their idea into motion

And so the deed had been done. Her father called his old friend, the judge, explaining the situation in distraught tones, and Judge Webster agreed to help. A new will was drawn up, notarized and couriered to the law firm. Marie and Brent made arrangements to bury the little boy very quietly, leaving the paperwork with his old friend, the judge. They dove off the sailboat and swam to shore where Howard Littman had hidden a car for them and left some money. And then they headed to Texas.

They changed their names. The judge helped them with everything—new identification, the purchase of the ranch, whatever they needed. With a supreme effort, they proceeded to make a new life for themselves on a ranch in a small town in the Texas Hill Country. The new baby arrived, a sunny, beautiful child with gorgeous sable hair who brought joy to everyone around her. And if an air of sadness hung over them, they did their best to ignore it. Life went on for all of them.

Nick was exhausted when he finished, but at least the telling had kept his mind occupied.

Five interminable hours passed before the doctor finally came to find them. Nick was as tense as a wire, exhaling the breath he'd been holding only when the doctor smiled.

"She's doing fine. We had to remove the spleen, but we were very careful how we did it and kept a constant supply of blood to the uterus. She and the baby are doing quite well. By the way, I can understand why the doctors told her what they did about her ability to conceive. There's a tremendous amount of scarring in the reproductive system that looks to be the result of acute endometriosis."

"That's what she said," Nick told him.

"All it takes is one tiny opening and one very strong swimmer, though, and apparently that's what happened." The doctor's face sobered. "The next challenge will be to see if she can carry to term and deliver successfully, without damage to herself."

"Is there a chance she won't?" Nick stared hard at the man, seeking some kind of reassurance.

"I can't make any promises, but I'd say with proper rest and care, she and the baby will be fine. They'll be taking her up to ICU in a moment," he went on, as if he had not just dropped a bombshell. "I want to monitor her there until tomorrow. Then we'll talk about moving her. I have to check on another patient, but if you'll come with me, I'll take you up there. You can see her as soon as they have her settled."

"Thank God. Thank God."

Nick kept repeating it to himself all the way to the ICU, Reno hard on his heels. Lindsey would be fine. The baby would be fine. He would spend the rest of his life making up to her for his lapses. He couldn't wait to take her in his arms.

"Just give us another minute, please," a nurse told him when he entered the ICU unit. "If you'll just wait right here?"

Nick could see them moving Lindsey from the OR gurney to a bed, checking her IVs, her vital signs, hooking her up to monitors. He looked at her and wanted to cry.

All my fault. She's already mad at me for God knows what. Will she see this as the final end to us? No, we're going to share a child. We have to be together. I'll find a way to make her see that.

****

Lindsey was drifting again, her body wrapped in pain but her mind suspended. People moved her, jostled her, and she wanted to cry out, only her mouth wouldn't work.

"Did you hear what the doctor said about the baby?" Nick's voice, piercing the fog surrounding her. "Complication doesn't begin to explain this. I have to do something."

Do something? What did he mean? Did he want her to get rid of it? No way was she having an abortion.

He certainly didn't need to be involved, but it was her baby and she was keeping it. Why couldn't she make her brain work?

"I think you've done it already." The same familiar voice, this time with a little chuckle.

"That's not what I meant. Listen, I need to call Stacy, but I can't use a cell phone in here. Can you go down to the pay phone and call her for me? Tell her there's been a change in plans and I'll call her later with more details. In the meantime, she should put everything we discussed on hold."

Lindsey bit her lip, trying not to cry out. She hurt, but the physical pain was nothing compared to the pain in her heart.

Stacy again. Why did he need to call her right now? Couldn't he at least wait to find out if she lived or died before getting back to another woman? He didn't want the baby, and he didn't want her. She wanted to roll into the fog and stay there forever.

When she opened her eyes again, Nick was sitting in the chair by her bed. When her lids fluttered, he reached forward to take her hand. "They'll only let me stay for five minutes," he said hoarsely, "but I had to touch you, make sure you were okay."

I'm fine, she wanted to tell him. You don't have to be concerned about me. Go to your Stacy, or whatever. She tried to speak, but she was still too drugged. The next minute she was asleep again.

She woke briefly several times during the next hours, always to see Nick sitting in the chair. One time she noticed there were fewer machines in the room and the room itself was larger. The next time she woke, she felt more alert. She was still in a lot of pain, but she felt more aware of her surroundings.

Nick was standing by the window, but she moved and the rustle of the bedclothes caught his attention.

"How're you doing, sugar?" he asked softly. "You gave us all quite a scare."

"Fine." The words came out as a croak.

"We're chartering a hospital plane to fly you back to San Antonio in another day. I called Ruben, who about took my head off when he heard you'd been shot. But he did give me the name of your doctor and I put a call in to him. He's going to make all the arrangements at Methodist Hospital."

"Nick?" Speaking was a huge effort for her.

"Yeah, sugar?"

She forced herself up from the fuzziness she kept sinking into, and the pain that stole her breath. "Get out."

"What?" His face lost its color. "What do you mean?"

Sweat drenched her body, the effort to speak almost more than she could handle. "Just what I said. Get out. Now." She swallowed and closed her eyes.

"Lindsey?" A woman's voice. The nurse? "Lindsey, I have pain medication for you. I'm injecting it into your IV. You should feel a difference in seconds."

"Lindsey." Nick again.

She felt herself falling down a long slide of clouds. "Go away. Please."

Someone came into the room behind Nick, and she heard the other male voice. Reno, she finally figured out.

"Come on, Nick. Let her sleep. You can talk to her

about this later.

****

Nick let Reno lead him out the door. He was in such a state of shock he couldn't even think. He thought he'd at least have a chance to explain things. To apologize to her, tell her how much he loved her. What the hell was happening? Outside, he sagged against the wall.

Reno literally had to prop him up. "She's just reacting to the pain and the medication," he said. "We'll try again when she wakes up. Lindsey Ferrell doesn't seem the type not to at least give you a hearing. I know your silver tongue. You can talk to her later."

Reno couldn't have been more wrong. When she woke again, they discovered Lindsey had left explicit instructions that she didn't want to see anyone. Not Nick, not anyone else. No matter how he shouted or threatened, Nick could not get past the hospital's formidable barrier.

Reno finally bulled his way in the next morning.

"I said no one in the room," Lindsey told him.

"I just want to talk to you for a minute, okay?"

She turned her face away from him. "There's nothing to discuss."

"I'm not going to get into anything that was said between you and Nick, who I admit can be a handful when he wants to be. I can tell you two things. First, he promised Quinn to take care of you and that's what he planned to do. He's beating himself up over what happened."

"I forgive him. Okay?"

"Second thing. You need to get back to San Antonio. You're in no shape to take care of yourself or to make any moves without assistance. The agency has arranged for a plane to take you back. Your doctor will be advised of your arrival time, and he'll be at the hospital to meet you. That is non-negotiable, so don't waste your energy trying to argue. You're a client, and you were hurt while under our care. We will take care of you."

He held out his hand to her, then withdrew when she ignored it.

"I know you're very angry at Nick right now," he went on, "and I don't blame you. In your position, I'd feel he let me down, too. But he feels worse about what happened than you do. He really needs to see you. Can I impose on you to give him just a few minutes?"

She shook her head. "Not today, not any day. I'll accept your offer of the flight because I don't seem to have a lot of choice, but I don't want him on the plane. Just tell him to stay the hell away from me. Now if you'll excuse me, I'm very tired."

The last thing she heard before she drifted off again was Reno saying, "Well, I tried, but somehow you've made a real mess out of this. I don't know how you think you're going to fix it."

Chapter Nineteen

The flight was accomplished with a minimum of distress. The doctor gave Lindsey pain medication just before she was moved. The two nurses on the plane did their best to keep her comfortable once they had her in place. From the plane, they transferred her to an ambulance to ferry her to the hospital.

Dr. Edberg, bless him, was waiting for her as promised. He followed the orderlies as they whisked her to her room, waited while the nurses checked her vitals, then examined her himself.

"Well, Lindsey, you've had quite a bit of excitement." He smiled down at her. "But you seem to have come through it well. Everything looks fine. We'll run some more tests tomorrow just to make sure, but it all looks good to me. And of course, we'll monitor your pregnancy carefully."

"Yes, my pregnancy." She closed her eyes, trying to shut out the pain of Nick's voice. She had tried so hard to block out his words the past few days, but they seemed to echo over and over in her head. "I guess we both got fooled, didn't we?"

"God has a way of taking over things when we least expect it," he told her. "Have you told the father?"

"He has nothing to do with this." Her voice was harsh and angry.

Edberg raised an eyebrow. "Well, he had a little

something to do with it. I take it there will be no involvement?"

"You can bet on it."

"Then it will be just you and me, Lindsey. We'll do our best to bring a healthy baby into the world. While you're here, I'll also get a plastic surgeon in to look at that cheek. Right now, I think you need sleep more than anything." He gave her a reassuring smile. "I'll check on you tomorrow."

She asked him to leave a No Visitors order except for Ruben or Mary, and he said he would.

They came, of course, fussed over her, and begged her forgiveness for hiding the truth for so long. But at least now a lot of questions were answered, like why the Ferrells had no relatives to interact with and why they never went anyplace outside Texas. And most especially why sometimes they looked so very, very sad.

Because even with the pregnancy, there was a sadness that hung over all of them, a sadness for the desperation her parents had felt, for the brother she'd never know, for the sister who was born with a madness that nearly destroyed all of them. But at the same time, joy for the child she carried, for the new life she could focus on.

Ruben, as implacable as always, asked no questions about Nick, nor did Lindsey mention him. Mary just pretended he'd never existed. The two of them constantly tried to cheer her up. Ruben even took a picture of Jingo and brought it to her room "to keep you company."

Her office was closed, at least for the moment. Quinn had taken care of everything, calling all her active clients to let them know what happened, giving the prospective ones some other recommendations. Mark finished what he could and delivered plans and sketches to the appropriate people. There was a temporary outgoing message on her answering machine. The office might open again, but Quinn didn't think it would be any time soon. He recommended Mark look for another position and promised him a letter of reference.

Lindsey had Quinn call Guardian several times to ask them to send a final bill. He reported Nick was a wreck and not dealing with life very well at the moment, and there would be no bill. Reno told him he had no intention of charging her anyway.

She spent most of her time thinking about the family she'd never known and wondering if there was someone still out there she could contact. Maybe her uncle existed someplace. When she got home, she'd go through everything again and do some Internet research of her own. It saddened her that her only living sibling, a sister she'd never known, had turned out to be a vicious killer who hated her. A bad seed, Nick said, and she had to agree he was at least right about that.

At night, she lay in bed trying to make sense of all that had happened. One minute she remembered the sweet words Nick had whispered to her, the intensity of their lovemaking, the tenderness he'd shown her, and wondered if she was wrong in her conclusions. The next minute she remembered the phone calls with Stacy and the hurtful words she'd overheard in the hospital, and the ache in her heart increased. Apparently, when he said they'd talk about the future, she thought it meant something different than he did.

She cried when she was alone, unwilling to subject herself again to Mary's scrutiny and Ruben's knowing gaze. The tears came hot and scalding, burning her cheeks, and she made no attempt to stop them. They were the first tears she'd shed since that awful night. She cried for what seemed forever, hoping it would ease the terrible tightness in her chest and the ache in her throat. But all it did was make her feel worse.

She was aware Nick had tried several times to see her, but she'd been firm in preventing that. Even Reno had tried to talk her into a conversation with him. She just couldn't take the pain of knowing he was off with another woman. And that he'd lied to her. Okay, not lied, exactly, but maybe misled her.

At the end of another week, when she was able to move around for short periods of time, Dr. Edberg examined her, ran some tests, and was pleased with the results.

"You'll have to take it very easy," he cautioned. "But with the right care, I feel confident this will be a successful pregnancy. You can go home tomorrow. Make sure you have plenty of rest but move around for short periods each day. You need to build up your strength. And probably no work until we see how you're progressing. I'll have the office call you for an appointment in two weeks. I've given Mary all the instructions. You can also decide what you want to do about plastic surgery."

"Nothing until after the baby is born." She was emphatic. "If it leaves a scar, no big deal."

She was more grateful to be home than she could have believed. She made it up the stairs slowly but under her own power, Ruben next to her for support.

Mary got her settled in bed, then left to make her some tea.

Lindsey looked out the window at the meadow and the horses grazing peacefully. She remembered standing at the fence with Nick, sharing a quiet moment with him. And with that came the memories of their wild lovemaking, the heights to which he took her, the things he did to her body, the feel of him driving into her so powerfully. Out of that wildness, a child had been created, a child he obviously didn't want.

Mary eyed her critically when she brought in the tea. "You'll have to talk about it soon, little one, or it will eat you alive. Here. Drink this tea. Tonight, I'll bring you a tray but tomorrow Ruben will help you downstairs for dinner. Doctor said you should make it downstairs at least once a day."

She left the room, giving no opportunity for argument. Lindsey lay back on the pillows and sipped at the tea—peppermint, her favorite. But nothing was going to help the pain that consumed her.

Mary fielded all of Nick's calls, reporting them to Lindsey but not saying anything else. Lindsey had been adamant about not talking to him. He sent flowers almost daily. Those she gave to Mary to keep at her house.

"That man's going to drive me out of my mind," Mary said, bringing up her lunch one afternoon. "You have to talk to him sooner or later."

Lindsey just shook her head. She rested a lot and increased her physical movements a little each day. Mary cooked all her favorite foods. Ruben even spent time playing cards with her. But she couldn't shake off the deep depression that gripped her. She lay awake at night, her hand gently touching her stomach, and tried to shut all thoughts of Nick Vanetta out of her mind.

Kate came nearly every day, cheerful at first, keeping everything light. Finally, one day, when Lindsey made it downstairs and they were sitting on the porch, Kate turned to her with a determined look. "I've kept Quinn away because he's like a bull in a china shop about this, but if you don't listen to me, I will bring him out. Lindsey, I can't begin to know what went wrong between you and Nick. I know he's a mess. I've never seen him like this. There's a man in love if ever there was one. And I think you feel the same about him. Whatever it is, you have got to talk to him."

Lindsey shook her head. "Not in this life. You can forget that."

"No, I'm not going to forget it. Whatever the trouble is, you have to get it out in the open. If it's not fixable, then you'll both have to come to terms with it. But this is stupid. You're wilting away here, and don't say you're not. I see it every day with my own eyes. Quinn says Nick is a human train wreck. Please, Lindsey, just hear him out and tell him what's on your mind. It's not good for the baby for you to be so emotionally distraught. If nothing else you need closure."

"I don't believe Nick's any kind of wreck," she argued. "If he is, it's because he's out carousing with Stacy, or whatever her name is."

"Stacy?" Kate had a curious look on her face. "What do you mean? What about Stacy?"

"You know, his latest toy? He didn't even have the decency to tell her not to call while he was with me. And the night I got shot, he had the gall to have Reno run and make a phone call to her about their plans. That was one snatch of conversation I wish I hadn't overheard."

"Exactly what did you overhear? Tell me word for word."

"What does it matter? Let it lie."

But Kate was not to be denied. She pried every painful word from Lindsey, questioning her in great detail.

"And what else did you 'overhear' on your bed of pain, when you were supposed to be out of it?" Kate continued to look at her strangely.

"He doesn't want the baby," Lindsey said miserably. "It would probably cramp his style. He lied about everything, right down the line. This was all a game to him, just like with his other women. He saw it as a way to have unrestricted recreational sex." She leaned her head back and closed her eyes. "I'm embarrassed enough about the whole thing as it is. Please, Kate, I don't want to discuss it any more. There isn't anything to say. I made a royal fool of myself, and I have to figure out how to get over it."

"All right." She sighed. "I have to pick up John, anyway. Quinn has him at the office, and I'm sure he's destroyed it by now. I'll see you tomorrow, honey."

Lindsey had dozed off in the rocker, warmed by the sun and caressed by a soft breeze, when she heard the crunch of tires in the driveway. She opened her eyes in irritation, annoyed that someone else was disturbing her. Quinn climbed out of his big black pickup and strode to the porch.

"I've had all I can stand today," she protested. "Please don't you start in on me, too."

He leaned his hips against the porch rail, crossed his booted legs at the ankles, folded his arms across his chest, and fixed her with a stare.

"Not today, Quinn. Please. I refuse to humiliate myself by breaking down into tears in front of you."

"No, Lindsey, you don't get out of it that easily. You might be able to push Kate away, but I've known you since grade school. I want the whole story, and I'm not leaving here until you tell me, so you might as well start talking."

She wanted to push him over the rail and run into the house. Except he was bigger than she was and she wasn't up to running away from anyone just yet. She certainly didn't want to relive her misery one more time, but Quinn was relentless.

"Do you know you'd make a good prosecuting attorney," she snapped at him in the middle of his diatribe.

"Yes. I used to be one, remember?"

He dragged every little fact from her, everything her mind wanted to block away. Finally, when she was done in from repeating everything on her mind, he looked hard at her again, then shook his head, a disgusted expression on his face. "Lindsey, I've known you since you had skinned knees and messy braids. You've done some dumb things in your life, but this one takes the cake."

She opened her mouth but no words came. Finally, she managed, "Exactly what do you mean?"

"I mean that it's a wonder you haven't pulled every muscle in your body jumping to conclusions." He stomped off down the stairs to his truck and climbed in.

"Quinn?" She wished she had the strength to run

after him. "Wait, what did you mean? Quinn? Get back here!"

But he was already pulling onto the road, gravel spitting from beneath his tires. Lindsey leaned her head back and let the tears come again.

Late the following afternoon, when she was lying down on her bed, reading, tired from the emotional dredging of the previous day, Mary came in to tell her she had a visitor.

"You know I don't want to see anyone. Whoever it is, tell them to go away."

"I think she'd do it, but I was rude enough to follow her upstairs," a strange female voice broke in. "Quinn said you'd probably kick me out, and I wasn't taking any chances."

The woman who walked into the room was lovely. Medium height with dark, almost black hair pulled back in a gold clip. A lush figure and black eyes that reflected shifting light. She was cool and sophisticated in peach silk slacks and a short-sleeved matching sweater that just set off her complexion. There was something very familiar about her, but Lindsey was sure they'd never met.

"Hello," the woman said, coming over to the bed. "I thought it was time we met and straightened out what seems to be a colossal misunderstanding. I'm Stacy."

Lindsey was simultaneously shocked and angry. How dare this woman march into her home? Why was she here? Did Nick send her for some strange perverted reason? What was this all about? If she'd had the strength, Lindsey would have gotten out of bed, slapped the woman, and shoved her out the door, but she was too weak to do anything but lie there and seethe.

"Stacy?" she asked, wishing she could disappear.

"Yes. Stacy Vanetta Morgan. I'm Nick's sister."

Lindsey was so astounded she couldn't even take the hand extended toward her. Her brain was whirling, and her mouth didn't seem to work.

"Never mind, you don't have to say a word." Stacy grinned. "I'll do all the talking. May I sit down?" Without waiting for Lindsey to say yes, she sat on the edge of the lounge near the bed. "I can't tell you how great it is to finally meet you. Nick hasn't shut up about you since forever, it seems."

"I don't understand." Lindsey stared at the woman, unable to get her brain out of first gear.

"When Quinn called yesterday, I told David, my husband, the only way to straighten this out was to come see you in person. Nick was wild to come with me, but I figured he'd make a mess out of everything like he's apparently done already. Reno's sitting on him until after we talk."

"Reno?"

"Yes, I had to call him to find out what really happened in the hospital. He's still as much at sea as everyone. I did get most of the conversation out of him, though. I apologize for coming so late today, but I couldn't leave earlier and it's about a ninety-minute drive from Austin where we live."

"You drove all the way here from Austin?"

I sound like a dope. I need someone to write my lines for me.

"Oh, no problem. I drive all over the place. Now." She crossed her legs and clasped her hands over one knee. "Let's work backward here, shall we? I understand you overheard my calls to Nick. And then

Nick asking Reno to call me when you were all at the hospital and somehow got the idea that I was his girlfriend. As you can see, I'm not. The call was to change arrangements he'd made, as he said. But the arrangements were for you."

Lindsey frowned. "This is all brand new to me and a lot to take in.

"Our folks have a big vacation place at Horseshoe Bend," Stacy continued. "Nick wanted to bring you there after everything was over. He thought it would be a great place to get you away from it all and give you time to rest. He asked me to make all the plans and let the family know. We're all really close, but Nick and I are twins so we're probably closer than the others."

Twins! Good Lord!

But that explained the familiarity she'd sensed. The resemblance was obvious.

"He never mentioned he was a twin," Lindsey said in a weak voice.

"Yes, well, Nick isn't always very good at communicating, which I guess is why we now have this problem. Anyway, we've all been dying to meet you." She flashed a grin that was a duplicate of Nick's.

Lindsey didn't know whether to laugh or cry. "How nice," she managed in a weak voice.

"No one ever thought Nick would settle down, so naturally everyone is curious about this fantastic woman he's fallen for so completely. We figured, after he caught your stalker, we'd assault you with all the Vanettas at once. If you survived that, you were a keeper." The grin disappeared. "But when you got shot, we obviously had to put that on hold."

"Oh. I see."

Lindsey didn't know what else to say. She felt like a total and complete idiot. Why hadn't she just asked Nick straight out who Stacy was, instead of letting her own insecurities back her into a corner? Because she didn't want to hear him make excuses? Lie to her? Only it seemed it wouldn't have been a lie.

But the baby…

"I have to tell you," Stacy went on. "My brother is a mess. He hasn't been to work. He went one day and was so miserable, Reno sent him home. He hasn't eaten, which for Nick is like saying he hasn't breathed. Mom finally went to his house and told him that, big as he was, she'd give him a good spanking if he didn't shower and shave and put on some decent clothes."

"But I don't understand," Lindsey said. "He's the one who doesn't want me, not the other way around. I heard him in the hospital."

Stacy cocked an eyebrow. "What exactly did you hear?"

"When he found out about the baby…" She looked up. "You know about the baby?"

Stacy nodded.

"I could hear him ranting and raving and yelling about how it just wasn't possible and what a mess it was and all that." To her embarrassment, she burst into tears. She pushed her glasses up on her head and rubbed at her eyes with tissues she grabbed from a bedside box.

"He sounded so resentful, like I'd trapped him or something," she sobbed. "I realized then that he hadn't meant any of the things he'd said to me. Or at least that's what I thought." She yanked more tissues from the box and swiped at a fresh cascade of tears. "I'm so crazy about him. I don't know what to do, and I'm sick that he's mad about the baby."

Stacy nodded but didn't say anything, waiting quietly for Lindsey to calm down.

"I really didn't think I could get pregnant, Stacy. Every doctor told me that. I don't even know how this happened. Nick said it didn't make any difference to him. I guess he was right, but I misunderstood. He doesn't want children at all. I sure didn't need him throwing it in my face, though. This is my child, even if he doesn't want it, and I'm not getting rid of it. It may be my only chance. And then I heard him talking to Reno about you and I thought…"

Another fresh flood of tears consumed her. Hormones. All pregnant women cried at the drop of a hat.

Stacy handed her the box of tissues. "Well, this is what my grandmother would call a fine kettle of fish. Quinn is right. This is a ridiculous situation, but I can certainly sympathize with you. Do you know Nick has no idea why you won't see him, and he's ready to come out here and kidnap you?"

"What?" She sat up straight.

Stacy held up her hand. "I know, I know. Lindsey, Nick is so in love with you he can't see straight. He's been driving us all crazy since he met you. All the calls were about the big family shindig at Horseshoe I just mentioned."

"For real?" Lindsey couldn't wrap her mind around it.

"That's right. He was so excited for the family to meet you. And by the way, he's thrilled to death about the baby, but he's worried sick about you. The doctor told him what a difficult pregnancy this was liable to be, and he's been scared to death something will happen to you. You're more important to him than anything, you and the baby."

Lindsey stared at her open-mouthed, her face still wet with tears. "But this is crazy. How did we get in this mess?"

"My guess is because his pride wouldn't let him ask what was wrong and yours wouldn't let you question him directly about the calls," Stacy said.

"Oh, God." Lindsey blew her nose, then took another tissue and cleaned her glasses.

Stacy sat on the edge of the bed and took one of Lindsey's hands in hers. "Being in pain in the hospital magnified things for you and even distorted them. It's easy to happen. You were in no condition to do anything but deal with the physical pain, but now I think it's time for the two of you to talk to each other." She leaned over and kissed Lindsey on the cheek. "I hope you don't mind. I feel like we're sisters already."

Lindsey levered herself off the bed, stood up, and gave Stacy a hug. "I can't thank you enough. I feel so idiotic about everything, and now you have to drive all the way back to Austin by yourself. I'm so sorry."

"Actually my husband is at Kate and Quinn's. I dropped him there, and I'm picking up pizzas to take back. By the way, I told Nick to give you until tomorrow to mull over all of this before he rushed over here."

"Thanks. You certainly have given me a lot to digest. Including my own stupidity in jumping to conclusions. Besides, I still tire easily. And I need some quiet time to figure out how to apologize to Nick for not having faith in him."

"I know he'll understand. He's not that dense. I'd get plenty of rest if I were you, because I have a feeling you'll be having a visitor before the sun is barely up."

"Thank you again, Stacy. I can't tell you what this has meant to me."

"Just keep that obstinate brother of mine in line." Stacy winked at her and was gone.

Lindsey had barely settled back in bed when Mary came into the room, trying hard not to smile.

"I knew I was right about him," she said, straightening the bed covers.

"Eavesdropping, were we?" Lindsey chuckled.

"Now, little one, don't you give me any of that mouth. I just came to ask if you wanted to come downstairs tonight or have me bring you a tray up here. And by the way, it does me good to see some color back in your face and a sparkle in your eyes. Will we be having a guest tomorrow?"

Mary's face betrayed nothing, but Lindsey would have bet every dollar she'd listened in to the entire conversation with Stacy.

Chapter Twenty

The sun had just begun to climb into a perfect blue sky the next morning when something caused Lindsey to stir. She shifted as a warm, nearly naked body slipped into bed beside her and arms cradled her gently. Her eyes flew open. She tried to sit up, but the arms held her in place.

"I think this is where we left off," a low voice said in her ear.

"Nick?"

"It better be. If you're expecting anyone else, they won't live to tell about it."

She shifted in his arms so she could face him. She was still sore, and she moved gingerly.

Nick picked up on it at once. "Am I hurting you?"

"No. I'm just still a little tender. You can touch me," she said impishly. "I promise I won't break."

"How are you really? And the baby. Is the baby okay?"

"We're both fine," she reassured him. "We're eating properly, taking all our pills, and doing the light exercise Dr. Edberg told us to do."

"Good." He kissed her nose. "You don't know how badly I want to be inside you right now, but I can wait because we've got the rest of our lives." He tilted her face away from him. "I should paddle you, you know. How in hell could you even think I didn't want you?

Both of you?"

"You said…"

"Like everything else, you totally misread and misinterpreted what I said. I was stunned, sure. You'd said over and over that every doctor told you this wasn't possible. But I was not unhappy. Oh, no, sugar. I'm definitely not unhappy. Just scared for you, wanting you to be okay."

"I'm fine. Really."

He was caressing her cheeks, her forehead, her shoulders, touching her as if he wanted to be sure she was real. "And why the hell didn't you just ask me who Stacy was?"

"Because I thought she was one of your girlfriends, and I'd sound like a jealous idiot interrogating you."

"We owe Quinn and Stacy a lot for getting us past this."

"Yes, we do. And by the way…" She tapped the side of his head with her knuckles.

"Ouch. What was that for?"

"For not telling me you were a twin. She's lovely. A class act."

"Classier than me, apparently. I seem to be the world's biggest screw-up."

"Shut up and kiss me," she said.

Which he did. Very thoroughly.

"How soon?" he asked.

She knew what he meant. "About another three weeks. We'll have to take it a little easier at first, but I'm sure our inventive minds can get around that."

He groaned. "I guess I'll be taking a lot of cold showers."

She gave him a devilish grin.

"And the baby?" Lines of worry creased his face. "It won't hurt the baby or anything?"

"If you'd like, you can come to the first obstetrician appointment with me and get it first-hand."

"Damn straight. And every appointment after that. I was scared to death when that doctor told me you were pregnant. I remembered everything you'd said, and I was afraid having the baby would kill you. I couldn't stand that." He kissed her again. "Yesterday was the longest day of my life. When I found out Stacy was coming to talk to you, I wanted to jump in my car and meet her out here. She got Reno to come to the house and practically hog-tie me. She said she wanted everything out in the open before I came charging in. I think she really wanted to make sure I hadn't screwed up big time."

"I know I've been an idiot, Nick, but when I heard you talking, all I could think—"

"Enough. We were both fools. But never again." He tilted her face up to him. "We have to talk about getting married. I'd do it tomorrow if we had the paperwork, but my mother claims she's in charge. I hope you don't mind. She knows you don't have any family. Of course, when you're better, we can try to find your uncle if you like."

She nodded. "And anyone else we can trace."

"Okay, then. That's a plan."

Lindsey sighed. "At least all the memories are finally silent. Thank the Lord for that."

Nick kissed her cheek. "Amen. Listen, my mother is hot to plan something with you, if that's okay. I don't know who you want to include or what's in your head—"

She touched his lips with her fingertips. “Shh. It’s fine. It will be wonderful. I will love having your mother plan my wedding. I think just the family and people like Quinn and Kate and Reno would be more than enough. After all, we are kind of putting the cart before the horse here.”

“Don’t even think about that,” he admonished. “Just being married is what’s important.” He hugged her again. “I love you, Lindsey. I nearly died when I thought I’d lost you. Don’t ever scare me like that again. Promise?”

“I promise.”

“I have orders from Reno not to show up at the office until I have my life straightened out. I think that’s going to take quite a few days, don’t you?”

“Oh, yes. Absolutely.” She didn’t think she could possibly get any happier.

About the Author

Known as the oldest living author of erotic romance, Desiree Holt has produced more than two hundred titles in nearly every subgenre of romance fiction. Her stories are enriched by her personal experiences, her characters by the people she meets.

After fifteen years in the great state of Texas, she relocated back to Florida to be closer to members of her family and a large collection of friends. Her favorite pastimes are watching football, reading, and researching her stories. She lives with her three cats, who love to sit with her when she writes.

~*~

Desiree loves to hear from readers.
www.facebook.com/desireeholtauthor
www.facebook.com/desiree01holt
Twitter @desireeholt
Pinterest: desiree02holt
Google: https://g.co/kgs/6vgLUu
www.desireeholt.com
www.desiremeonly.com

~*~

To chat with Desiree Holt and other Wild Rose Press authors of erotic romance, join us at www.groups.yahoo.com/group/thewilderroses.

Also Available

Moving Target

Guardian Security Book One

By Desiree Holt

http://a.co/5q5Ikjj

They're trying to kill her, and she doesn't know why…

Kathryn Holt knows only that she has to get far away as fast as she can. In a frantic, cross-country odyssey, she transforms from pliable Kathryn to feisty, determined Kate Miller, staying one step ahead of the killers on her trail. Then Fate delivers her into the hands of a dark knight with a tortured past. The safety he offers is as tempting as he is.

After having his perfect life ripped apart, recluse Quinn sees protecting Kate as his chance for redemption. He never plans on wanting the guarded beauty, never mind falling for her. Denying the explosive chemistry between them is useless, and as danger closes in, he must fight to expose the killer or risk history repeating itself.

Also Read

The Last Resort
By Ember Leigh

http://a.co/1vWNxfy

Rose Delaney is a baby bounty hunter, rescuing children from fugitive ex-spouses. All she wants is to return a recovered child to its mother and get back to her regimented solitary life. But when a snow storm leaves her and baby Emmy stranded, Rose has no choice but to lean on the ruggedly handsome rescuer, who thinks the baby is hers. Holed up in their mountain resort-under-construction and unable to contact Emmy's mother, Rose's priority is hitting the road—even if Garrett's erotic touch entices her to ride out the storm.

Construction boss Garrett Galo loves his job, but he never imagined a perk like being snowbound during a whiteout with the sassy brunette he just rear-ended. He's learned to stay away from women who want a family, especially when they come with a kid in tow. When passionate nighttime encounters flare between them, Garrett begins to question what he'd risk to keep Rose.

This isn't the time or the place for romance—but will five days on a mountain make these loners reconsider giving in to love?

Thank you for purchasing this
publication of The Wild Rose Press, Inc.
If you enjoyed the story, we would appreciate
your letting others know by leaving a review.
For other wonderful stories, please visit our
on-line bookstore at www.wilderroses.com.

For questions or more
information contact us at
info@thewildrosepress.com.

The Wild Rose Press, Inc.
www.thewilderroses.com

Stay current with The Wild Rose Press, Inc.
Like us on Facebook
https://www.facebook.com/TheWildRosePress
And Follow us on Twitter
https://twitter.com/WildRosePress